A Killer in the Crystal Palace

THE KIER AND LEVETT MYSTERY SERIES
BOOK 1

DEB MARLOWE

DRAGONBLADE
PUBLISHING, INC.

ARE YOU SIGNED UP FOR DRAGONBLADE'S BLOG?

You'll get the latest news and information on exclusive giveaways, exclusive excerpts, coming releases, sales, free books, cover reveals and more.

Check out our complete list of authors, too!

No spam, no junk. That's a promise!

Sign Up Here

www.dragonbladepublishing.com

Dearest Reader;

Thank you for your support of a small press. At Dragonblade Publishing, we strive to bring you the highest quality Historical Romance from some of the best authors in the business. Without your support, there is no 'us', so we sincerely hope you adore these stories and find some new favorite authors along the way.

Happy Reading!

CEO, Dragonblade Publishing

Prologue

The Great Exhibition
London
June 1851

HIS NERVES WERE a tangled wreck, twisted with fury and twinges of panic. Still, none of it disturbed him as much as the twice-damned heat.

London lay under the thrall of a hot and dry summer. The Crystal Palace, home to the Great Exhibition and naught but a giant, overblown conservatory, held all that heat and threw in the warmth generated by thousands of visitors. They were packed in, marveling at the collected artistry and technological achievements of the world over each other's shoulders.

He occupied the emptiest space in the whole place, but the air was hot and still and stifling in here. The stump of his ruined arm itched abominably, as it always did when he perspired, and his hiding spot smelled of musty, dead elephant.

Understandable, as he was crouched beneath the stuffed animal that graced the stall from India, hiding in the folds of fabric that fell to the ground from the highly decorated howdah upon the creature's back. He'd dived in here because he'd been spotted and then pursued. Discreetly, but with foul intent. Oh, there could be no doubt of that. And so he stayed, sweating and agonizing and plotting his way out of this unholy mess.

The afternoon wore on. The Great Exhibition closed at six every evening, before the light faded. The hour approached and the noise and bustle lessened as the crowds began to file out. He waited out the trickle of footsteps and murmurings as the exhibitors soon followed. The background scent in the air faded as the great fountain in the barrel vault was shut off and the perfumed water stopped flowing.

Silence crept in with the dark, but the heat remained. He tore off his cravat and coat and curled up, staying put until all sound faded, until he could not tolerate another second of the heat and smell and suspense. Driven out from behind the rich fabrics, he scurried over to rest against a weaponry display, sucking in the slightly cooler air and listening for a footstep or the cock of a pistol.

But he heard only the sleepy chirping of the birds perched in the trees left to grow through the open-roofed bits of the glass building. Nearby, the cage that housed the Koh-i-Noor diamond during the day caught the fading light, looking wan and empty. He stared at it, thinking. The diamond had already been lowered into its safekeeping place. How soon would the guards be back around this way? There were too many treasures to be left unattended. It was impossible to get away with any of the safely contained and wildly popular jewels, but there were other riches here. Riches of industry, of imagination, of the future. Prince Albert and his like could crow about sharing, learning, and advancement, but he knew—it was competition that fueled this exhibition and that he knew how to take advantage of.

He was out of time, though. He would collect the item that would serve his own needs, and he would get out. Out of this cursed glass palace, out of London, out of England.

Tossing his coat over his arm, he rose and moved stealthily down the British nave, navigating the dark and judging his progress with all of his senses. Leaving India, he entered the

Canadian display. He knew this spot because of the darker bulk of the birch-bark canoe hanging overhead and the tropical smells coming from Trinidad and Tobago's display of colonial produce next door. The Medieval Court came next, and he stepped carefully around the heavy furniture and display cases of yet more valuable jewels and gold plates and goblets.

Almost there. He passed into British Furniture, and his heart began to race. The japanned piano stood on his left, and he was there.

He slipped past the tall case clock and into the stall. Here it stood: a marvel like he'd never seen. An automaton so intricate, so detailed, that he'd held his own breath when he first saw it, waiting for it to breathe. Though unfinished, it was fascinating. It was a young man, with a porcelain face, wearing the clothes of a gentleman. When he was awakened with the turn of a crank, he moved and blinked, and his hand reached out to pick up a set of pasteboard cards. His other hand tapped the table, as if to communicate with a dealer or another player.

He'd been filled with wonder and longing from his first glimpse. He could literally feel his own phantom limb lifting those cards, fanning them out. Restored. Whole. A man once more.

That glimpse had changed everything, exploded his plans— and the plans of others. Others who were looking for him.

The time was now. He had to remove his treasure. In the dark and with one hand it would not be easy, but he would take it and make his escape. There were others who could replicate this work. He'd made inquiries. He had names. He had to believe they would be as talented as this woman, who wrought magic with her nimble fingers and saw straight through to a man's soul.

He explored the masterpiece he'd watched her laboring over these last weeks. Touching it gently, he sought a seam or an obvious spot of separation. The whole thing was a miracle, but it was the arm he needed. The arm with its articulated joints and its ability to grasp something as thin as a playing card.

A footstep. He froze.

Waiting, he strained to hear anything else. Long minutes passed. He heard no further sounds of any kind.

He went back to work. After a few fidgety moments, he managed to detach part of the arm, but it made a creaking sound of protest.

More footsteps. They were moving quickly toward him. Panic had him in its grip now. He grabbed the arm and yanked. The whole figure fell over with a great crash. Holding on to his awkward prize, he ran.

There was an exit at the end of the nave. He pushed through and emerged into the courtyard where great collections of rocks and minerals sat about. Beyond them loomed the boiler house that powered the machinery of the exhibit, quiet and menacing. He'd tarried long enough, and the moon had risen, casting strange shadows. He was headed toward a large pile of coal, thinking to hide, when someone stepped out from behind the tall column of Cornish granite.

He skidded to a stop.

The figure moved closer.

He blinked in surprise. "You!"

"What a disappointment you've turned out to be, Walter."

"I don't care what you think of me!" He shook his head. "No more. I'm finished with you. I'll not do your bidding any longer."

His nemesis reached out and plucked the arm from his grip.

"Give it back," he said roughly.

"You fool. For this, you betray me? If only you had done as you agreed, I would have bought you a hundred arms. Arms of silver, or of gold, if you wished."

"You don't understand. This is a technical triumph. With this, I could hold a fork or a set of reins. I could play a hand of cards. I could be normal again!"

"Neither magic nor science will make you normal again." His former employer held the arm aloft and tore a bit of machinery from the inside—a caged gear attached to a long metal arbor.

"No!"

"Can this make you feel again? Allow you to touch again? No." Eyes narrowed, his nemesis growled. "Do as you were bid. My plans are set and time is limited. Finish the job and I will reward you, still."

He shook his head. "I cannot. You should not. Such a mind. Such unique skill…"

"She is a complication that cannot stand."

"No. So much good she could do. You should not take that from the world."

"Idiot. You are bespelled. I will—"

He didn't wait to hear and lunged for the arm. His opponent growled and danced back, holding it out of reach. He followed and jumped, getting a grip on the narrow end. They struggled. Though he had but the one hand to fight with, he managed to hold on—until he was grabbed from behind and dragged away.

His chest heaved. He didn't even look back to see who held him. His opponent's face had gone white with fury. Long experience told him that nothing good would come next.

"You are nothing. No one." Fury and contempt hit him like a wave. "If you will not serve me, then you are of no use to anyone on the face of this earth."

Moonlight flashed on the long metal arbor. The slim metal spike stabbed him deep in the junction of shoulder and neck.

He gasped. His nemesis pulled the arbor free and watched while hot blood spilled down his front.

He fell to his knees and clapped his one remaining hand over the wound, but the blood welled between his fingers and each breath began to come harder. He looked up into that impassive face, unbelieving.

Sharp words. An order. He could not make them out, but his opponent turned and walked away. He was on the ground, gasping for breath, when rough hands began to drag him toward the boiler house.

The world had gone dark, and he'd breathed his last before they reached it.

Chapter One

London, England
Several Months Earlier

The first time he saw her, he knew her for an artistic genius.

M R. NIALL KIER was determined to be heard.

"I don't know what it is you think I can do," Mr. Grant insisted. "All of these selections were meant to be handled by the local committees. The spots are filled. The plans are made."

"Yes, well, the local committee in Alnwick did not deign to see everyone who showed up. We all dreamed of being chosen for the Great Exhibition, but they tired of evaluating submissions and went down to the pub instead." Niall kept his expression neutral and his tone urbane, but the gentleman across from him must have sensed something of his fury and of all the subsequent frustration he'd endured, for he shifted slightly in his seat. "I came all the way to London because I must be heard and seen." Niall cleared his throat. "I have learned that Mr. Charles McLean was recently added to the list of exhibitors in this fashion."

"Yes, I've heard of it as well. I am on the panel, Mr. Kier, but I'm not what you might call...prominent. I'm not sure I could achieve the same result." Mr. Grant sighed. "I'm not sure just what I can do for you, sir."

"You can come over to the window." Mr. Grant's office, as befitted a successful architect and a member of the Royal Commission of the Great Exhibition, smelled of ink and leather and featured, besides several fine bookcases, a wall of high, wide windows. The view looked out behind the building onto a small courtyard.

Niall stood and waited for the gentleman to precede him. "I've studied the Royal Commission's views on what the Exhibition is meant to showcase. You wish to highlight Britain's manufactory might, her economic prowess as well as the artistic soul of our nation. With respect, sir, my work represents everything the prince and your commission are hoping to show the world."

They'd reached the window. He gestured, and his associate, waiting outside, whipped the covering off one of the pieces he'd placed there earlier. It was a standing screen of three panels, done in intricate iron scrollwork. The design, however, was not a usual one of random curls and swirls.

"Good heavens," Mr. Grant breathed.

Niall was rather proud of the piece. One panel featured a recognizable—and flattering—depiction of the diminutive figure of the queen. She held a scepter in one hand and extended the other benevolently over the isles of Britain, a representation that stretched over the remaining two panels, showcased several major landmarks, and was surrounded by gently lapping water.

"The prince will buy it at first sight," Mr. Grant whispered.

"I would be happy to gift it to His Royal Highness," Niall told him. "*After* the Exhibition."

A brisk knock sounded upon the door. It opened at once, and a woman strode in. "Forgive me for barging in without an appointment, Mr. Grant, but the matter is urgent. I have come to request..." Her words trailed away as she stared at Niall and pursed her lips, obviously surprised at his presence.

He could echo her reaction. Niall's experience with women was extensive. He'd known and charmed them in England and abroad. Rich and poor. Young and old. From the lowest orders to the highest. But this woman?

She was…new.

Stunningly beautiful. That was a man's first impression. Thick locks of deep walnut brown and large, dark eyes. Her close-fitting coat and wide skirts were of rich forest-green wool. Instead of a bonnet, she wore a tiny black hat perched atop her gathered curls. On the brim sat a fan of green lace, pinned there with, of all things, a jauntily placed drafter's compass.

"Well. I see I am not the only one to be inspired by Mr. McLean's good fortune," she said, glancing out the window. "Very well, Mr. Grant. At least you are already in the correct frame of mind." She made a half-turn back toward the door. "Come in, Turner."

A man entered. Tall and lean and soberly dressed, he carried a box that looked to be of considerable weight. Even as Mr. Grant began to protest, the newcomer set it down on a desk and unlatched the locks fixing the top to the base.

The woman stepped over to it. "My name is Miss Levett, sir. I was unfortunately—and likely purposely—delayed, and I missed the chance to submit my work to the Exhibition committee."

"Another one?" sputtered Mr. Grant. "This cannot continue. I really do not see—"

"I promise you, I have not come to waste your time," she interrupted. Without fanfare, she lifted the top off the case.

Niall and Grant stared.

"Yes, yes. It's a very nice model," Grant began.

"It is not a model," she said.

"It's an automaton," Niall said, moving closer to the finely crafted replica of a three-masted ship. He glanced up at her. "You made this?"

"I did. Let me show you what it does."

Niall looked it over, taking in all of the intricate details, while she retrieved a fanciful key from her reticule and inserted it into the machine. She turned it, and the mechanism started.

Music played. A sea shanty, he recognized. The ship tossed as waves of differing sizes rolled by. The finely articulated sails billowed and furled as if filled by sea air. A tiny captain strode across the top deck, and a sailor scrambled up into the rigging. The Union Jack flapped. As the song wound to an end, a mermaid popped out of the waves and blew a kiss toward the stern of the ship.

It was a stunning accomplishment. There were no other words for it.

"If you toggle this switch," she said casually, "a different shanty will play."

Niall stared at her. "You built this?"

She nodded.

He pursed his lips. She was the most beautiful woman he'd ever seen, and he realized suddenly that her beauty might just be the least interesting part of her.

"I..." Mr. Grant looked helplessly between them. "I don't know what to do."

"Allow me to make your decision easier," Niall said smoothly. "Come back to the window, sir, if you please. I believe this will be exactly to your taste." He gestured, and the tarp was drawn off the second piece he'd set up outside.

Grant drew in a breath. His eyes widened and he took a step nearer the window.

Niall knew he'd judged his man correctly. He'd heard Grant had a sentimental attachment to his birthplace in Scotland. The grand set of gates outside were meant to cater to it.

The two sections met in the middle and seamlessly formed the shape of a thistle. Across the black iron pikes on either side stretched a scene crafted of wrought iron, representing a Highland glen with a mountain rising behind and a loch and castle in the fore. Above the top rail, a scrolled figure of a stag rose on one side and a unicorn on the other.

Grant turned away from the window. "You're in. The gates can be part of your exhibit, but afterward I want them installed at my house in Craigshook."

"Your offer includes both of us, I hope." Niall inclined his head toward Miss Levett.

"Yes, curse you." The gentleman looked toward the woman. "Do you have a father or husband who might stand for you, Miss Levett?"

Her chin went up. "My father has passed on. I have no husband, but neither do I have need of one. My work is my own, sir."

He sighed. "That won't make it any easier."

One of her fine brows rose. "I can envision an automaton of a Scottish castle, with the flag flying in the wind, a working gate, men on the battlements, and a fine stag drinking out of the loch. Perhaps that might make it easier?"

"Damn the pair of you. Fine. Both of you. Leave your work here, all of it. I'll call a meeting here tonight. The committee will agree to it; I'll make sure of it."

"Thank you, Mr. Grant." Niall gave the man a small bow. "You will understand, I hope, if I leave a man of my own outside of your offices, to keep watch?"

"Certainly." Grant rubbed his brow. "We'll find room for you both, somehow." Very formally, the architect shook Niall's hand, and then Miss Levett's. "Welcome to the Great Exhibition."

The second time she saw him, she knew he must have the creative soul of Hephaestus...

However, he most definitely did not share the Greek god's physical disadvantages. Where the mythical god of forge and fire was reputedly twisted and lame, Mr. Niall Kier was...formidable.

Kara found him not at his display inside the Crystal Palace, but outside in Hyde Park. As sales were forbidden inside the Great Exhibition, some of the exhibitors had set up vendors' tents and tables out here, next to the hawkers of souvenirs and geegaws graced with illustrations of the grand building. Out here, a steady flow of goods and money changed hands.

Mr. Kier's stall currently held several stunning fire grates.

One was done in a lovely scrolled pattern. Another was garden-themed, shaped and decorated with metal blooms and vines that would never shrivel in a fire's heat. There was also a large case of finely wrought jewelry, including several brooches and watch fobs featuring a delicate compass rose.

More interestingly, Mr. Kier also had a small forge set back behind his tent. It was an ingenious contraption constructed of a shallow coal pan and a bellows that he worked with a foot. Right now, though, he was at the anvil, pounding metal into submission. Several ladies had gathered, drawn by the sight of him hammering away wearing only a kilt and large linen shirt. His unfashionably long hair had been pulled back into a queue. Sweat gathered on his brow and gleamed on the bit of chest that showed at the open neck of his shirt.

The ladies tittered and sighed—and Kara didn't blame them. He was magnificent.

He was also extremely focused. He looked to be flattening small disks of metal. Bases for the brooches, perhaps? She waited nearly fifteen minutes as he moved between forge and anvil. At last, he glanced over and noticed her. He blinked, stopped, set his tools aside, and approached, wiping his brow as he came.

"Miss Levett. Good day."

"Good day to you, sir. I hope you'll forgive the interruption. I came because I wished to thank you."

"You are more than welcome." He grinned. "For what, though, may I ask?"

"You didn't have to push Mr. Grant to include me that day. I do appreciate it, though. It cost me less effort than I expected to convince him."

"Your work convinced him. You belong here," he said.

"Thank you. As do you. I've never seen such functional pieces so creatively designed."

"I've seen the longcase clock you are exhibiting. I could pay you the same compliment."

She didn't blush like one of those other young ladies might

have done, but it was a near thing. Her life was busy and rewarding in its own way, but it did not generally include kind words from sweating, vital men. Perhaps she should take mental notes of her reactions to him. Such details might prove useful at some later point.

"I brought you a gift to show my gratitude." Reaching into the specially crafted bag at her waist, she brought out a small figure and set it before him.

He looked surprised but bent down to inspect it.

She showed him how to turn the small crank at the bottom. The tiny blacksmith banged his hammer at an anvil, then moved to circle a scrolling jig, turning a small piece of metal with him.

"Remarkable." He looked enchanted. "He even has my hair."

"It's a small thing. I might have made him a little more elaborate, but I've been occupied drawing plans for commissions, as I'm sure you have."

"Indeed. The Exhibition has been as good for business as I'd hoped."

"I have heard of the demand for your compass rose talismans."

He grimaced. "Is that what they are calling them?"

"I heard a man say he wouldn't set out to sea without one. And also, that they must be made by your own hands and not an assistant's?" She raised a brow. "It is your touch that lends them their protective charm, it is whispered."

He rolled his eyes. "They only say that because word has got out that I have managed to survive not one, but two shipwrecks."

"Ah, no wonder they call you the son of the sea king." Standing so close, it was easy to understand all the gossip surrounding him. She could feel the heat coming off him. He smelled of coal smoke and honest sweat, with a fresh citrus tang beneath it all. His dark gaze was intense and made her feel...*seen*. It was all most interesting.

He snorted. "I don't mind making them, but it is the bigger commissions that truly interest me. There is so much more scope for intricate designs."

"I feel the same." She hesitated. "It's the other reason I had hoped to speak with you."

He looked surprised again, but waited for her to continue.

"I wondered if you knew of a skilled wire worker? So many of them are focused on wire-weaving looms right now and are not able to produce what I need."

"What are you looking for?"

She handed him a slip of paper. "These are the specifications."

He looked it over. "Thin, but with such strength." He drew in a deep breath. "A difficult task."

"So it seems." She sighed. "But essential for my latest project."

"It will require someone who still knows the old ways—and knows metal." He frowned. "I might know someone who could do it. He won't come cheap."

"Cost is no issue," she said briskly. "If you would give me his name?"

"No. He's an odd sort, and particular. Reluctant, as well as private. I'll tell him of your request and see if he'll take up the challenge."

She blinked, disconcerted. "Oh. Very well, then. Thank you." She turned to go but stopped and looked back.

He nodded. "I'll do my best. And I'll be in touch."

There was nothing else she could do. Returning the nod, she went on her way, analyzing as she went. Fascinating. She'd never met a man who combined such skill, talent, and sheer physicality. Nor had she ever felt such an attraction. She didn't know which part of him interested her more.

Data, conjecture, and hypotheses scrolled in her brain as she made her way inside. A social experiment based on her own reactions would be fascinating, indeed. So many factors: proximity, exposure, shared interests, different beliefs and backgrounds—it would be a puzzle of enormous proportions.

She shrugged as she entered the building. An interesting topic to be sure, but she doubted there would be time or opportunity to explore it.

But she did hope he could obtain that wire.

The third time he saw her, he had to save her from an accusation of murder...

Niall yawned as he entered the Crystal Palace, bracing himself for another long day. He'd been up late last night. His apprentice, Gyda, had spoken to a prospective customer yesterday—and the gentleman was interested in Nordic designs. At last. Niall had been waiting for such a chance. He'd been awake half the night, sketching out ideas.

He pulled dust covers off his exhibits, folded them away, then went into the aisle to look it all over. The roll of metal in his coat bumped against him as he moved. He'd obtained the wire Miss Levett had requested—with no small effort. He had to admit, he looked forward to giving it to her.

He stretched and yawned again—and paused when something shiny caught his eye. Something small and out of place, on the floor near the extremely long model of the Liverpool docks.

He strolled over to pick it up. It was a metal gear, an inch in diameter. He cast about and spotted another, sized larger, near the door at the end of the nave that led to the courtyard.

He started for it, but was brought up short by a sharp cry behind him.

Miss Levett stood frozen a few feet from her exhibit space. She looked feminine and beautiful in a gown of deep blue, with short, lace-edged sleeves and a wide off-the-shoulder decolletage of the same lace. She was missing the black leather belt he'd noticed her wearing each day at the Exhibition—one side was lined with several pouches where she kept tools and who knew what else. But it was the look on her face that stole his attention. Her expression was a mask of dismay.

"My *Gambler!*" she gasped. "He's gone."

Niall knew she meant the intricate automaton she'd been

working on during the Exhibition. The crowds had flocked to see it, and they had marveled to see her fashioning small bits and pieces at the workbench she'd set up. He glanced down at the gear in his hand and headed toward her.

He slipped past the long clock and into her space, then heard her breathe a sigh of relief as he drew near. "Oh, thank goodness. He's only fallen." He hurried to help her as she knelt over the heavy piece. She looked up at him, distressed. "His arm. It's not here."

He held out the gear he'd found. "This was beneath the model of the docks." He stood and looked back to the outside door just as it opened. A boy crept in, bent over, searching. He gave a cry of victory and pounced upon the gear before disappearing back outside with it.

"I'll be right back," Niall said to Miss Levett. He followed the boy out to the courtyard.

Stopping in his tracks, he gaped. There was not just one, but a great gaggle of boys coursing through the space. Street urchins. How did they manage to get in? He shook his head. They had their ways, just as street rats did in every city he'd traveled in. A crowd of them, all sizes and varying degrees of filth, were gathered around the boiler room. Niall sighed. It would not do for them to interfere with the boiler and all the mechanics it ran inside. He set out to scatter them.

They were too excited to run from him, though. They sounded like a pack of starlings, chattering and paying him no mind at all.

"Give it over," a larger boy snarled. He backed up, raising something aloft. "Cor!" he crowed. "Still blood on it, ain't there?"

Niall grabbed his wrist. "What have you got there?"

The boy struggled wildly. "Leggo! Leggo!"

Niall held on. "Not until you tell me which of you destroyed the lady's automaton and turn over the rest of it." He took the object the boy held. It was a lantern gear attached to a long rod. Shocked, he realized the urchin was right: nearly dried blood coated the long arbor.

"We didn't do nuthin'!" the boy cried.

Niall let him go. The boy scampered away as his friends took up the cry.

"The bloke were already dead when we found 'im," someone insisted loudly.

"Ain't just a bloke," another scoffed. "He's a gentry cove. Just look at 'im."

"Dead?" Niall repeated.

The crowd of boys parted. A man lay inside the boiler room, bloody and already stiff.

"Holy Mother of God," Niall whispered.

One of the lads crouched down to tug at the man's glove. Niall realized they were right. The body was dressed in fine linen and a costly embroidered waistcoat. He wore no coat, but a quality one of superfine material had been tossed across him.

"Here now, step away. Leave him alone." Niall would be damned if he allowed the poor dead sod to be looted as well as murdered.

Murdered. And the deadly weapon looked to be...

"Here 'tis!" The call came from beyond the slabs and piles of minerals, from the edge of the courtyard. The smallest boy yet emerged from beneath a fence, and several others ran to meet him. "Tried to hide it, didn't they?" His tiny voice sounded triumphant. "But I scrounged it!" He was clutching the missing arm from Miss Levett's automaton.

Damn it.

The lad Niall had gripped earlier snatched the limb from the smaller boy. "It's from the lady's mechanical man," he called out. "P'raps she killed the cove." Shooting Niall a dirty look, he clutched his prize and headed inside the building.

A man passed him, coming out. "What's all this?"

Niall recognized him as one of the furniture exhibitors. He beckoned the man over and grimly indicated the body.

The man gasped in horror.

"I found this lot surrounding him, just a moment ago. It looks like he's been dead for some time."

"Get away, guttersnipe!" The furniture maker hauled away a persistent boy crouched over the corpse. The boy resisted, hanging on, until the dead man's glove came with him—and so did a wooden hand and a length of wooden arm.

"I knew it didn't look right," the boy said in triumph. He wiggled away, but Niall grabbed the artificial limb before the lad could escape with it.

He looked down at the poor dead man's empty sleeve. He must have lost his arm just beneath the elbow. "What a damned sorrowful mess," Niall said. "We need to see if any of the police have reported in yet this morning."

"I don't believe their shifts start this early," the furniture maker said. "They'll want to keep this quiet, though."

"You are right about that. They won't want this tarnishing the exhibit's shine." Niall sighed and handed over the wooden arm and hand. "Will you stand guard over him while I go find someone to report this to?"

He turned to go as the furniture maker nodded, but found a group of exhibitors gathered behind him.

"Saints alive," someone breathed.

"Stay back until the police have been here," he said loudly. But people were streaming into the courtyard while others gathered at the doorway, whispering. He pushed his way through, but even inside there were people talking low—and staring down the nave toward Miss Levett's exhibition spot.

"Perhaps it were a lovers' quarrel," someone said.

"No. You heard the boy. Saw the contraption." A man brandished the mechanical arm. The boy hadn't held on to his treasure long. "Someone tried to steal her mechanical man."

"Did she kill him over it, then?"

"What else could it be?"

"Nothing else has been touched, has it?"

Men looked up and down the nave, confirming the theory. A

dark muttering began to rumble among them.

"I knew it was a bad idea to include a woman here."

"They should have kept the ladies to their embroidered linens."

"Whoever heard of a lady clockmaker? Let alone these other strange creations."

"Did you hear the fellow who damned her for trespassing on God's territory?"

The volume of their discontent rose a notch.

"She'll likely get away with it."

"We should confront her now."

"Let her know we know what she did."

Damn it all to hell.

Niall strode quickly down the nave. He would have to move fast.

Chapter Two

K ARA CROUCHED DOWN, one arm full of gears and armature. She was reaching for more pieces, spilled all under her workbench, when Mr. Kier came rushing back.

She stared, fascinated, at the hard-edged scowl that had re-placed his normally tranquil expression. It suited him, whatever dark emotion that he was ruthlessly controlling. He looked implacable, a granite mountain of determination. It crossed her mind that she wouldn't wish to be on the opposing side of all that cold, formidable control.

"Come." Grasping her arm, he hauled her upright. "Forgive me, but you had better leave, and quickly."

"What? Leave?" She pulled away. "I cannot. I must find out what happened here. I have to find the arm that's gone missing from this piece."

"It's right down there, in that crowd." He nodded toward a group of men gathered around the courtyard door. "I don't think you are going to get it back."

"Why ever not? Of course I must have it back." Here she was, opposing him already, just after questioning the wisdom of such a thing.

"That mechanical arm was found just beyond the courtyard outside." He lowered his tone. "And inside the boiler room was found a dead man."

She gave him a level look. "A dead man did not steal the arm from my *Gambler*."

"No. A man stole it and then he was killed." He held out his hand. "With this."

Kara stilled at the sight of the arbor topped with a lantern cage. "That is mine. It's from the *Gambler's* arm."

"It was used to stab the man in the neck." He indicated the blood coating the metal rod. "It's long enough to have gone deep."

He leaned in, and she caught his scent. Something with bergamot and cedar, tainted by the faintest whiff of smoke. She shook her head to free herself from such distractions.

"And the dead man wore an artificial arm and hand," he announced.

That caught the attention of the wayward part of her brain. She banished thoughts of his scent and the warmth of his hand upon her. "Are you saying a *one-armed man* was murdered?"

He nodded.

She dropped the armful of parts on her workbench. "Where is he? The boiler room, you said?" She turned to go, but he moved to block her.

"It's not a good idea," he warned. "Tempers are…uncertain."

"You don't understand. A one-armed man? I have to see him." She slid sideways past him and moved quickly down the nave.

The crowd near the door saw her coming. Hostility shone in their narrowed eyes and curled lips. She could almost feel the icy touch of their distrust.

"In a hurry, isn't she?" someone remarked as she headed for the door.

"Thinking someone else out there needs a stabbing, do you?"

She ignored the snide remarks and the men who made them. She hurried outside and had to push through to get to the boiler room. One man stood on guard, keeping the milling crowd away from the body. He held an artificial limb in his arms, but she slipped past him to get a clearer view of the dead man's face.

A shiver moved down her spine. Niall Kier followed, stepping up close beside her. Bleak foreboding dropped over her as she looked up.

"It's him."

"You know him? Who is he?" Kier asked.

"No. That is, I don't know his name. But he's been watching me. I've seen him several times, lurking across the aisle, near Lord Ross's telescope. He always stared so intently. Relentlessly. Especially when I was working on the *Gambler* figure."

"He didn't approach you?"

She hesitated, but he was clearly already involved, and she wanted to get to the bottom of this and might need help doing it. "I believe he did, but not as himself."

"What does that mean?" Kier frowned. "Not as himself?"

"He dressed differently when he engaged with me. He wore whiskers and a cleric's collar."

The man who had been guarding the body spoke up. Kara thought she recognized him as one of the exhibitors from the British furniture section of the nave. "I saw that clergyman. He confronted you, calling down all the fire and brimstone he could summon."

"Yes. He lectured me and anyone who would listen about the evils of trusting in machines instead of God."

"He didn't like you making a whirligig that looked like a man. He accused you of challenging God Himself."

"And you think this is the same gentleman?" Kier asked, scowling down at the body.

"He wore a set of great, bushy whiskers and slicked his hair into a different style, but his jaw was the same, as is the color of his hair, his height and build." She gestured toward the empty sleeve. "And they both were missing the same limb. What are the odds of that?"

"You noticed it? The missing arm?" Kier glanced down again.

"I didn't spot it on the body. One of the urchins did."

"I've worked with men who have suffered amputations before. I know the signs." She glanced over at the man holding the wooden arm. "It was far more noticeable in his clergyman persona. You saw him berating me. He gestured wildly with his left hand, but did you ever see him use both? Or the right hand?"

The man frowned, thinking. "No. I didn't. Now that you describe it, I can see that left hand waving in my mind's eye. But not the other."

She held out her own hand and was surprised to find she still held several of the gears and pins she'd been gathering. She hadn't yet donned her utility belt, so she held them in her palm as she reached for the arm. "May I?" He handed over the artificial arm, and she ran her fingers over it. "Willow. Carved to resemble his true limb." She knocked against the back of the device. "A lower-cost option."

"Don't you go disparaging good English wood and craftsmanship." The rude fellow who had taunted her inside pushed his way closer. He'd taken off his coat and cradled her metal figure's arm in it. He thrust it forward. "Not when you spend your time creating such godless work."

"You cannot compare the two," she replied. "Men with an amputation of an arm or hand face a difficult decision. Do they use a mechanism such as a hook, that looks and acts as a tool? Or a facsimile of a human hand? Right now, the only choice is between form or function. I have tried to reconcile the two in the past, but what you hold there is just clockwork, not such an attempt."

She reached for the metal arm, but the scowling man held it away from her. "That one is made of metal," she explained. "It is not suitable to be worn. It is only fit for my *Gambler* figure. He is purely meant for amusement."

"And was it amusing for you? Murdering this fellow?"

She reared back in shock. "Don't be ridiculous. I didn't end this man's life. Why would I?"

"He did call you a godless jezebel," the man guarding the body offered.

"Name calling is hardly reason for murder," she said wryly. "And in any case, I have been called worse."

"No doubt you have," the oaf from inside rasped. "Did he ask you to make him a new arm? Did you refuse? Did he not have the blunt for it? He must have resorted to stealing it, and you struck him down."

"That is nothing but absurd conjecture."

"She's just said she didn't know the man. Had never spoken with him," Kier said.

"I never spoke to him when he looked like this. Nor really when he was dressed as a curate. I just listened to him shout."

"You can tell the police just that and we'll see what they say." The sour man thrust his coat and the metal arm at one of his companions. He gestured to another, and the man stepped in front of Kier. The oaf reached for Kara, gripped her wrist tightly, and pulled her close.

Kara had learned early—and the hard way—never to tolerate a bully. A woman alone, without husband or family, and with much to lose, she knew she was vulnerable. A great deal of her life had been spent taking steps to protect herself.

When the scoundrel grabbed her, her instincts kicked in. Covering the man's knuckles with her hand, she swung her arm around, twisting his arm and shoulder and grabbing his wrist with her other hand. Twisted awkwardly, he was now the vulnerable one. She pushed him down and quickly stepped back.

It was a motion she'd practiced a hundred times, but she'd forgotten the metal pins and gears she still held. One of the sharp edges sliced through the linen of his shirt and through the flesh at the top of his wrist, too. He landed on one knee and looked up at her in disbelief. Blinking at the red line of the cut, he held his wrist high. "You see! All of you? She assaulted me!"

Growling, he rose to a crouch and launched at her.

Kier struck the man blocking him aside and moved quickly to

defend her, but there was no need. Kara waited, balanced on the balls of her feet, and when the oaf drew near, she ducked beneath his swinging arm and moved aside just enough to allow him to lumber past her. She also swept his feet with one of her own and sent him crashing into the crowd. There were curses and complaints as he stumbled and fell into the crowd. He lay there, breathing heavily and glaring at her while blood welled, coloring the white linen of his sleeve red.

"You think you are a cunning wench, don't you?" he wheezed. "Do you think to murder me next?"

"*You* grabbed *me*, sir. There is a crowd of at least twenty here who witnessed it. You are a bully and a blowhard. I have never harmed a soul in my life, nor would this incident have happened had you kept your hands to yourself."

Kier blew out a breath of exasperation. "Enough of this! None of us holds any authority here. Nor will we win favor by turning this into a scandal."

"He's right," the man guarding the body agreed. "The directors will wish us to keep this quiet."

"The Exhibition is turning out to be a great success, despite the months of criticism leading up to it," Kier reminded them all. "It's a jewel in England's reputation—and a boon to our business-es. Do we wish to be a part of dulling that shine?"

Kara was relieved to see the crowd muttering and shaking their heads.

"Then let's return to our positions. This good man will keep the scene clear for the police." He gestured toward the man who had been standing over the body.

"And what of her?" the oaf demanded. "She's dangerous!"

Kier's gaze lit up with dark humor. "Since you are frightened of the lady, I will take her and escort her to a magistrate, where she can tell her tale and answer any questions."

The bully heaved himself to his feet and grabbed back his coat and her metal arm. "I'll be keeping this. And I'll be telling my own story."

"As will all of us," someone said from the crowd. "And you don't come out so well, trying to manhandle the lady."

Others murmured their agreement.

Someone hissed at him. "Shame!"

Kier offered her his arm. She took it and, chin lifted, let him lead her through the press of bodies and back into the Crystal Palace.

Chapter Three

NIALL'S MIND WAS awhirl as he led Miss Levett along the British nave, past the fountain, and out into Hyde Park. This incident was not going to go well. All the possible impacts and complications swirled in his head like sparks flying from the forge.

It would be better if he did not involve himself.

And yet... Glancing over at Miss Levett, he noted her calm expression and the set of her shoulders, straight as an arrow—and he felt for her. He knew the cost of presenting an impenetrable façade to a cold, harsh world.

"Odin's arse," he said under his breath. "If only that hadn't plummeted from bad to worse."

She turned, and amusement smoothed the faint wrinkle between her brows—the only sign of turmoil she hadn't been able to suppress.

"Odin's *arse*?" she asked.

He sighed. "My apologies. My assistant has a varied vocabulary. It seems I've picked up a few bad habits."

"Why Odin's *arse*, though?" She sounded genuinely curious.

"Well, it used to be Odin's eye, but she worried he might be sensitive about it, having traded it away."

Miss Levett's brisk pace faltered. "She? Your assistant is a woman?"

"She is," he said agreeably.

"And she works in the forge with you?"

"She does."

Miss Levett blinked and then resumed walking. "Interesting."

"No more interesting than the way you handled that oaf of a furniture maker back there."

She kept her gaze fixed on the people strolling near the Serpentine as they grew closer.

"I've never seen anyone move like that in an altercation. Your every motion was smooth and efficient. Where did you learn such a thing?"

"Various teachers."

"Teachers. But how? Why?" he asked.

Hesitating, she pursed her lips, and he thought she would rebuff him for his impertinence. Instead, she drew a deep breath, stopped, and met his eye. "I come from a very wealthy family. The first time someone tried to abduct me, I was eleven years old."

"The *first* time?" he repeated woodenly.

She nodded. "It was the only time they succeeded in taking me. My father saw to that. He started my training once I was home again." She shrugged a shoulder and started to walk again. "But I enjoy it. I've kept on with it, even after he passed."

"Your training." She was going to think him a fool, the way he kept repeating her words, but she kept surprising him. "Who trains you?"

"Anyone who can help me think, fight, move, or escape. I've learned from celebrated pugilists, tawdry magicians, champion marksmen, and even a particularly dirty fighter I saw in the street."

He walked in silence for a moment, absorbing that extraordinary notion. But then he cleared his throat. "It stood you in good stead today. In the short term. But you must think in the longer term of what happened today. They are going to come down hard on this murder case. One way or another."

She nodded but didn't speak.

"That buffoon back there, he isn't going to make it easier on them."

"No. His sort is never quiet by choice."

Niall frowned. Calm was one thing, but indifferent was another. "You understand that the prince and the scientists and industrialists need the prestige of a grand success. They will not allow—"

She cut him off with a glance. "I am not a fool, Mr. Kier. If possible, the authorities would bury this crime completely. The likelihood of that is small now." She shook her head. "If they cannot keep it quiet, they will need to demonstrate swift and decisive justice."

"They won't concern themselves with true justice," he warned.

She sighed. "I am an easy target, it's true. But I might be a troubling one, as well. A killer arrested—and a woman? The papers would seize upon such a story. But a lady with connections to the peerage? Heiress to a fortune? The sensation would be irresistible. The city would be plastered in lurid headlines. It would be the last thing the authorities would wish for."

He raised a brow. "It might be enough to protect you. But it might not."

"I agree. If there is pressure from the press, the populace, or the Crown, they might just find it expedient to arrest me."

"I hate to say it, but I fear you are right." He nodded ahead at the busy junction of Hyde Park Corner. "We can get a hack over there, but you should not go home."

Her mouth twitched. "You don't actually propose to take me to a magistrate?"

He grinned. "I do, if only to be able to answer truthfully if asked. But do not worry; it's not what you think. He is not a proper sort of magistrate. You'll be safe."

She shook her head. "I will only be safe when the killer is

caught. Unfortunately, I do not trust that the authorities possess the ability or the interest to do the job correctly."

"Nor do I." They had reached the crowded intersection of streets. "There's a hack just there." Pointing, he tugged her toward it. "You need to stay hidden for a time."

"No. I need to find the killer."

His hand fell away. "You? *You* need to find the killer?"

"Who else has so much at stake?"

"But...how? We don't even yet know *who* was killed! How do you propose to find the killer?"

"The same way that the police should do it. Through reason and investigation and thoughtful deduction."

He stood for a moment, at a loss. It had been a calculated risk, taking a spot as an exhibitor, but it was one he'd been willing to make. He'd been but one out of hundreds of exhibitors, easily overlooked. But this? Messing about in a situation sure to interest the people, the government, and the Crown? Interfering with an official investigation? It could be courting attention from exactly those he needed to avoid. It would be foolish. It would be better if he did not involve himself.

But could he abandon her? He thought not. He didn't even wish to, truth be told. She was so intriguingly direct, so startlingly different from the significant women in his life. And more vulnerable than she believed. He would simply have to find a way to stay out of sight in this matter. In the shadows, where he belonged.

He heaved a sigh, then shook his head. "Do you know, of anyone, I do believe you might just be able to do it." He turned to wave at the hackney driver. "Let's get you settled and we'll discuss how to begin." The driver caught his signal and nodded. "There. He'll take us. Let's go."

She didn't reply. Niall swung around—but she was gone.

He startled, darted around the couple who had moved in behind him, and searched frantically through the intersection.

And found no sign of her.

Damn it all. He cursed further, in his head, as he stalked to the hack.

"Where can I take you?" the driver asked carefully. Apparently, Niall's temper was showing.

He stood a long moment in thought, then climbed up on the step. "Mayfair," he said shortly. "Berkeley Square."

≫≫≫⟪⟪⟪

IT TOOK A good while to find the man she needed to speak with. In normal circumstances, Kara would ask Turner to locate him. Her butler-turned-lab-manager-assistant and closest friend was often forearmed with an encyclopedic treasure trove of information she needed. He was also impressively quick at discovering what he already didn't know. But Turner was back at Bluefield Park, and she judged it unwise to return home just now.

She was perfectly capable of doing her own digging about, though, and by midday, she stood outside a shop on Catherine Street, staring at the sign.

Mr. Harry Boggs
Bootmaker
Tool Repair
Surgical Mechanic

She brushed off a twinge of guilt. It hadn't been kind of her to ditch Mr. Kier earlier, and in such a fashion. He seemed a genuinely nice man, and she believed he wished to help her.

But time was of the essence. She'd had a target and needed to move quickly. Honestly, he was a bit of a distraction. All that gorgeous masculinity—it threatened her focus, tugged at her awareness. She couldn't afford any dulling of her senses right now. She couldn't let him slow her down.

And she'd never yet met a man who could keep up.

With a shake of her shoulders, she let herself in the shop and stood a moment, sorting through the assortment of smells. Leather, oil, hot metal, and…wood shavings?

A volatile combination.

To her right stood a display of men's boots, spread over several shelves. She stopped to examine them.

"I do apologize, but we have no ladies' footwear." A man had looked up from his work. A wooden form sat next to him, draped in leather, but he was holding two twisted shapes of metal. As she watched, he glanced down, holding the pieces together and frowning at the comparison. "Most of my business is done with laborers," he said, obviously distracted. "Those boots are all for working men."

"Yes. I see how you've varied the form according to function," she called back. Leaning in toward the display, she nodded. "Your work looks very fine." She glanced back at him. "I might be interested in a couple of pairs of over-the-knee boots. The men who work my cider press must wade through the pomace, as well as deal with the mules who turn it."

He looked gratified as he set down the curiously shaped pieces of metal. Each was thin and round at the bottom, with a hole like a washer, but a thick stem rose out of it and curved to the left, while another, shorter branch curved to the right, near the top. He dropped his hands when he saw her watching, and picked up a file. "Get me the measurements and I'll have them ready for you quickly enough."

"I will." She moved farther into the shop, passing by a rack of refurnished tools and stopping when she spotted a glass case containing several limbs. A short leg and another with an articulated knee. Three arms. One of carved wood, very like the one the dead man had been wearing. Another that was purely functional, with the capability of attaching several different tools, according to need. But the third—that was the one that drew her. An idealized artificial hand, encased in leather. This was very close to one she had created herself not so long ago. She bent down to examine it.

The shopkeeper, trying to focus on the metal piece he was filing, noticed her interest. He set it all down and drew closer.

"Have you found unraveling to be a problem?" she asked, pointing down to the seams dissecting the leather shell, suggesting fingers.

The question surprised him. "Yes. It's vexing."

"I agree. Even more so when you separate the fingers." She tilted her head. "It's a horizontal joint with a spring plate?"

He blinked. "Yes, it is."

"I found it the best combination to allow the 'fingers' to curl in until they meet the thumb."

He looked impressed. "Yes. But there is still so much refinement needed. Another spring movement in the last joint of the thumb, I think, will help in holding a pen and perhaps actually allow writing."

"It will, but you are right, there is still a long way to go." She met his gaze. "Having to manipulate the spring catches externally is cumbersome and slow."

"It is. And awkward in company." He frowned. "Have you a relative who has lost a limb?"

"No. Why?"

He shrugged. "I find it is the most common way that men become interested in surgical mechanics, though I never met a female with the same interest." He cleared his throat. "My brother lost a leg in a mine."

"I'm sorry. It was a tenant for me. An agricultural accident. I have a bit of experience with clockmaking and other engineering. When he was pronounced healed enough, we began to experiment with making an appendage that would be the most useful for him."

He stared. "Forgive me, but are you the baron's daughter? Miss...Levett, is it not?"

"It is." Smiling, she clarified, "Or I am." She inclined her head. "And I presume you to be the Mr. Boggs indicated on the sign outside?"

"Indeed." His eyes had gone wide. "I have heard of your work. You are part of the Great Exhibition, are you not? I have heard tales of your case clock, your sailing ship, and of your automaton. People have raved over them."

"It is very kind of you to say so." She met his gaze directly. "The Exhibition is why I have come. There has been an incident."

"An incident?"

"A murder. A man involved was wearing a wooden arm of your creation."

"Mine?" He drew back, his expression darkening. "How could you—"

"I saw the maker's mark on the piece," she interrupted.

He frowned. "And you recognized it as mine?"

"No. However, I am good friends with Dr. Balgate." The crusty old surgeon had been a friend of her father's. Known for his skill with difficult wounds and tricky amputations, the old man knew nearly everyone who worked with amputees. "He knew your mark. And I see it repeated on the pieces in your case."

Boggs sighed. "My clientele for such work is small. The sad truth is that I can almost guess who is mixed up in such trouble."

"The number on the piece was thirty-four."

He closed his eyes. "Who has he killed?"

She had to force herself to stay calm and not move toward him. "What is the man's name, Mr. Boggs? The man who wore that carved arm?"

"Mr. Walter Forrester." He frowned. "Is he not cooperating?" He slumped onto a stool. "It's like him, isn't it? I'll never see the money he owes me now."

"Forrester," she repeated. "What do you know of him? Has he family? Friends? You must at least have record of his address."

"I know he lived just off the Lambeth Road when he ordered the limb from me. He's since slunk out of there without paying his rent, as I discovered when I sent the bailiffs after him. They have yet to discover where he's hiding now."

"And before? His family?"

He made a face. "Country gentry, I believe. From somewhere in Shropshire." He raised a brow. "I hope you are not consorting with the man, Miss Levett. He is a bounder and no fit companion for someone like you."

"I am not. It appears that Mr. Forrester stole an arm from my automaton during the night. He was found outside the Exhibition this morning. Someone pulled a long arbor from the arm and stabbed him with it. I'm sorry to say that he is dead, sir."

"Good heavens," he breathed. He looked genuinely shocked.

"Gossip is already spreading. Some are saying that I must have confronted and killed him during the theft."

"I wouldn't blame you, if you had. The man could tempt a saint."

"I did not kill him," she said firmly. "He was watching me closely, though. Several times I noticed him standing down the nave and staring quite directly."

"If your automaton is half as brilliant as I've heard, then I am not surprised to hear it. He wanted a new arm. A better one." He nodded. "It's beginning to make sense now. This was a new obsession, you see."

"New?"

"Yes. When he first came to me, he only cared about making the limb look natural. Proportional. A match for his remaining arm and a good fit for his gloves. Perhaps it was the Exhibition that set him afire for something better." He shrugged. "He came back, wanting another. One that could function more like a real hand." He gestured at the one in the case. "More intricate than that one, he insisted."

"I imagine you refused to take on the project?"

"When I had yet to be paid for the first? Of course I refused. I make the bulk of my income on my boots, in any case. The appendages are something I began to dabble in when my brother was in need. I don't make enough money on them to speak of."

"I don't understand why your Mr. Forrester stole the arm

from my automaton. It's nothing like a piece I would make for an amputee. Completely unusable in such a way."

"He wouldn't know it. He likely wouldn't believe it if you told him. He spoke often of being 'normal' again. He wouldn't wish to hear anything contrary to that dream."

"Perhaps he meant to have the workings adapted? Would he have taken the arm to another surgical mechanic? Do you know if he consulted with anyone else?"

"He asked for recommendations. I declined to give him any, as he still owed me."

She sighed. "Well, you have given me something to begin with. At least I know now who he was."

Boggs frowned at her. "I find it surprising, Miss Levett, that you are here ahead of the police."

"Well, as one who has already been informally accused of the crime, I find I might be more motivated than the authorities."

"I see."

"They will likely come to you, eventually."

He didn't look as if he liked the notion.

"I hope you will answer them as you have me, sir."

"I will, of course." He hesitated. "Don't waste a moment mourning Forrester, miss."

"Though he was clearly troubled, he was still a fellow man. And he had his life stolen from him. I would mourn anyone in such circumstances. As I hope we all would."

"Yes, of course. And I will take leave to mourn the guineas he owed me."

"I appreciate your help, sir." She turned toward the door. "I should go."

He escorted her. "I wish you good luck, Miss Levett. I'm afraid you are going to need it."

Chapter Four

I T WAS ONLY fitting that the most elaborate door in the square would grace Lord Stayme's home. Nothing plain or understated for the viscount. His door was elaborately carved and polished—and equipped with a new knocker, too, since Niall's last visit.

He laughed at the cheeky monstrosity. Two dancing nymphs adorned the sides of the metal oval, both bare of breast, with flowing hair. Their raised arms created the top. Each had a leg raised and entwined with her sister's, forming the grip, while a leering face grasped their knees and peered out from between them.

Rolling his eyes, Niall grabbed the brash thing and knocked briskly. Anyone unfamiliar with Lord Stayme would be forewarned, at least.

The impassive butler greeted him with a nod. "Welcome, Mr. Kier. If you'll step in here, I shall see if his lordship is at home."

"He'll see me, Watts," Niall assured the servant as he stepped around him. Ignoring the anteroom, he headed down the hall toward his lordship's study.

It was a sign of his standing here, as well as the butler's wisdom, that Watts did not argue. "I shall bring tea," he intoned.

Niall swung the door open and stepped into the room without hesitation. Flooded with light from the midday sun, the study was done up in the highest taste, with the most expensive materials, by a most discerning eye—just like the thin, debonair, older gentleman who sat at the ornate desk.

"Niall, my boy!" The viscount's look of surprised pleasure turned to shocked disapproval. "Bollocks and blazes, boy! When was the last time you cut your hair?"

Niall winced. "When was the last time you minded your own business, old man?"

Stayme laughed. "I've been mucking about in everyone else's business far longer than you've been growing your hair. Far longer than you've been alive, in fact. And well enough that I have, eh? Or where would you be today?"

"I might not be here at all, and well I know it." Niall took the seat opposite as the door opened and Watts came in with a tray. "I don't often say it, but I do appreciate it."

Stayme watched him while Watts poured. "Bring us some of the good brandy from the cellar—there's a good man, Watts." The viscount sounded pensive. "I think perhaps we shall need it."

The old man leaned back with his cup and peered at Niall over the rim. "Now, what's this about? I've sent no word. All remains calm and quiet—despite your decision to flaunt yourself at the Exhibition."

"I'm not *flaunting*," Niall protested. His mouth quirked. "I saw you on opening day, in the queen's procession. I saw the moment you spotted me. You didn't so much as meet my eye—and I am grateful."

Stayme laughed. "You are welcome, dear boy. But is it wise? It's not like you to be so...flagrant."

"It is a calculated risk." Niall hardened his gaze. "I know I am bound by agreements that I did not make, but I mean to live my own life, and I will make the best of it. I stick to my sphere but will not pass up opportunities."

"Of course, of course," the viscount said. They both fell silent as Watts entered with the brandy and added a liberal pour to their cups. "Thank you, Watts. Leave it, if you please."

Niall appreciated the smooth warmth of the liquor. "I didn't come to explain myself. I came for information."

He'd managed to surprise the old man. "Above and beyond our usual arrangement?" Stayme asked. His eyes narrowed. "That I offer as tribute to your charming mother, as you know. Anything else will cost you, just the same as anyone else."

"I can pay. And in your favorite coin."

The viscount laughed. "I doubt you even know what that is."

"Oh, I do. I have a very juicy story to tell—and it's one no one else yet knows."

The old man's eyes lit up. "I'm listening."

"There is trouble at the Great Exhibition."

Stayme leaned forward. Niall could see the questions bubbling.

"An incident." He held his silence for a beat. "A murder."

The viscount grew serious. "Tell me everything."

Niall told the tale.

Stayme listened. He asked several questions. Once Niall had finished, the old man sat back, fingers steepled, lost in thought. "Levett's girl," he mused. "She's a curious one." His gaze sharpened. "Is it her you wish to know about? Or do you wish my help in identifying the dead man?" He raised a brow. "Juicy as your tidbit is, it will buy you one, but not both."

Niall tamped down a surge of frustration. How he would love to hear everything Stayme knew about Miss Kara Levett. He shook his head and paused a moment to ask himself why he was going to so much trouble. He didn't quite know the answer. He knew only that she fascinated him. An heiress. Her own words. But so different from women he'd known who had possessed any measure of wealth or any modicum of power. Deep intellect rather than shallow understanding. Interest in the world rather than self-absorption. And he felt as if he'd only scratched the surface of her. She was unique. She made him feel as he did in the presence of a great masterpiece, full of awe and appreciation and possibility.

Yes. He wished to help her. And that meant curbing his curiosity and prioritizing.

"Discovering the man's identity should be easy for you, my lord." He raised a brow in challenge. "Young. Blond. Enough money to pay for expensive tailoring and the knowledge of where to find it. One arm. I should think you likely know him already."

"Well, I do not. Not right off." Stayme frowned. "But I do have an inkling..." He rose and approached a bookcase. One entire shelf was lined with handsome leather-bound volumes marked with numbers on the spines. "You are wise, indeed, to recognize the resource you have in me, my boy." He ran a finger along the row of books. "Let me think...last spring, was it not?" He pulled out a volume and brought it back to the desk. "Yes. It's a vague memory only, but...yes. The Countess of Darham's garden party on the river."

Craning his neck, Niall could see the book was a journal, all in neat, bold handwriting.

"I spoke that day with Lord Peter Norwood."

Niall straightened. "Brookdale's son?"

"Brookdale's *heir*," Stayme corrected him. "And you may wipe the dismay from your face. He is not your victim. But he was attending with a friend—a young blond gentleman. I might not have noticed him, beyond noting his pretty face. But someone made a snide remark about his inability to row out with the young ladies." He made a face. "The comment was not made to me, but, of course, I heard it."

"Of course you did." The uncanny man heard everything, one way or another.

"I had to ask about the lad, then, didn't I? He'd lost his arm in a boating accident when younger. A shame. He was quite handsome."

Niall leaned in. "His name?"

Stayme peered down at the journal. "Here it is. Forrester. Walter Forrester." He ran a finger to a thin column at the side of the page. "Minor gentry. Family apparently has a reputation for bad behavior, out there in the wilds. No blood ties to the peerage, but he'd formed a close bond with Lord Peter. Thick as thieves, it was reported. Perhaps you can learn more from him."

Niall drained his cup and closed his eyes to appreciate the burn of the brandy. "I will find him." His tone gentled as he eyed the gentleman he'd known since he was in leading strings. "Thank you, old man."

Watts entered as he rose. The butler handed a folded note to the viscount. "One of your young runners just brought it in from Whitehall, sir."

"Hold, my boy." Stayme held out a hand before Niall could take his leave. "You might wish to speak to your Miss Levett first." He glanced up. "It seems Scotland Yard is now looking for her."

KARA CAME OUT of the secret door into Turner's rooms at Bluefield Park and was surprised to find the butler gone and the suite empty. She moved through to the outer door and eased it open. Listening a moment, she could hear no one moving in the long corridor. All lay quiet, as it should at this late hour. The servants would have long since finished their dinner. She could hear the faint murmur of voices from the servants' hall, but no indication of anything unusual.

Satisfied, she left the way she'd come and continued on up the hidden passage to her own rooms. These were unlit as well, but she didn't need light to navigate them. After closing the hidden door behind her, she crossed the sitting room, reaching for the bellpull—only to freeze as a deep voice emerged from the dark.

"Don't ring. And don't light a candle or lamp."

Her pulse jumped into a gallop. Moving carefully, she lowered her arm and turned. A large, shadowed form was seated on her favorite chaise. She inhaled discreetly. Citrus and cedar and a tinge of smoke.

Her tense muscles relaxed. "Well, Mr. Kier," she said easily, "you may force me to revise my thinking." He had surprised her. It didn't happen often. Might he, indeed, be a man who could keep up with her?

"Have I?" He sounded just as casual, as if invading a woman's private apartments, lying in wait, was a normal occurrence. "In what way?"

"Never mind."

He waited a beat, but she didn't give in to the silent invitation to elaborate.

"Miss Levett," he said carefully, "have there been many people in your life who find you infuriating?"

"A great many." She pursed her lips. "Have there been many in yours who find you annoyingly persistent and apt to push in where you don't need to be?"

"None at all."

"Well, you can start counting today."

He laughed. "I will."

She sighed. "I am aware I owe you an apology, sir. I was unpardonably rude this morning, leaving you that way. But surely you could have waited until next we met?"

"I'm not here for an apology, Miss Levett. I am here to warn you. There is a police inspector awaiting you in your drawing room."

He stood, and she saw his indistinct form move to stand to one side of the west-facing window.

He'd surprised her again.

"Thank you," she said. "I did spy the constable lurking at the gate, which is why I had the hackney drive on around. I did not know of the inspector's presence below, however. It seems Scotland Yard is several steps behind, but not as slow as I expected." She paused. "I am surprised that Turner, my butler, was not here to apprise me of the situation."

"I instructed him to pack a portmanteau for you. I asked if he could get it out without anyone knowing, and he said to tell you he would leave it in the wood."

"You told him—" She stopped. A rare occurrence—finding herself at a loss. She found she didn't much enjoy it.

"Yes, well, he found me in the passageway as I was searching for your rooms. After we finished brandishing weapons at each other, we talked about your situation."

"Weapons?"

He nodded. "Curious, that your butler carries a pocket pistol." He paused. "But perhaps a good thing after all."

She drew a deep breath. "What do you want of me, Mr. Kier?"

"I wish only to help."

"But why?"

He hesitated. The answer came at last, low and with a rough edge of emotion. "I'll say only that I found myself in trouble, once, through no fault of my own. If I had not had help, I would not have survived it."

She let out a sigh and sank into a chair. "What is it you are looking at out there?"

He turned toward her. She caught the gleam of moonlight in his eye. "It's your decision, whether to accept my help or continue on your own, but you should know this—there's something more afoot here."

"More than murder and me being suspected of it?"

"I think so. I made my way past the police posted outside easily enough, but I wasn't the only one to do so."

She straightened. "What do you mean?"

"Someone else has been waiting for you. Someone who knew about your alternative entrance."

"What?" She rose, coming to stand near him and peer outside.

He pointed. "A man was perched up on the roof of that outbuilding."

"The cider house." Feeling the weight of the look he gave her, she explained, "The press is in there, as is the other equipment and storage for casks." She stared out again. "How do you know about the other entrance?"

"Because I was watching him, quite as closely as he was watching for you. The man barely glanced toward the house. All of his attention was focused on that section of hedge, where we both saw you come through. He held his position until you entered the farthest outbuilding."

"My laboratory."

"He didn't wait for you to come out, but scurried down, crossed behind the laboratory, and left through the hidden door you used. Presumably, he went to report your arrival to someone—and not to the police, or they would have been in there or up here by now."

He was likely right—but what did it mean? The police were here because of reports from that buffoon from this morning, surely. Who else would be interested in her whereabouts?

"Since you never did emerge from your laboratory, I assume there exists a tunnel between the laboratory and the house?" He nodded toward the hidden door she'd come through.

"Yes, but I would ask you to keep that bit of information to yourself. Very few know of it, and I prefer to keep it that way."

"Of course." Folding his arms, he leaned a shoulder against the wall. "That spy might not know of it, still, but by now someone does know you are here. Whether you choose to accept my help or not, I would urge you to leave. Sooner or later, whoever set that watcher on you will arrive. Or perhaps the inspector downstairs will wish to be sure you are not hiding away up here."

He was right, of course, and she was sorely tempted to accept his offer. To give herself a moment to think, she whirled away. "You are correct. I should go. Just let me check to see that Turner didn't miss anything vital."

Kier followed her but stopped at the threshold of her bedroom. "One thing more," he said as she bent to run her fingers over the objects in her desk. "I've discovered the name of our one-armed victim."

She straightened up and stared in his direction. "What? You did? I discovered it as well."

They both spoke at once. "Walter Forrester."

She could barely see him, but she grinned and knew, somehow, that he must be smiling too.

There it was. A moment of connection that stretched out between them. And right then, her thinking shifted and she knew. There was more here than her unusual attraction to a large and masculine male. Perhaps he would turn out to be the one who could keep up with her. Perhaps he offered a challenge she hadn't even known she longed for.

"How did you discover him?" he demanded.

She slipped a couple of pencils into the pouch at her waist. "I will tell if you will."

He raised a brow at her deliberately cheeky tone. "Very well. I consulted a Society catalogue."

She frowned. "I was under the impression that Forrester was minor country gentry. Not the sort to be found in *Debrett's*."

"It wasn't *Debrett's*. More of a walking, talking, insult-slinging sort of reference."

"I see." She was impressed that he was not without his own resources.

"Forrester might not have had blood ties to the *beau monde*, but the young man had ties of friendship. Enough to make him known." He leaned against the doorjamb. "And you? How did you discover him?"

"I saw the maker's mark on the carved wooden arm this morning."

"You knew it?" He sounded surprised.

"No, but I have my own curmudgeonly guide to the world of mechanical surgery."

"Ah."

There it was again. A longer-than-usual moment of mutual appreciation.

"You did not happen to discover Forrester's address, did you?" he asked.

"Unfortunately not."

"Well, then." He straightened. "I do think we should see you safely away from here. Allow me that much, at least."

She nodded. "Very well, Mr. Kier. Let us go." She reached for a heavy wrap from her wardrobe. "In fact, I believe I will accept your offer of help."

"Excellent." He sounded altogether satisfied.

She let him have his moment of victory. "Yes. I think that together, we might just accomplish something."

Chapter Five

NIALL COULDN'T SEE how she'd triggered the hidden door.

"Stay here a moment," she ordered him.

He heard the rustle of skirts and the strike of a match. Faint light illuminated a small square room, covered in wood panels but otherwise bare, save for a small shelf.

She took up a miniature lantern, turned back toward him, and reached high. Behind her, a door in the back wall creaked open. He saw darkness—and a stone staircase curving down.

"Close the door and come along." She spun back and started down.

Hurrying, he followed.

They passed the landings of two more short hallways, ending in doors. One more level down and they emerged into a tunnel.

The lantern cast a small circle of light. He could see only that the floors were stone and the walls brick, but there was plenty of headroom, and he thought they would be able to travel two abreast.

She set off, and he moved beside her, admiring the construction as they went. These must be truly old. Dating from the build of the place, surely. Yet the stones were even, with no sunken spots or damp seeping through walls.

She noticed his attention. "Bluefield was originally an abbey," she told him. "One of my ancestors donated a warship to Queen Elizabeth's armada. The *Bluebell* was fast and maneuverable and showed well against the Spanish. In appreciation, he was gifted the abbey."

"I'm surprised there wasn't also a monetary donation," he murmured.

"Oh, there was, a sizeable one, indeed. But that was later, and that's when he was given the title and the estate in Sussex. But that all came after Bluefield Park had been renovated. When my ancestor arrived here to inspect his prize and make plans to turn it into a home, he found the tunnel that ran from the office of the abbess to the stables. He had it shored up and extended into a system of passages. They lead to several spots on the estate and one beyond the main park, in the bluebell wood he had planted in the ship's honor."

He nodded. "Tunnels and escape routes were useful in those times of court intrigue and assassination plots. But you said it remains a secret now. How is it also so well maintained?"

"With careful discretion. We keep a small number of stone-masons along with our gardeners. They have plenty of work, shoring up buildings and fences and ha-has, here and at the other estates and farms. But it is the head mason who is traditionally inducted into the secret and into the responsibility of keeping the tunnels sound."

"A trusted employee, indeed."

"Yes, and well rewarded for his loyalty. In fact, for the last nearly one hundred years, the position and the secret have passed from father to son in the same family."

He considered it all as they walked on, moving easily within the small circle of light.

"Do you still intend to take me to your magistrate?" she asked eventually.

"I think it's the wisest course."

"Why?"

"For multiple reasons. First, I know him and I trust him." She heaved a sigh, and he stopped to grip her arm. "I would trust him with my own life," he said, meeting her somber, dark gaze. "And I am aware I am trusting him with yours."

After a moment, she nodded. "As I have decided to trust *you*, Mr. Kier, I suppose I cannot quibble."

"There are other reasons," he said, letting her go and continuing on. "Towland is a true believer in justice. He will not be swayed by political pressure or hope of advancement. He will listen to your story and he will hear you."

"I hope you are right."

"Any objective person considering the facts will see you are blameless, or at the very least that the accusations against you are nothing but conjecture. He will make a report of his findings and opinions, and you will have an ally within the justice system— and the ability to truthfully tell anyone who asks that you have already answered the questions put to you by the authorities."

She pursed her lips. "Those are very good reasons."

"I know."

She chuckled. "You do not indulge in false modesty. It's a rare characteristic, but it's one I admire."

"Because you also eschew it?"

"Why else?" She grinned. "Such a waste of time."

The tunnel began to angle upward, and they climbed the gradual slope until they came to another set of stairs. At the top sat the promised portmanteau.

"Oh!" She frowned. "We've missed Turner."

"He probably went to check on the waiting police inspector."

"Very likely." But a wrinkle remained between her brows as she faced the door carved into a stone wall. Again, he missed her trigger, but suddenly the door shifted, just a bit, enough for her to get her fingers along the edge of it. "Will you help? It's heavy."

It was, but it was also well maintained. Once they got it moving, it swung open silently. She blew out the lantern and left it on a shelf similar to the first. He picked up the portmanteau and stepped through after her.

They emerged into a small space. A cave of sorts? The light was dim, though he knew the moon was bright outside. When she closed the door, it merged seamlessly with the rock.

"Where are we?"

"Near the river."

"I can smell as much." He heard the breeze moving through trees as well.

She took a step forward and one to the right and disappeared. She'd rounded a corner, and as he stepped around, he saw the small space was part of a shallow cave or indentation in a rocky outcropping. He moved out to the edge of it and looked back. You could not tell that small space existed, even from so close.

"Remarkable."

"It is. And quite useful." She gripped his arm as he turned. "Be careful where you step. It's best not to leave footprints."

"Understood." He hefted the portmanteau. "Now, how close are we to the village?"

"A bit of a walk, but not so bad." She set out, watching where she placed her feet. "Let's go, though. I gave the jarvey the price of a meal and told him I'd meet him at the tavern."

KARA KEPT HER expression even as a footman admitted them into a very fine townhouse on South Audley Street.

"I sent word earlier," Kier told the servant. "He should be expecting us."

"Indeed. He will see you in his study, sir."

Their footsteps echoed off the cold marble and around the stately entry hall. Just a few steps down the passage, though, the footman opened a door to announce them. A voice bade them enter, and she stepped into a very different atmosphere, indeed.

The room was warm and welcoming, the walls rich with carved paneling, leather-bound books, and bright art. A fire crackled, its light gleaming on the polished surfaces of several musical instruments, the most impressive of which was a tall, curved harp. The magistrate himself rose to his feet as they entered, not from his massive desk, but from a stool placed before a stand of music, where he'd been playing what looked like a very old lute.

"Niall, there you are. You are later than I expected." Approaching, he gave Kara a nod. "And you must be Miss Levett. Welcome."

"Thank you." She was oddly reassured by his warm smile and wondered if he was as charming as he first appeared.

"Miss Levett"—Kier stepped forward—"May I present Mr. Arthur Towland, magistrate of the police court at High Street, Marylebone."

"A pleasure, sir. Mr. Kier speaks highly of you."

"As I do of him," Towland said. "Welcome to my home."

"Thank you. Your home is beautiful."

Towland laughed. "Oh dear. Your face is as transparent as glass, Miss Levett. I can see you wondering how a police court magistrate can afford to live like this."

"Forgive me, sir. I don't mean to offend."

"But you are curious, I can see." He waved her farther into the room. "I don't mind sharing. Actually, my case is similar to yours."

"I am even more interested now, sir."

"We are both cadet branches of great families. Granted, I am several lengths further from the trunk of the family tree. Where you are the daughter of a baron, my grandfather was the third son of an earl. He had the audacity to make his own way in life, rather than hanging about, hoping his brother would take pity on him. He invested in shipping and became a wealthy man, if unfortunately tainted with the stink of trade. His son, my father, followed in his footsteps and developed an early interest in the railways. And so I found myself a young man with no need to work, but with an abhorrence of idleness."

"Another similarity between us, sir." She inclined her head.

"Excellent. In my case, I studied the law and became a barrister, intending to go into politics, perhaps stand for the Commons. But somewhere along the way, I discovered I prefer to more closely serve the people, in a more hands-on approach to justice. And so, you find me here."

"But is here a suitable place for us to talk?" she asked.

"As no formal charges have been placed against you, I can see no objection. Come, let us get comfortable and we can begin."

She glanced around as she took the seat he indicated before the fire. Kier moved to lean against the mantelpiece. As Mr. Towland sat across from her, she smiled at him. "Are you Ancient Order of Druids, sir? Or United Ancient Order?"

He stilled. "You are perceptive."

She glanced toward the triquetra inlaid in the wooden table between them, and to the elaborate trim of oak leaf and acorn framing the mirror across the room. "If I had to guess, I would say Ancient Order of Druids." She gestured toward the harp. "They have kept to the tradition of encouraging the appreciation of music, have they not?"

"They have. And you would have been correct, had you guessed years ago. But when the Great Secession came, I split away entirely and created my own sect, the Order of Druidic Bards." He sat back. "How is it that you are so familiar with the supposedly secret orders?"

"My family business began long ago with ironworks. That led naturally to manufactures. We own several of each now. There are always lodges in and around such industries. My own father was a member of the grand lodge here in London."

"Yet you were not."

"No. They've none of them seen fit to invite women. Yet." She smiled. "However, I was quite an industrious snoop when I was younger and fascinated by the very idea of the society."

Towland laughed, and Kier nodded toward his friend. "There are women who have been accepted as members of the Druidic

Bards."

"By which statement, I can also conclude that you are a member," she replied.

Kier raised a brow. "I told you, did I not?" he said to the magistrate.

"Unusual, you said. I begin to think that it was a vast understatement." Towland looked to her. "I think we should begin, Miss Levett." He steepled his fingers. "Tell me. From the beginning, please."

He let her speak without interrupting, and she told him all, holding back only the bit about Kier waiting for her in her rooms at Bluefield Park. The magistrate listened closely, and when she had finished, he went back to the beginning to ask for details, clarifications, and answers to questions she hadn't considered.

As they reached the end again, he heaved a sigh. "Your story rings true to me, Miss Levett, but it is the lack of anyone who can confirm your whereabouts that night that is troublesome. Can you think of no one?"

She shook her head. "I keep rooms close to the park for those nights I don't wish to ride all the way out to Bluefield Park after a long day at the Exhibition. I stayed there that evening, but saw no one."

"Not even a maid?"

"No, sir. I am quite capable of dressing myself." She sighed. "Usually I would speak with the lady who runs the coffee house downstairs, but she had closed early."

"As I said, that is the one thing that might give you trouble."

Kier straightened. "One thing more," he added apologetically. "Forrester was apparently close with Brookdale's heir. We should probably speak with Lord Peter, and soon." He gave her a shrug. "There was no time to tell you before."

She didn't have time to respond as Towland nodded and leaned in toward her. "Tell me," he said. "What would you have done had Forrester approached you outright and asked for a new appendage? Clearly, he did not have the blunt to pay for it."

She gave him a sharp look. "I have resources, sir. And skills. Like you, I am not one to stay idle. I have worked with difficult amputee cases before. Dr. Balgate has made such work his specialty, and he's come to me before with complicated stumps or desperate situations, because he knows I like the challenge and that I am happy to help to improve someone's lot in life. If Mr. Forrester had approached me openly, I would have begun work for him that very day."

"Why do you think he did not approach you? At least, not directly."

"I don't know," she said honestly.

"I think the answer to that is at the heart of the matter," Kier said. "His behaviors—staring at you from afar and disguising himself to harangue you—are not rational or logical. Not on the surface. We must discover what was spurring him, driving him from beneath."

She nodded her agreement. "It's also how we will find who killed him and why, I believe."

Towland drew a deep breath. "In your childhood snooping, Miss Levett, I assume you found that most members of the various orders of the Druids are simply looking for brotherhood, camaraderie, and a place to belong. They enjoy wrapping it up in a bit of flavor, in ceremony and ritual."

"Yes, save for those that are also looking for security and assurance, as from a benefit society—dues paid in with the guarantee that they and their families will receive assistance if they fall ill or die in poverty."

"All true. But there are those of us who are genuinely interested in the culture and learning of the old Druids, so far as we can discover. They were said to believe in the spirits of the natural world. It is intriguing to think of the spiritual nature of trees and mountains and rivers, but I am interested in the spirits of people. I don't mean that in the religious sense, but more along the lines of character. All of that to say—I like your spirit, Miss Levett. I think you are right. I believe your account and believe you innocent of involvement in the young man's death."

"Thank you." Something in her relaxed a small bit.

"I also believe you should indeed investigate Forrester while you can. I can tell you now—word has come down from on high. You are wanted for questioning, and you are a priority."

"She's wanted for appearances," Kier interjected.

"For a possible scapegoat," she said tightly.

"I'm ashamed to admit it might be true," Towland said. "I will do what I can. I will report our conversation in detail and my assurances that I believe you innocent."

"Will it go hard on you? If you don't bring me down to Whitehall?"

"No. My understanding is they want you questioned. I have done so. But there is an undercurrent. It is also understood that this needs to wrap up quickly."

"And it is quicker to find us than to start cold and discover the truth," Kier said bitterly.

She felt quite suddenly heartened and warm at his use of *us*.

"Just so. Keep looking. Find all you can, but stay in the shadows." Towland looked to Kier. "Niall, you were right to be careful. I'm not sure what will happen once she's in custody."

The magistrate had only confirmed their own conjectures, but still, his words chilled her. This was truly happening. To her.

Towland stood. "I would love to offer you tea and settle in for a good chat, but we should maintain every appearance of professional detachment. You were here, you answered all of my questions, and you departed under Niall's protection. My servants will be able to honestly confirm it." He gave Niall a significant look. "No one will know if I suggest you take her to the White Hart and tuck her away there." He went to his desk and took out a paper similar in size and weight to a bank note. She thought she saw the image of a stag printed upon it, his antlers dripping mistletoe. "Give this to Hywel when you arrive. There will be no questions, and he will see to her every need."

"Thank you." Niall clasped hands with his friend.

"If you find yourself in trouble, don't hesitate to go to The Grove. Bring Miss Levett, should you need to."

"I hope it doesn't come to that."

"Continue to be careful, my friend," the magistrate advised. "And be prepared. They will be coming to you next."

Of all the things Kara had thought and heard during this long, difficult day, that was the one that disturbed her the most.

Chapter Six

THE HOUR WAS late, but in this section of Mayfair, the dinners, balls, and soirees were still in full swing. They caught a cab easily. Niall gave the inn's direction and sat back against the worn seat.

"Thank you for convincing me to speak with your friend," she said quietly. "You were right. It was the wise thing to do. I think it will buy us a bit of time."

"You are welcome."

She stared out of the window, her hands clasped together.

"I understand you did not wish to mention our meeting in your chambers, but unfortunately, it left the existence of that other watcher out of the tale," Niall said.

Miss Levett continued to stare out the window at the passing night.

"We don't wish to forget him. He was not with the Scotland Yard men."

She gave a slight shake of her head.

He studied her profile. This cold detachment had descended on her after Towland's confirmation of their worries. "That man could have something to do with those hidden forces at work on Forrester."

Still nothing.

"Do you not agree?"

"No. I mean, yes. Of course I agree." She sighed. "It's just…" She breathed deeply. "There are always eyes on me. I sometimes feel like a caged animal in a traveling show. Fortune hunters, business rivals, matchmaking matrons with impoverished younger sons to marry off, young ladies who wish to crush my spirit or bask in the glow cast by my fortune…and the list goes on."

"Add in how many kidnapping attempts?"

"Four."

Three of which she'd fought off or eluded. The scope of everything they were facing suddenly loomed larger. He frowned. "Do you often go into Society?"

"Not often. Occasionally."

He straightened suddenly. "I know we mean to keep our profiles low, but is there someone, friends or loved ones, whom we should contact? Even if just to let them know what is happening and that you are well?"

"Oh, yes. When I am settled, I should send a note to Turner. He'll need to take my place at the Exhibition, I suppose."

"Turner? Your butler?"

Her shoulders stiffened. "Turner is more than a butler. He is my assistant and also my friend."

"Of course. Anyone else?"

"I should perhaps contact my man of business. We've several projects ongoing."

"What of family?"

"No. There's only my cousin. He might be in Town by now. He meant to bring his betrothed at some time during the Season. There's no need to bother him, however."

"You are not close?"

She shrugged. "We are friends. But not terribly close."

The carriage slowed. They had arrived at the White Hart. As he helped her disembark, he could not stop thinking of what she'd said. So many eyes upon her, but did none of them *see* her?

The hack ambled off, and for a moment they stood alone beneath the inn's painted sign. He took up her bag but paused and set it back down. "Miss Levett," he began quietly, "is there a chance that this is less about Forrester and more about you?"

The question stopped her short. She tilted her head up, and her eyes glittered in the dim light from the streetlamps. "About me?"

"Can you think of a reason someone would try to make it look as if you murdered a man?"

"No! Who would do such a thing? Why would they?"

He waited.

She paced a few steps away, and then back. "I understand why you are asking, but honestly—no. It would take a great deal of ill will to do such a thing. And there's the rub. No one cares that much." She swept a hand before her. "Behold, sir. A young woman who fits precisely nowhere. Not in Society. Not in business circles. Not in the scientific circles my interests might involve me in." She sighed. "Oh, they all watch. They stare and judge, as humans are wont to do with anyone showing differences. None of them know precisely what to do with me, but they don't hate me."

He nodded. "Understood. I have only one further question. Who would stand to benefit if something disastrous happened to you?"

She stared up at him. "I presume you mean my cousin?"

He spread his hands.

"No. Joseph and I don't live in each other's pockets, but we spent a good deal of time together as children, and we are friends. He is Baron Camhurst now. He has the title and the entailed estate in Sussex since my father's death. Joseph is easy to like, if a bit bland of personality. He enjoys the agricultural aspects of running Camhurst Place. He has an interest in a specific breed of cattle, although I cannot remember which one. He likes his hunting and his horses, and pursues a couple of pet issues in the House of Lords. He is...content. Legally, he has no right to the businesses or my father's fortune. Those came first, and from the beginning, they have never been part of the entail."

"That is an…unusual arrangement."

She gave a bitter laugh. "That ancestor received the title from a woman whose life was plagued by the issue of primogeniture. He knew better than to place all his eggs in one basket. The separation of the business and the title was written into the letters patent and has been the way of our family for generations. Joseph has not been trained for it. He would not be skilled at managing it all or seeing to the work that it generates, nor would he enjoy it. He is happy to leave it to me."

"Fine, then. I had to ask." He took up the bag. "Let's go in."

They found the desk in the entryway unmanned, most likely due to the ruckus sounding from behind the closed door to the taproom. "Hywel must have gone to settle whatever is going on in there." He gestured. "We will wait a moment."

She nodded, but she'd fixed her gaze on the floor between them. As he watched, she squared her shoulders and looked up.

"Mr. Kier, you've been so kind. You are clear-minded and concise in your thinking. Your help has been invaluable. I know you offered it freely, but perhaps you will have thought further about it by now. It is likely best if you do, and we part ways here."

Niall stilled as outrage stiffened his spine. "Excuse me?"

"Please. I'm so grateful, but I'm sure you will need to get back to your exhibit and to your business."

Various angry replies piled up. He was still sorting them when Hywel emerged from the taproom and spotted them. The small, dark man looked harried, but he tried to rally.

"Mr. Kier! How can I help you?"

Niall swallowed back all those sharp retorts. "Good evening, Hywel. This is Miss Levett. Towland has sent her." He laid his order's emblem on the desk.

Eyes wide, Hywel swept it up. "Indeed. A very great pleasure it is to meet you, Miss Levett. We will do all we can to make your stay a pleasant one. Our Woodland Chamber is ready and waiting."

He winced as a crash sounded from the taproom.

"Go on," Niall told him tightly. "Give her the key and I'll take her up."

"Thank you," the innkeeper said. He turned to Kara. "I do apologize. Jenny, our maid on duty this evening, is busy dealing with the mess inside, but I will send her up directly to see to your needs." He handed her a key, bowed, and hurried around them and through the taproom door.

"Come on, then," Niall told her shortly.

"I apologize if I've offended you," she said in a whisper as they climbed the stairs.

He guided her to the right and down to the end of the hall. She was distracted by the carved images on each of the doors. He understood. They had fascinated him his first time here. They passed a stone well. A cherry blossom. A circle of standing stones. He stopped in front of the last door. A grove of trees had been carved into it with fluid lines. He knew the chamber inside was large, comfortable, and welcoming.

Unlike his expression.

"I meant nothing untoward," she began. "Honestly. You have been kind. You have used your contacts to come to help my cause, and now you've found me a safe place to stay. I appreciate it more than I can say. I just don't wish to take advantage."

"I offered you my aid, Miss Levett. I meant it then. Neither my offer nor my intentions have changed." He knew he sounded stern and unyielding, but it was how he felt. "As you have failed to understand me, let me explain. I may not be within a branch's reach of a great family tree, but I am a man of honor. I would no sooner abandon you now than I would drag you down to the river to throw you in."

She started to speak, but he held up a hand.

"I know you are an accomplished lady. A woman of intelligence and vast capability. I do not doubt that you could likely weather this crisis without me. But there is no need for it. I have offered; you have accepted. Let us pool minds and resources and get through this as quickly and easily as possible. I assure you, I will ask nothing from you in return."

"I didn't think you would," she said quickly. "It's just, I don't wish you to neglect your work—"

He closed his eyes, and she stopped.

"My work." He paused. "I think I should return to the Exhibition tomorrow. All the better to appear as if my situation is back to normal, I think. You should stay hidden, though. We will speak to Lord Peter, but he's a young buck of the Town. He'll likely not even rise until well after noon."

She breathed deeply. "Very well."

He gave her a curt bow. "Now, if you are finished insulting me, I will bid you goodnight."

She reached out and grasped his arm. "Women have honor as well, you know."

His resentment ebbed a little. "Yes. I am aware of it."

"It's just…I am not skilled at accepting help." She hesitated. "I don't have many friends. Though we don't truly know each other, if feels as if a friendship could develop between us."

He softened further. "Yes."

"I heard what Mr. Towland said about them coming for you." Her mouth quirked. "It didn't feel wise to expose a new friend to persecution."

"Nor is it acceptable for me to leave a new friend alone and in possible danger."

She sighed. "We are at an impasse, then."

"It does appear so."

She let go. "We seem to have run the gamut of a great many experiences and emotions in one day. In light of it, why do you not call me Kara?"

"Thank you. I will, if you will call me Niall."

"Goodnight, Niall."

He stepped back, turned, and looked over his shoulder. "Goodnight, Kara."

THE SUN HAD barely inched over the horizon, but still painted the sky with broad strokes of crimson as Niall made his way to the Crystal Palace. He'd been at sea too many times, with superstitious seamen of every nation, to eye the brilliant sunrise with anything but trepidation.

Red sky at morning, sailor take warning.

He meant to be among the first exhibitors to arrive, if only to avoid the questions and stares he was sure to face today. A fairly successful strategy, as only a few others were venturing in now. He collected a couple of distant nods and felt the weight of several speculative stares as he moved on, but he wasn't truly surprised until he came down the nave toward his exhibit.

A man waited there, bent over a display case, examining the jewelry and small pieces. Niall slowed, taking the man's measure as he went. The fellow was big, though not as tall as Niall. Broad shoulders and long arms. The sort of man you'd want on your cricket team, though he looked middle-aged and going soft with it. He had the small paunch and the bright, crisp linen that spoke of a woman's care.

"Good morning," Niall called as he drew close. "You've come early. Most of the exhibits will still be unmanned."

A pair of birds swooped past as the man turned. "Ah, but I've had the chance to see a few things unmolested and without the crowds pressing in on me. I've been promising to bring my wife to see it all. She'll be all atwitter now that I've been inside, and I'll have to bring her along that much sooner."

Niall nodded and swept past him, stepping into his space and removing the first dust cover. "I daresay she won't be disappointed. I don't think any attendee has begrudged the price of admission."

"No, not that I've heard." The man eyed him closely. "You are Mr. Niall Kier, then? I rather thought so." He gave a formal nod. "I am Mr. Lionel Wooten, inspector with Scotland Yard."

Niall nodded in return.

"There is some fine and delicate work here. I've heard much of your compass rose talismans." He leaned in again. "I know a sea-mad boy who would go wild-eyed over the stories behind them."

Impulsively, Niall reached for the keys in his pocket. He opened the case and drew out a fob with the compass rose. "Please, take it for him."

Wooten drew back. "No. No. It wasn't intended as a hint, Mr. Kier."

"Nor did I think it was, but if a boy has the scope and imagination for such dreams, he should be encouraged."

The inspector's eyes widened. "Wise words. Thank you, then. I shall be glad to encourage him."

Niall handed it over. "Here investigating that poor man's murder, are you? I hope you can manage to keep the matter quiet."

"Ah, so you see the wisdom of keeping this from turning into a lurid headline affair?"

"I do, and so I told this lot yesterday morning." He gestured around them. "All of those months of the press bellyaching and naysaying and predicting disaster. It was a triumph for Prince Albert and his committees to have the Exhibition come off so well. It would be a shame to tarnish it now."

"That is the refrain, yes," Wooten said wryly. "I understand you found the body early yesterday morning?"

"No. A horde of street urchins found the body," Niall corrected him. "I found them—and tried to keep them from prying, prodding, and looting the poor sod until the authorities could arrive. Unfortunately, some hotheads caused a bit of a dustup."

"I heard about it."

"I hope you can manage to keep those blokes quiet."

Mr. Wooten's tone grew bland. "I believe they have been sufficiently cowed."

"Good."

"Tell me about the dustup, as you so aptly put it." The inspector pulled out a notebook. "What was it all about?"

"Honestly?" Niall eyed the man. "It was about some weak men who don't like being confronted by a woman who is demonstrably smarter and more talented. They saw the chance to knock her down a peg or two—and they took it."

"You don't subscribe to their theory? That she confronted the thief as he attempted to steal the metal arm and killed him in a fit of passion?"

"Not for a moment," Niall declared. "First, it makes no sense. That body, when we found it, was not freshly killed. The blood was nearly completely dried on that arbor. He must have been killed in the middle of the night. And believe me when I tell you, sir, we spend long days here, endlessly smiling and speaking and pressing flesh. At the end of the day we are exhausted and want nothing but to go home."

"Might the lady not have decided to work on her automaton figure that night?"

"Here? The patrolmen would have known she was here, were that the case. And I daresay Miss Levett has a superior workstation at home. Word is, she can afford it."

The inspector made a note.

"But the real reason I know it's rubbish is because I was here when she arrived yesterday morning. Actually, I was right there." Pointing, Niall told the inspector about the scattered gears. "I saw her arrive. I saw her face when she was a good ten feet away and noticed the empty spot where her automaton should have been. She was shocked. Dismayed."

"It wasn't put on for show?"

"No. She was truly distraught. She thought the whole figure was gone, until she rushed in and found the rest of it shoved beneath some furniture."

"I see. Tell me about the altercation outside."

Niall did, in detail.

"Do you perhaps know any of the boys who were out there yesterday?"

"No, although I would recognize a few of them, should I see them again."

"And when it was over, Miss Levett left, under your escort?"

"Yes."

"You said you were going to take her to a magistrate?"

"Yes."

For the first time, the inspector allowed a note of disapproval to show. "It would have been better if you did as you said, sir. We've seen no sign of the girl since she left with you. We wish to speak with her."

"So she can be sufficiently cowed?"

Wooten ignored his sarcasm. "If you see her again, I ask you to bring her down to Whitehall. She's wanted for questioning."

Niall frowned. "I'm unsure why you've taken this tone, sir. I did do just as I said. She's answered your questions."

That did surprise the inspector. "Excuse me?"

"I told them all I would take her to a magistrate, and so I did." He hoped like hell Wooten didn't ask *when* he'd taken her.

"*Which* magistrate?"

"Mr. Towland of Marylebone Police Court. He questioned her extensively. It's my opinion that he believed all she said and thinks her an unfortunate victim in this affair."

"Towland? Why take her to him?"

"I know the gentleman."

The inspector waited, pencil poised.

"He commissioned a set of gates for me, for one of his properties. I believe him to be a fair man."

Wooten pursed his lips. "I've certainly heard the same. Cannot bribe a man like that, eh?"

Niall did not answer.

"Did you stay while she was questioned?"

"I did."

"And then?"

"And then I put her in a hack and I went home." He did not add that he'd also climbed into the hack.

Wooten eyed him closely. "Have you seen her this morning?"

Niall looked down toward her exhibit space. "No."

"Do you think she'll be in today, then?"

He shrugged. "Most women wouldn't, would they? But she doesn't bear much resemblance to the women I'm acquainted with."

"I heard she's a pretty piece," the inspector ventured.

"Then you heard wrong. She's stunning."

"I heard that, too." Holding his silence for a moment, Wooten watched Niall re-lock the display case. "You haven't asked about the dead man's identity," he said quietly.

Niall looked up in surprise. "Have you found out who he is, then?"

"No. Not yet."

He let his shoulders slump, as if in disappointment. "Oh. Well, I'm sure you will discover it, but I do hope you find his killer."

"We will." Wooten flipped his notebook closed and tucked it away. "Thank you for your cooperation, Mr. Kier. I believe I'll leave a man here to see if Miss Levett decides to return, while I go and have a word or two with Mr. Towland."

"Give him my compliments, if you will. And my thanks again for seeing the girl."

"I will. Thank you again for the compass rose."

"I hope it inspires the lad."

"As do I." Wooten nodded. "I like you, Mr. Kier. But I've been at this for a long time. Long enough to spot a man with secrets."

Niall gave a bitter laugh. "Every man has secrets, Inspector Wooten."

"True enough. True enough. Good day to you."

Niall watched him go for a moment, then turned back to his dust covers.

Chapter Seven

"I BELIEVE YOU can trust him," Turner said, his mien serious. "I've been looking into him. Not much is known, but everyone I've spoken to insists he is an honorable man."

Kara's butler had arrived early this morning with a trunk of clothing, her post, and other necessities. She'd felt an immediate and enormous sense of relief. Nothing seemed quite real until she'd discussed it with Turner. They'd had a hurried cup of tea in the parlor attached to her room and caught each other up.

"I'm glad your sources confirm it, but I've already decided to trust Mr. Kier." She smiled to reassure him. "So far, he's more than earned it. We are to speak to Lord Peter about Forrester today. I'll send word of what we discover."

"Shall I return to Bluefield after the Exhibition closes?"

She could see the strain this last day had caused him. Sometimes she forgot how much older he was. "I suppose so. You should try to act as if everything is going on in usual fashion."

"What should I say if Inspector Wooten returns?"

"I hope he will not, but if he does, you can tell him that I sent word that I would be staying with friends for a few days."

He donned his coat and gave her hand a squeeze.

"Don't worry so," she told him. "We've dealt with these situations before. We're prepared."

He shook his head. "This is different."

"Still. We are up to the challenge, Turner."

He drew a deep breath and nodded his agreement before he left.

Kara went to the trunk. After unpacking quickly, she began to dress. Mr. Kier—Niall—had said he would send word to her this afternoon, but she had no intention of wasting the morning.

She managed to confine her hair neatly into a couple of braids and a heavy knot at her nape, then passed regretful fingers over her favorite bonnet. She loved wearing the unique piece. The specially customized drafter's compass spoke volumes about who she was. But she was meant to be blending in right now. She chose a larger, duller bonnet instead, hoping to conceal more of her face. She'd just taken it up when a knock sounded on the door. Expecting the maid, she called permission to enter.

It was not the maid.

A sharp-featured blonde swept in, eyeing Kara with obvious curiosity. "Good morning!" She raised a brow. "Well! Niall has spoken of you several times, but he never said you were beautiful."

Kara blinked, unable to summon a proper response. The woman wore a tightly fitted jacket, made of alternating panels of cobalt-blue wool and rich brown leather, stitched together with a heavy, decorative herringbone pattern. Her matching blue skirts swirled as she turned to go into the parlor. "I've never actually been in this suite of rooms. Very nice, indeed."

Kara followed as the woman took a seat at the small table where the tea dishes still sat. Grinning at her, she spoke again. "Pardon my manners. I forgot to introduce myself. I am Gyda Winther. I work with Niall."

Comprehension dawned. "Oh! You are his assistant?"

"Is that what he is calling me now?"

"You work in the forge with him, he said."

"I do."

Kara dropped the bonnet and went to sit across from her. "I

have a great many questions I'd like to ask you."

"About Niall?"

She frowned in surprise. "No, Miss Winther. About you. About your work, and your life."

Miss Winther grinned. "Call me Gyda, please." Her slanted eyes and defined bone structure gave her the look of a mischievous vixen. Her gaze wandered over the things Turner had brought, from the small collection of tools on the desk, to the pile of mail and invitations heaped on the side table, next to a set of open notebooks, filled with columns of numbers and notes about business. She looked back to Kara. "I have a couple of dozen questions I'd like to ask you, too." She stood. "But not now. I've yet to see my bed, and I must rest before I take over for Niall this afternoon at the Crystal Palace." Heading for the door, she said over her shoulder, "Niall says he will meet you here at half past two."

"Wait. You'll see him before then, before he leaves the Exhibition?"

"Yes."

"Then tell him not to come all this way. I'll meet him at the coffee shop on Adams Road, off Upper Seymour. It's a short walk from the park."

"Very well, then," Gyda answered with a yawn.

"It was a pleasure to meet you," Kara called after her. "Good day!"

"Goodnight!" Gyda called back.

With a grin, Kara took up her bonnet again. The maid came in, and Kara sent her downstairs to arrange for a hack.

Traffic moved quickly, and she soon found herself disembarking at the door of a solid, comfortable-looking townhouse on Red Lion Street.

The footman who opened the door looked surprised to see her.

"Good morning, Creech," she said briskly. "Has Mr. Moseman left for the office yet?"

"Good morning, miss. No." He glanced nervously over his shoulder. "The family is still at breakfast."

"Excellent." She breezed in, forcing the servant to step back. "I shall join them."

"But miss! I should warn you—"

Too late. She was through the breakfast room door before he could finish. She removed her gloves as she continued in and greeted her man of business. "Good morning, Moseman." She swept on, smiling warmly at his wife. "Joanna, good day to you." Their pretty adolescent daughter grinned at her as she tweaked her braid. "Harriet." Then Kara calmly turned to stare at her cousin hovering at Mr. Moseman's shoulder. "Joseph! Whatever are you doing here?"

Instead of answering, he glared down at the man who helped her run her businesses. "You said she was not here!"

"Nor was she." Mr. Moseman gestured in her direction. "As you can see, she's just arrived."

Her cousin looked back at her. "Is it true? Have you just arrived?"

"Of course. I often come here to breakfast."

As usual, Joseph was easily distracted. "Why?"

"Why? Because I can speak to Moseman without interruption." She smiled at their hostess. "Because Mrs. Moseman's cook makes the most excellent sweet buns." Taking a seat next to Harriet, she grinned at her. "And because young Miss Moseman always knows the best gossip, and which salons and soirees have a scientific slant, or some other good reason to attend." She wrinkled her nose. "Honestly, Joseph. You know Mr. Moseman is my right hand. The Exhibition is showing how advanced our society is becoming, but we haven't come so far as to allow a woman like me to head up the family businesses and manufactories."

"I should say we haven't," he said, disapproving at the very notion.

She sighed. "But you know I have a hand in the direction of

the companies. We often discuss the work here before the start of the day." She tilted her head up at him. "But you have not answered my question, Joseph. Why are you here?"

"I am looking for you, of course!"

"He's been spinning a horrendous tale about your being taken up for murder," Mrs. Moseman said. "Tea, dear?"

"Yes, thank you."

"Tea? Tea?" Joseph was clearly overset.

The footman had followed her in. He pulled out a chair, and her cousin sank into it.

"Joseph prefers coffee, Creech," Kara informed the servant.

"Yes, miss."

"How calm you are," Joseph marveled. "While I've been in a tizzy since last night when the police arrived, looking for you and asking if you might have strangled a one-armed man."

"Of course she did not!" Harriet said stoutly.

"Thank you, dear." Kara smiled at the girl then turned to her cousin. "In point of fact, the man was stabbed, not strangled, but I had nothing to do with it."

"Strangled. Stabbed. Dead, isn't he?" Joseph waved a hand. "And if you weren't involved, then why was Scotland Yard at my house looking for you last evening?"

"Because, before he was killed, the man stole the arm from the automaton I've been working on at the Exhibition. They had questions for me. I spoke with a magistrate and answered them. Now they are free to look for the real killer."

"Thank heavens." Mrs. Moseman sighed. "I hope they find him quickly."

"As do I," Joseph said fervently. "They said you have built another of your machines—and this one looks remarkably like a real man. Why should this fellow steal the arm and not the whole thing?"

Kara shrugged. "Presumably because he wanted to use it as a model for a limb for himself? More pressing is who killed him, and why."

"More pressing is where you have been," Joseph declared. "The police inspector said you were not at home last evening, nor had you returned when I rode out there at the crack of dawn."

"I spent the night at the residence of a friend." Not a complete lie, if she counted Niall Kier as a new friend. And Gyda Winther, as well.

"It must have been so unsettling for you, my dear," Mrs. Moseman said gently.

"It was, but I hope it will be over soon."

"Yes," Joseph agreed. He sipped his coffee. "It's not done, Kara, getting involved with murder and gallivanting around Town. You must take better care. Let me tell you, it's most unsettling, having a police inspector come to your home. And in the middle of a dinner party, no less!" He shook his head. "My betrothed and her family were in attendance, and they were quite shocked."

"I am sorry, Joseph, to have worried you." Kara gave him a fond glance. "And I hope your Miss Bailey is not too put off. I know you care for her."

He flushed a little. "Yes, well, she is a most comfortable sort of girl. Always knows just what to do or say. Indeed, it was her notion that I look for you here."

"How resourceful of her."

"It was. I was so scattered, I had no idea where to look. It seems you are always at Bluefield, Kara."

She nodded. "Yes, but it seems now I am always at the Exhibition. You must come and see me there."

He considered. "It would make a good outing." He was still caught up in his nostalgia, though. "I hope we can visit you at Bluefield, as well. Audrey would like to see the place." He smiled, his composure recovered. "I have so many fond memories of running about there with you. And I've never yet seen a bluebell wood so glorious."

"Of course, you must bring her for a visit. I'll have Turner arrange it. And we will make more memories, Joseph," she assured him.

"First, we will make memories at my wedding. Audrey wishes to speak with you about it. I was meant to tell you so, if I found you."

"Well, both of your duties are discharged." She reached into the bag at her waist and pulled out her notebooks. "But now, I must speak with Mr. Moseman. We have business matters to discuss, and he will be anxious to be on his way."

"Very well." He rose, gave his thanks, and made his good-byes.

"Come, Harriet." Mrs. Moseman rose after he was gone. "You know how these two get. Let's see to your lessons and let them discuss the aging smelting buckets at the ironworks."

"No, today it is contracts with shipping companies," Kara corrected her cheerfully. She turned to Mr. Moseman. "If Cardea Shipping wants fittings that will hold their new ship together, they will have to pay our price. If they go with Ashworth's, they will get what they pay for."

She slipped into the familiar cadence of their business dealings and, for a short while, let herself forget all of the drama of the last twenty-four hours.

⟫⟫⟩⟨⟨⟨

IT WAS A day like most Niall had spent at the Exhibition—warm, crowded, full of smiles and introductions and chatting about forging and metalcraft. The case of his highly decorated blades received a good deal of attention today. He exchanged cards and discussed possible custom work for the future—and tried to surreptitiously discover who the hell was watching him.

He felt the weight of it off and on all day. The prickling of skin and the rising of small hairs. Someone was studying him. He could not find a sign of the culprit in the crowds.

He considered it might be Turner, Kara's butler. But he

glanced down the nave several times when the crowds permitted, and the man looked as busy as the rest of the exhibitors and oblivious to anything else.

Niall took advantage of a slight lull around noon to go down and speak with the man.

"Good day, sir." The servant gave him a formal nod.

"Good afternoon, Turner." Niall cut to the heart of the matter. "I assume she's informed you where she's staying?"

Turner nodded. "I saw her there this morning."

Alarm rose. "Good heavens, man. You weren't followed, were you?"

"Absolutely not." Turner gave him a quelling look. "I've been looking after my mistress for a very long time."

Niall gave him a look of sympathy. "I'm beginning to understand all that such a statement implies. Did she tell you of the watcher on the cider house roof?"

"She did." The butler looked troubled. "I don't like it. It doesn't feel the same. It feels as if something else is brewing."

"Something complicated."

Their eyes met. "Yes."

"She's lucky to have you, Turner." Niall extended his hand.

The butler eyed him, then slowly grasped his hand in a firm handshake. "I sincerely hope to be able to say the same of you, sir."

Niall walked back, thinking it made sense that Turner would be slow to trust. He approved. *He* felt protective of Kara, and he'd only known her for a short time. Still, it had been a good while since he'd had to prove himself to a man. He didn't doubt Turner would come around eventually.

The crowds grew thick again, and it seemed like no time had passed, but suddenly Gyda arrived.

Niall glanced at the time. "I thought you might be early, but I think instead you are late."

"Not late. Your Miss Levett proposed a different meeting spot." She told him of their conversation, then gave him a knowing look. "You never told me what a stunner she is, Niall. Don't you trust me?"

"Gyda," he said in a warning note.

She rolled her eyes. "Oh, no need for worry. I think I might find I like her. In fact, I quite look forward to getting to know her, but there's no heat to it."

Niall refused to show or even acknowledge the low level of relief he felt. "You'll be comfortable taking it all on again this afternoon?" He quirked a brow at her. "I knocked, but you were not in your room when I left early this morning."

"I'm perfectly able to smile and sing your praises. In fact, I expect a gentleman to visit today in order to inspect my shield. He's thinking of ordering one for his study." She gestured toward her pride and joy, a splendid shield she'd constructed herself in the Norse tradition. It was large, with a studded iron boss and an iron rim carved with runes. Painted blue, it bore an elaborate design of Odin's ravens. Far too heavy for actual battle, it was a triumph of personal meaning for Gyda. Niall had been proud to add it to his exhibit.

"Excellent. It will the first of many you will commission before all of this is over."

He took his leave and set out, weaving through the throng. As he left the British nave and passed by the perfumed fountain, a small figure darted out and fell in beside him.

Niall glared down with a baleful eye. One of the boys from yesterday morning's events looked solemnly back up at him. The smallest boy, the one who had dragged the metal arm from hiding and had it snatched from him.

"I'll save you the trouble," Niall told him. "My pockets are empty. What kind of fool do you think I am, to mingle in this crowd every day with full pockets?"

"I ain't 'ere to be dippin' in yer pockets, sir."

Niall made a noncommittal sound and waited.

"I seen that police inspector talkin' to ye this mornin'."

He nodded.

"He wrote a lot of marks in 'is book."

"I imagine he wishes to keep his thoughts clear and organized."

"Thing is, lots o' folks are sayin' the pretty lady killed that nob. Some say you 'elped 'er. Or did it fer 'er."

Niall sighed. He supposed the gossip was inevitable.

"But I know it ain't true," the lad said fiercely. "I know 'tweren't ye, nor the pretty lady. And so I'll tell 'em, no matter what Tom Ratter says." He leaned in, his dirty face earnest. "Ye can count on me, sir."

The boy gave a nod and stepped back. It took only seconds for him to melt into the crowd.

Niall stood a moment, staring after him and forcing the flow of people to part around him. With a sigh and a shake of his head, he moved on, out into the park.

Chapter Eight

KARA STOOD BACK a bit from the balcony windows, watching the street intently. Because of the slant of the street and her vantage point on the third floor, she could see a wide swath of Adams Street, leading from Upper Seymour.

Minutes ago, she'd seen Niall down there, making his way from the park. He'd had a tail, but he must have realized it, for he'd gone on without stopping. She wondered if he had the skills to lose his follower, but staring down now, she realized it likely didn't matter.

It wasn't Niall she watched for now. She guessed he would likely try to come in the back of the building, if at all possible. But she had her eye on a fellow across the street, casually smoking in a doorway a little way down the block. He was tall, clean, and dressed in nondescript clothes. But he'd been there for quite a while, and he betrayed himself by occasionally glancing up at the upper-floor windows.

And there it is.

A man in a slouched hat walked past the man she watched, pausing long enough to say a few words before moving on. The tall man gave no answer, but he crushed his cigarillo against the wall behind him and straightened.

Kara went to the door of the room she waited in. Leaving it

open, she crossed to the railing and stared down into the stairwell. It took only a moment for Niall to appear.

"Hurry," she called quietly.

She watched in appreciation as he raced lightly up the stairs, taking them two at a time. He wasn't even winded when he reached her, although his face was alight with curiosity.

"The woman in the coffee shop downstairs pulled me into the kitchen and sent me up here. What is this place?"

She didn't answer. "Quickly." She pushed him through the door before shutting and locking it. He stared around at the parlor, done comfortably up in shades of blue. "Come. Stand here. Far back enough so that you won't be seen. Look there."

"Where? What am I looking for?"

"See him? The bearded blond man? He just stepped away from that tobacconist's shop."

"Ah, yes. I see him."

"Look at how he walks. As if he owns the city." She wrinkled her brow in disapproval. "A dead giveaway. Police detective, I'd wager."

"Wait. What? I was followed from the park, but not by him. I gave the man the slip."

"Look, there's another." She pointed in the other direction, where another man was on the move. The pair of them met in the street and came resolutely on toward the coffee shop entrance below. "The police must have discovered my connection to the building."

He looked around. "What *is* your connection to the building?"

"I own it." He stared blankly, and she hurried on. "They must have posted a watch on it, or perhaps a watch throughout the area." She sighed. "Why are they wasting such resources on me?"

"They spoke to me this morning. I had hopes once they talked to Towland they would move on to tracking down other clues."

She sighed. "I'm guessing they need to show some sign of

progress, even if it is in the wrong direction." Frowning, she headed toward the balcony. "Well, I'm not going to take the chance they will settle on me."

He beckoned. "Come. Let's try to get down the stairs and out the back before they get past your friend in the coffee shop."

"No. Someone saw you come in the back. They got word to the men out front. They'll all be down there by now." She pushed back the heavy drapery at the side of the window. "We'll go this way."

She took up a tall, sturdy board that had been hiding behind the thick drapes. Carrying it out onto the small balcony, she maneuvered the end through the decorative iron trim at the top of the railing. She pushed the board through until it crossed over several feet of empty air and reached the same spot on the railing on the next balcony over. It took a bit of juggling, but she got the far end through the rail over there. Reaching over to push down on the board, she made sure it was firmly settled, then turned back.

Niall's jaw had dropped when he realized the trim on the railing had been constructed purposely for that function. "I would never have seen it without the board," he marveled.

She held out her hand. Automatically, he took it and steadied her as she stepped up onto the broad rim of a strategically placed planter and then onto the board. Keeping to the middle, she moved lightly across and stepped down onto the other balcony. "Come," she said.

He followed quickly and moved her aside as she began to pull the board across, hauling it over himself. She opened the balcony door and let him through. Stepping in after him, she watched him glance around at the room remarkably like the one they'd just left, except in shades of green.

Sweeping the drapery aside, she motioned for him to put the board in place.

He did—and then he stared hard at her.

"What was that?" he asked.

"What?"

"That! What we just did? You *planned* that?"

"I prepared," she corrected him.

"Four attempts," he murmured. "Four attempted kidnappings and you evaded three. I begin to see how you did it."

"Yes, yes," she said. "I am sure you are thinking that my character has been warped by such considerations. I have heard it before. There is no time to argue about it now."

"I wouldn't dream of arguing," he returned indignantly. "We all have incidents in our pasts that have shaped us, but I agree, now is not the time to detail them. I do wish to know what advantage we gain from that little stunt, though. One set of rooms is much like the other. Literally, in this case." He glanced around again. "They will search them all, looking for us."

"Ah, but you did not notice that the apartments we just left were the last in the passageway?"

He stopped to think. "You are right, by Jove. But how—"

"Simple," she interrupted. "This large building at the end of the block looks like a single structure from the outside, but the interior is divided into two separate edifices. They are looking for us in that building." She pointed. "We will go down and out onto a totally different, intersecting street and be long gone by the time they figure it out."

"Good heavens, you are diabolical," he said, all admiration.

Kara laughed. "Indeed. I can be, when it is warranted." She crossed to the door and opened it. "I suspect the same can be said of you, sir."

He offered his arm as they swept into the passageway. "I can think on my feet, I do admit. But this sort of calculation is in a class of its own."

"Thank you," she said briskly. "I will take that as a compliment."

"As it was meant," he assured her.

"Now." She looked up at him and couldn't hide a smile. "Lord Peter lives in Portman Square, correct?"

He nodded as they started down the stairs.

"We can walk from here, as long as we move quickly. Let's go beard him in his den."

"Yes," he said with a wry twist of his mouth that she quite enjoyed. "Let's do."

>>><<<

"I'M VERY SORRY, but Lord Peter is not at home."

The footman began to close the door. Before Niall could respond, Kara had stepped forward and smiled sweetly at the young servant.

"Forgive me," she said gently. "But perhaps you might be able to help me?"

The boy, dazzled, paused. Niall couldn't blame him. Kara's dark eyes sparkled. She leaned in, and the boy must have caught her odd but delectable scent—flowery soap and apple blossom and some faint note that might be metal filings.

"I have rather urgent business with Lord Peter. Might you tell me where I could find him this evening?"

The young footman flushed and shook his head. Behind her, Niall held up a gold guinea.

The boy turned redder still and looked nearly as longingly at the coin as he had at Kara. "I cannot," he said miserably. "It could be the end of my position here."

Kara drew breath to speak, but Niall stopped her with a hand on her arm. He pointed a finger at the footman. "You. Don't move. Stay right there."

Pulling Kara away, he escorted her down the walkway toward the pavement. "Hold right here a moment. Don't go anywhere."

He went back to the footman.

"Honestly, sir, I cannot—"

"Do you see that lady?" Niall asked.

The boy looked. "Yes."

"She is a lady. A peeress. Beautiful, isn't she?"

The answer came as a vigorous nod of agreement.

"She is also an heiress. Her fortune is said to rival the queen's."

"Never say so!"

"They all vie for her attention—the matchmaking matrons of the *ton*. Every mama with a lordling to marry off or a younger son searching for a wealthy bride—they all want an introduction. Now, think. Don't you believe that both Lady Brookdale and Lord Peter would welcome the chance to speak with the lady? And just imagine if she and Lord Peter did come to regard each other kindly. Perhaps they might even marry. Wouldn't the lady then recall fondly the footman who helped her in the beginning?"

The boy's eyes had gone wide. "Aye...perhaps she would."

"Well, then. I imagine Lord Peter is at his club now. But where might he plan to go later? To the theater? Out with friends?"

The footman wavered. Niall silently offered him the coin.

After a long moment, the boy snatched it up. He leaned in and spoke low. "Lady Brookdale and her older daughter are expecting Lord Peter's escort to the Loudins' ball this evening, but you didn't hear it from me."

Niall stepped back as the boy closed the door, then he went to Kara.

"Did you convince him?"

Niall told her, then gave a sigh. "We'll have to lurk outside Lord Peter's club, I suppose, and try to catch him between engagements."

"No, that will never do."

"Well, I cannot get into the club, and you certainly cannot, either."

"He will never confide in us if we accost him in the street."

"What, then? We shouldn't wait, not with Scotland Yard chasing you like a wanted criminal."

"We will talk to him where he feels safe, comfortable. We'll speak to him at the Loudins' ball."

He blinked. "And how are we to get in?"

She grinned up at him. "With my invitation, of course."

He stared down into that gorgeous visage that had lit up with wicked amusement. She flew in the face of everything he knew about women.

Suspected of murder. Pushed out of her home and the Exhibition. On the run, looking for a killer, and still she managed to laughingly rejoice in her ability to get one up on him—and make it seem a moment of camaraderie, instead of sharp and jagged triumph.

Oh, he was going to have to be so very careful with this one.

Chapter Nine

Kara recruited the White Hart's maid to help her prepare for the ball. Jenny was delighted. Fortunately, whatever mystical status Mr. Towland's paper had bestowed upon Kara, it was enough to keep Hywel from objecting.

A lucky stroke, because Jenny proved to be proficient with hair tongs and cosmetics.

"It comes of having five sisters, miss," the maid said matter-of-factly as she tucked a last hairpin into Kara's larger, shinier, and curlier than usual coiffure.

"Good heavens, five sisters? The chatter must be deafening."

"Lawks, yes, miss. It does get loud. But there's lots of fun, too. And always someone to teach you what you don't know. We share everything. Gossip, clothes, money, rooms—even, occasionally, boys." She grinned.

As an only child, Kara couldn't even imagine such things. It sounded intriguing and slightly alarming.

"And now I will share something with you, miss." Reaching into her pocket, Jenny pulled out a small jar. "You've already applied your cold cream?"

Kara nodded.

"Well, then. Just a bit of this rosy balm will do wonders." Jenny held up a hand as Kara began to protest. "I promise, I know what I'm doing. My oldest sister is married to an apothecary, and she makes this herself. The secret is quality ingredients and the lightest touch, so the color is just barely there." She dabbed a bit on Kara's lips and cheeks and smoothed and smoothed until, Kara had to admit, the bloom of color looked entirely natural.

"Now, a bit of powder on your neck and shoulders and you will shine like a swan amongst the geese."

The maid took the mirror from the vanity and stepped back so Kara could view herself. Her skin did glow against the royal blue of her Spitalfields silk gown. "I don't think I've ever looked so well," she told Jenny. "You have a gift. You should be applying for a position as a lady's maid."

"I did consider it," Jenny admitted. "But it sounds dull, the same thing every day. And I've no wish to be part of a stuffy, prudish downstairs set. I prefer the variety and liveliness of the White Hart."

"Well, I am grateful for your talents and for Mr. Hywel's leniency. And I should be even more grateful if you will take me along your sister's shop so that I might make some purchases."

"Oh, miss! That would be grand. Our Ellie would be beside herself, and ever so happy to help you."

Kara ran a measuring gaze over the girl. "Perhaps you might enjoy a bit more variety this evening, Jenny."

The maid looked interested.

"It would not be the thing for me to arrive at the Loudin ball alone with Mr. Kier. Lacking any other chaperone, I could, at the very least, bring you along as my maid. They will send you below stairs for the duration, and you could see a stuffy downstairs set up close."

Jenny let out a long breath, considering. "I would dearly love to see a society ball, miss. And Hywel has already brought his niece in to cover for me this evening." She nodded. "Yes, I think I should like the chance, thank you, miss. But I should ask permission first."

Kara nodded and turned back to the mirror as the maid ran

out. She breathed as deeply as she was able. Her evening corset was far more restrictive than the one she wore for daytime, but it certainly created a curvier silhouette. She could scarcely wait to see if Niall would react to it.

Her heart fluttered at the notion, and she paused to take note of it. She'd attended any number of society balls and was experienced with making an entrance, but she'd never felt such a shivery feeling of anticipation at the idea. She took a moment to enjoy it.

Leaving the room at last, she encountered Niall approaching the main stairwell from the opposite passageway—and promptly forgot to watch for his reaction, as she was entirely knocked askew by her own.

Good heavens.

He was dressed formally, his broad shoulders showcased in a black coat and his skin showing bronze against crisp white linen. But instead of breeches, he wore a kilt of red, green, and black. He wore black dress shoes, and his long, firmly sculpted legs were covered only by woolen socks.

She had to drag her gaze away.

She was gratified, though, to look up and find him suffering a similar fixation on her enhanced curves. He flushed and promptly bowed in an attempt to hide it. "You are strikingly lovely tonight."

"As are you." She still hadn't recovered herself. "I did not expect the kilt." She stopped. "Although I should have. I saw you wearing one at the forge that day, but it was a different pattern of tartan."

"Yes. We Kiers are a sept of Clan Kerr. That was the hunting tartan. This one is for formal events."

"But you've no accent."

He laughed. "My mother would be pleased to hear you say so, but I can put on a proper Scottish brogue, should you wish me to."

"Perhaps another time." Staring at the gold cuff links that

adorned his dark coat, she mused at the strangeness of the situation. On the one hand, she felt as if she knew a great deal about Mr. Niall Kier—and the sort of man he was. But now she was struck by how much she didn't know. It should have disturbed her.

Instead, she found herself caught up by the sight of his hands.

He stood silent, waiting.

Her mind cast back. He had the speech and manners of a gentleman. He'd always dressed with utter correctness—except for that time at the forge. And yet, like an artist whose fingers often carried the telltale stain of paint, she realized she'd grown accustomed to the faint tinge of coal dust about his fingers and nails.

But not now. The sight of his immaculate manicure made her feel…something. Both touched and bereft at once.

"Shall we go down?" he finally asked.

"Ground walnut shells," she blurted out.

"Excuse me?"

"I read somewhere that ground walnut shells added to soap can remove stubborn stains."

Color rose in his face, and she hoped she hadn't insulted him. Again.

"Yes. It does. In situations like this, I prefer to decide myself what to say about my work. I don't wish for my nails to announce it for me."

"I'm sorry. I don't mean anything disrespectful." She took his arm, and they started downstairs. "I hope you don't think I believe you should be ashamed of your work."

"Whatever you think, I am not," he said firmly.

"Good. You are an artist. Your talents are unique and bountiful. You have much more to offer the world than the majority of the guests that will attend Lady Loudin's ball this evening."

He stopped as they reached the bottom, and she was caught again. His brows arched beautifully over his slightly slanted eyes. When he frowned, they pointed right along the ridges of his aquiline nose.

"Thank you."

She told him she'd asked Jenny to accompany them, and he informed her that he'd asked the innkeeper to arrange for an unmarked carriage. It was waiting, and as soon as the maid arrived, having changed into her best dress, they were off. Jenny chose to sit up top with the driver. Niall saw her seated and climbed in after Kara. He sat silent, but Kara's brain had found a suitable distraction.

"Where do you get your soap?" she asked. "With the walnut shells?"

He'd folded his arms, and his hands were tucked away out of sight. Oh dear. She had made him uncomfortable.

"I make it myself."

"Do you?" She was even more diverted. She'd always found such processes to be interesting. She peppered him with questions.

He answered them in good humor until he gentled his tone and said softly, "Why are we speaking of soap, Kara?"

Her gut tightened at his insight. "Because I'm nervous," she admitted.

"You? Nervous? In the last couple of days, I've seen you face down a physical assault, put a bully in his place, evade Scotland Yard's best, and dance across a board three stories above the street. And you are afraid of a bunch of aristocrats at a ball? I refuse to believe it."

"Well, you must. When I go into Society, it's like engaging in battle. You'll see. I need all of my reserves." She sighed. "But will you distract me a little, until we get there?"

"How?"

"I don't know. Talk. Tell me something."

He hesitated.

"Tell me about your forge at home."

"Ah, now *that* I can talk about all night." She could hear the smile in his tone. "I have a little house. It's set on a cliff, not far from the sea. My forge is separate, a little outbuilding at the edge of a meadow. I can look out and see the wind blowing the grass. Flowers. The small creatures that feed and live there. And when my back has gone stiff or my arm gives out, I can walk to the cliff and stare out over the water and drink in the salt air."

"It sounds lovely."

"Aye. It is." He sounded reflective now. "Don't you miss it? The time alone with the idea in your head and the fire in your belly? The build of pleasure as your creation forms beneath your hands? That intense relief when you finish and you've birthed something new into the world?"

"Yes. That is it, exactly," she marveled. "I do miss it. It's why I set up my workbench and started working on my *Gambler* at my exhibit."

"It's a good idea. I try with my wee forge, but it's not the same." He leaned forward as the carriage began to slow. "Here we are."

She looked out at the crowded street. "To battle we go."

They had timed it perfectly, just as she'd planned. Not so late that their hostess had abandoned the receiving line, but late enough that only a few people stood waiting ahead of them. Kara saw the moment when Lady Loudin spotted her, and noted the speed with which the couples before them were shuffled through.

"Miss Levett! Welcome. I was so glad to receive your reply to our invitation."

Kara gave a perfect curtsy. "I do apologize for the lateness of my response, but I'm afraid my schedule has been dominated by the Exhibition of late."

The countess's face showed her complicated reaction to the mention of Kara's highly unusual association with the event. "Of course. My son Randolph has visited. He told me of your...display. It sounds most interesting."

"Oh, my gadgetry is nothing compared to some of the wonders to be seen. But may I make you known to my friend, Mr. Kier?"

"Of course. Welcome, sir." Lady Loudin cocked her head. "But have we met before this? Your face seems quite familiar."

"I wish I had been so fortunate." Niall's smile clearly charmed the lady. "But I've spent most of the last few years abroad. Unless...have you also been traveling?"

"Heavens, no." She frowned. "You have the look of someone I know. That must be it." She waved a hand. "I'll figure it out eventually. But do come in. We shall have a splendid evening."

Kara pulled Jenny forward. "Our plans were confirmed so late, I was forced to bring along my maid as chaperone. Is there a place for her, if it's not too much trouble?"

"Not at all," the countess said graciously. She waved a hand, and a footman garbed in livery of sunshine yellow stepped forth. "Take the girl downstairs and introduce her to Davies." Lady Loudin smiled at Kara as they headed off. "My own maid will see to her."

"Thank you so much, Lady Loudin," Kara said.

The countess took a significant pause. "And Miss Levett, I hope I may introduce you to Randolph later?"

"It will be my pleasure." Another curtsy, and they moved on before the countess could see the lie in her face. She hoped to find Lord Peter, ask her questions, and be gone long before Lady Loudin tried to match her with her son.

They followed the flow of guests toward the ballroom entrance, but Kara tugged on Niall's arm. "Let's stop in here first?" She indicated an anteroom filled with tables, covered in delicate offerings of bite-sized finger foods. A steady stream of yellow-liveried footmen kept the tables full, even as guests moved through, filling small plates. "If we linger here until after the first dance, we likely won't have to be announced as we enter the ballroom." She shuddered. "I hate that."

He nodded in agreement. "One of the few times it's perfectly acceptable for a whole host of people to turn and gawk at you."

"Ghastly."

"Well, it's no hardship to stay here, is it?" Niall headed for one of the tables. "Are those veal baskets?" He took up a pastry and popped it in his mouth. "I haven't had one of these in years." He held one up. "Here, try one."

She looked distrustfully at it. "What is it?"

"Delicious." She hesitated, and he leaned down toward her. "Kara, there's trouble enough in the world, and plenty of it heaped at our feet."

He loomed close. She could feel the warmth of his breath on her cheek. His eyes were kind, and his mouth twitched into a grin at the corner.

"And yet," he continued, "we should be wise enough not to ignore the pleasures. Peaceful moments. Beautiful scenery." His grin widened infinitesimally as his gaze dropped and ran over her. "Art. Music. Good food." He offered her the pastry once more.

She opened her mouth, and he popped it in.

The taste flooded her tongue. Flaky pastry, meat, spices. But it was the look in his eyes that held her fast. His enjoyment in witnessing hers.

"Very well done, aren't they?"

She nodded.

He grinned approval and reached for more. Kara hastily stepped away, pretending to peruse the selection. Why did she feel so very different in his company? But she knew the answer. He awoke places in her that had been long asleep. Now they were moving, stretching, peering about in curiosity.

And she liked it.

She tried a small bit of toasted bread spread with herbed cheese. Delicious. But she would have to be selective. The tightness of her corset kept her from indulging herself—as did the need to stay as light, mobile, and agile as possible. It was a constant concern, a hum of caution permanently abuzz in her brain. And a reminder of why they were here tonight.

She decided she could indulge in one tiny fruit tart before they moved on, but as she brought it to her mouth, her elbow was nudged by a guest reaching behind her. The burnt cream on the top wobbled and dropped onto her bodice.

"Dash it," she said.

The gentleman apologized profusely. After reassuring him, she turned to where Niall had discovered a plate of sweet pastries and was happily stuffing himself. "I'm going to the ladies' retiring room," she told him as she wiped at her bodice. "I'll meet you back here shortly."

"Shall I escort you?"

"No. I'll ask a servant for directions." She waved a hand at the sweets. "You should be well occupied."

He nodded and kept chewing as she headed for the stairs.

Fortunately, the silk came clean. She tidied herself and stepped out of the parlor set aside for such purposes, only to bump into someone coming in.

"Oh, pardon me."

"Do excuse me," echoed the other young lady. Kara turned to go, but the other woman suddenly gasped in surprise. "Miss Levett?"

"Oh, heavens. Good evening, Miss Bailey."

Her cousin's fiancée stared at her in shock for a moment, then grabbed her arm and pulled her down a dim passageway. "Whatever are you doing here, Miss Levett?"

"Enjoying the evening. Or, at least, I hope to. I've only just arrived."

"But...but..." The girl seemed unable to recover from her surprise.

"I assure you, I was invited," Kara said wryly.

"Yes. Of course! I just..." Miss Bailey lowered her voice. "The police came looking for you last evening at Joseph's home. They spoke of murder!"

"Yes. Joseph told me they were looking for me there. Fortunately, I had already spoken to a magistrate and answered the questions they had for me."

The girl stared at her blankly for a moment, then drew a deep breath. "Oh. Good, then. All to the good. We can put such unpleasant notions behind us."

She spoke with such relief that Kara wondered just what the police had said when they interrupted that dinner. "How well you look this evening, Miss Bailey," she said smoothly, sure that a compliment would go a long way toward making her cousin's betrothed more at ease. And it was the truth: the girl was dressed expensively, with her wide pink skirts covered in layers of dainty lace.

"Thank you." Miss Bailey gave herself a little shake. "I am glad to see you. I've been wishing to speak to you."

"So Joseph said. Is he here this evening?"

"Oh, no. He's at a committee meeting tonight. One of his causes is coming up before the Commons soon."

"Oh? Which one?"

Miss Bailey threw up a hand. "I don't truly know. Something about troop supplies? In the east, perhaps?"

"I see."

"We don't need him, in any case. I hoped to speak with you about the wedding."

Kara's insides chilled. "Oh?" *Please don't ask me to participate.*

"We would both love for you to take part in the ceremony. I would ask you to stand up with me as one of my attendants."

She tried to keep the horror out of her expression. "How kind of you to ask. Have you settled on a date, then?"

"Not yet. I must first undertake a thorough examination of Camhurst Place and see what must be done before we invite guests. We shall settle on a week sometime this summer, I should think."

"Oh dear." Relief flooded her. "I'm afraid I will still be fully occupied with the Exhibition."

Surprise made Miss Bailey pause. "Will you?" she asked pointedly. "I thought by then you will surely be tired of the project."

"Tired?" Now Kara was surprised. "No. It's a great honor to be included. And a great opportunity."

"I'm sure it is." Miss Bailey sounded a bit sour. "I know my father thought so."

"Oh? Does he have an interest in one of the exhibits?"

"No. He invested in land in Greenwich. Parkland and gardens along the river. It would have been an ideal place in which to host the Exhibition. Perfect in every way. He put it forth to the committee as the most likely spot, but they barely considered it and instead built that monstrosity right in the midst of Hyde Park."

"Oh dear. He must have been disappointed."

"To say the least. But he's not the sort to be defeated so easily. He's deep in plans to renovate the place now. He'll recover his investment soon enough."

"I'm glad to hear it."

"In any case, I think they are making too much of the thing. All those months, the papers predicted disaster, plagues, riots, an invasion of foreign rabble. Now they cannot praise it enough." She sniffed.

"I think we must all be glad their pessimism did not bear fruit."

"Yes. We must." The sour note had crept back. "I suppose."

"So many people worked so hard to bring it all about. It is good to see it a success and England poised as the vanguard of an alliance with so many great nations."

"Yes, yes," the girl said impatiently. "And yet you cannot think to miss Joseph's wedding for such a thing. He is your family. Your only family. They won't miss you for a week or two."

"Perhaps I can manage to get away—for a few days," Kara relented.

"Fine. Good." Nothing in Miss Bailey's demeanor matched her words. She looked thoroughly annoyed with Kara. "My mother and I will be shopping while we are in London, looking for ideas for my wedding finery. Perhaps you will join us?"

"I will see what I can do."

"Excellent." Miss Bailey turned back toward the retiring room. "We shall send word. Now, if you will excuse me?"

Kara let her go and set off to find Niall. It didn't bode well for future family relations that she far preferred to go and ask questions about a murder rather than spend more time with her cousin's betrothed.

Chapter Ten

NIALL LISTENED TO Kara's account of her run in with her soon-to-be cousin-in-law. Silently, he lamented those last few pastries, but when was the last time he'd had a graze at such a posh buffet? "I give her credit for trying to befriend you," he told Kara after she finished. "But she doesn't sound pleasant."

"We just do not have much in common," she replied on a sigh. "But that is not her fault. I think that, in general, we'll get along." She grinned. "Likely we'll get along better the less we see of each other."

"Sometimes family goes that way." He said it with the complete confidence of experience.

She'd caught the intonation. For a moment he thought she would ask, but she gave a shake of her head. "Let's focus. I heard the music change. The dancing has begun. Let us go see if we can spot Lord Peter."

They moved into the crowded ballroom. Lady Loudin had invited everyone of any pedigree left in the city—most of them still here because of the Exhibition—and they had come. The room was awash in costly fabrics, fabulous jewels, and wagging tongues.

Though her name had not been announced, Kara still drew a good deal of attention. Stares and sidelong glances lingered on her. Men nodded and ladies gave small, finger-waggling waves, and more than a few people approached to greet her, compliment her, or ask about the Exhibition.

Niall watched her respond to it all and grew ever more fascinated.

He'd had two significant women in his life. Both had been beautiful. Both had wielded their beauty as a weapon, as a means to extract what they wanted from the people around them, from life.

Kara outshone them both. With her creamy skin and wide, dark eyes, her luxuriant chestnut locks, and that petite figure that stole a man's breath away, she could have easily beaten them both at their own game.

And yet her demeanor could be described as the opposite. He saw no evidence of such games. She spoke directly and answered any questions forthrightly. As far as he could tell, she was completely unaware of how comely she was. She seemed not to notice the sparks of desire and appreciation in the men or the hints of envy from the women.

Not that she lacked detractors or those who thought to knock her down a peg or two. But he greatly enjoyed watching her handle those, as well.

They were nearly halfway around the ballroom when she gave him an exasperated glance. "Here comes another one. Get your pocket watch ready." She indicated a tall, haughty woman approaching.

"Good evening, Lady Bertley." She introduced Niall, but the lady dismissed him after a moment's glance. He guessed she must have only daughters of marriageable age, judging by how she felt free to condescend to Kara.

"It is not quite the thing, is it?" Lady Bertley asked after a moment's conversation. "I speak, of course, of your questionable decision to take part in the Great Exhibition."

"Come now, Katherine," the lady's escort chided her. "Surely it is not so bad as that."

Kara smiled her thanks at him, but Lady Bertley was not done. "Oh, but I think it is. A woman of your position, Miss Levett? It's most...unusual."

"It is," Kara readily agreed. "I wish I could say the same about your comment, but I cannot. I've heard the same tired, barely disguised, and completely uninformed censure three times." She held out her hand, and Niall obligingly handed over his watch. She consulted it. "In just the last eight and a half minutes."

The gentleman at Lady Bertley's side hid a laugh behind a cough. He looked to Niall, who merely shrugged.

"It appears none of them have had any effect," the lady said sharply.

"No. But I do wish you all might consult a bit and come up with some variety of complaint and veiled insult."

"I doubt different wording would sway you to good sense." Lady Bertley's tone was growing nastier.

"It would not," Kara acknowledged. "But at least it wouldn't bore me." With a nod, she moved on. Niall bowed to the sputtering woman and her openly chortling escort then followed.

"Let's just complete a circuit around the ballroom and then check the cardroom," Kara muttered. "I am not familiar with Lord Peter or his sister, but I would recognize his mother. I've yet to see her tonight."

They continued on, and their next encounters were short and pleasant enough. Niall caught sight of Stayme across the room, but the old man merely raised a brow at him before returning to his conversation.

Just as they were nearing the ballroom doors again, Niall heard someone call Kara's name. A lilac blur whooshed past him, and suddenly Kara was spinning, laughing, and smiling into the face of a lovely young woman.

"Kara! I couldn't believe it when I heard you were here!" The woman cast a sharp eye at her. "I thought you were done with Society?"

Niall stared at the stranger's softly rounded face. Her blonde hair was crowned at the back of her head with a row of pearls, then twisted in a rope down her back. It was an unusual hairstyle, one he'd never seen before. But why did she look so familiar?

"And I thought you were done with England," Kara replied. "When did you get back?"

"Only days ago. I've scarcely even unpacked. But I had to come, didn't I? Everyone in the world is talking about the Great Exhibition. I had to see it for myself. And now I hear you are in the thick of it?"

"I am, in more ways than one." Reaching out, Kara touched his sleeve. "Eleanor, if I may, please allow me to introduce a friend—"

"Mr. Niall Kier."

The woman had taken a step back. She said his name with a speculative note even as she ran an eye of appreciation over him. Ah, yes. He'd seen that before. The memory snapped into place.

He bowed. "Mrs. Braddock. A pleasure to see you again."

Kara blinked. "You two know each other?"

"We do," Eleanor affirmed. "We met only the once, in Rotterdam." She glanced at Kara. "I assume you two met at the Exhibition?"

"Yes, but how did you know?"

"I've seen your friend's work. We met at a party given by a very rich merchant. Mr. Kier had just finished installing the most fabulous scrolled metal shelves throughout the man's wine cellar." She smiled up at him. "Ingenious, really. You can read the label without disturbing the wine."

Niall smiled. "Mrs. Braddock is being modest. The party was designed for the unveiling of a painting she did for the host." He gave her an encouraging nod. "It was stunning, and Dhr. Tasman was suitably proud."

Mrs. Braddock gave a little curtsy, and Kara's eyes widened. "Eleanor, how wonderful! You are truly making your way into a career with your art!"

"It was a fun little commission. The gentleman is descended

from a famous explorer. He wished to commemorate one of his ancestor's discoveries. I was happy to do it, and it did turn out well."

"It was a triumph in itself, and the gentleman was very happy with it." Niall glanced between the two women. "But how do you two come to know each other so well?"

"What? The two most unconventional young women in the ranks of Society? Of course we know each other." Mrs. Braddock laughed. "Whom else should we talk to at these functions?"

"Oh, don't listen to her," Kara said with a laugh. "We met when we were—what was it? Fifteen years old?"

Her friend nodded.

"We were both at the Royal Academy Exhibition. I was caught up in a stunning landscape that depicted Bodmin Moor. I was drawn in to it, pulled in by the rocks and the rolling hills and the brilliant sky and a single, twisted tree. I gradually realized all of the other attendees had moved out of the room, save for another girl, who was similarly entranced with a seascape nearby."

"We introduced ourselves and promptly got into an argument over which form of art was more interesting—landscapes or seascapes."

"We were both passionate and eloquent in our defense," Kara recalled fondly.

"It was quite the most stimulating conversation I'd ever had with another girl of my age," Mrs. Braddock said. "I was so pleased to find someone that cared about art. So refreshing to find a girl not obsessed with fashion, hair, or marriage."

"Who won the argument?" Niall asked.

"We converted each other, and ended up again on the opposite sides of the issue. We've been friends ever since."

He laughed.

"Oh! And since we are speaking of art, and of my art in particular," Mrs. Braddock said, "you must come and see my latest work. I insist. I cannot wait to show it to you. I plan on creating quite a stir with it."

"Well, now I am intrigued," Kara said. "But yes, of course I wish to see it. And you, in turn, must come and see me—both of us—at the Exhibition."

"Oh, you can be sure I will. I've lately been in Dusseldorf, studying with the masters at the *Kunstakademie*, and even there, there was talk of nothing but the Exhibition. Even as I headed home, I met a great many people traveling for the same reason." She waggled her brows. "In fact, I crossed the channel with a charming group of gentlemen from Berlin. I believe they will be exhibitors as well, come to replace the men who have been here for weeks already." She gave Kara a look of concern. "But who will give you a respite, my dear?"

"No one," Kara said cheerfully. "I will manage my own exhibit all the way through, and be happy to do it. It is a wondrous opportunity."

"Not to mention, it's the single most exciting place to be right now."

Kara made a face. "Spread a little of that enthusiasm through here, won't you? Half the room finds my participation a disgrace, and they are happy to tell me so."

"Oh, do not give any of them a second thought." Mrs. Braddock raised a brow at him, and Niall appreciated the vision she made, the transparent lace lining her off-the-shoulder bodice swinging a little as she bent to speak in Kara's ear, yet loud enough for him to hear. "You have a fine escort, a fortune, and your freedom. Who cares what they think? What more can you wish for?" She stood straight. "Except for more of my company, of course."

Kara laughed.

"I'm utterly serious. Here we are, at last, both of us free from mourning and at last taking the first steps on our chosen paths. Even Grandmama agrees—" She stopped suddenly. "Oh, but there's the answer to your troubles."

Niall had an inkling of what she meant and had to thrust aside a stab of alarm. He knew who Mrs. Braddock's grandmama was, just as everyone else did. No one else, though, had as much reason as him to avoid her attention.

"Grandmama will take up your cause," Mrs. Braddock rushed on. "And then no one will dare speak a word against you."

Kara wore a doubtful expression. "I rather thought Lady Abbington might agree with the rest of them."

"Absolutely not," Mrs. Braddock declared.

"I'm not sure Kara requires anyone's help," Niall interjected. "She's handled herself beautifully tonight, and as you said yourself, ma'am...why should she care what they think?"

"You are absolutely right, Mr. Kier. Or more to the point, I am right. But there's no denying that everything goes easier if Society is not against you. Especially if you are a woman."

"And it might be best to build up some public favor, in case I need it later," Kara said quietly.

"Also true," Mrs. Braddock replied. "Who knows what trouble you might get into, if given the chance?"

Niall exchanged a glance with Kara.

"In any case, Grandmama will be on your side, Kara, dear."

"But I had the notion she was very traditional. She was so adamant about your marriage..." Kara's words trailed away.

"She had her reasons, and most of them were good ones. No. I know she will champion you. I will recruit her myself, and we'll see what these gossiping biddies have to say when she's done with them."

"Her influence might be helpful," Kara admitted.

"Well, it does extend far, but not everywhere." Mrs. Braddock's eyes had widened, and she nudged Kara to turn and look. "Oh dear. Here comes someone even Grandmama cannot convince to see sense. I'm sorry to abandon you to him, darling, but he's already called me a shameless hussy once this evening." She embraced Kara warmly. "Come and see me, and make it soon."

The woman slipped away, and Kara turned to Niall. "Let us

go and search out Lord Peter." She took his arm, and they nearly made their escape, but an older gentleman stepped into their path.

"Young lady," he said by way of greeting.

Kara stopped and forced a smile. "Lord Latham." She made the introductions. "Lord Latham was a friend of my father's," she explained.

The gentleman ignored Niall completely. His frame was rangy, his limbs long and thin, but he possessed a daunting paunch in his middle and his complexion was growing redder by the moment. The color climbed to his temples, where it ran a ragged line of contrast to the pale skin of his bald head. "I was a *very* good friend of your father's," he said, his tone irate. "Enough to shudder at what he would feel if he could hear what is being said of you here tonight."

"About the Exhibition?" she asked, incredulous. "You think my father, of all people, would object to my participation?"

"Of course he would. As would any father," he thundered. "Preposterous, the idea of it."

Niall could only imagine what the gentleman would say if he knew about the murder and her tenuous involvement.

"Horsefeathers!" Kara declared. "Sir, you knew my father well enough to know he would have been first in line to secure an exhibit space. He would have gloried in the chance to show off his manufactures. Were my father still alive, I would still be at the Exhibition every day. The only difference would be that our space would have at least doubled!" She pointed a finger at him. "You cannot deny it."

"Nor do I. But that picture is vastly different from your taking part alone. And what is this rumbling I hear of your creating a metal man? It is beyond the pale. Unfeminine."

"Nonsense!"

"Ungodly," he insisted. "And unnatural."

She drew back, affronted. "You know Father would disagree with you on this as well. He would say the only unnatural thing would be for me to ignore the gifts that have been bestowed upon me. Be it God or nature, whomever you credit, I have been given a quick mind, nimble fingers, and a well of creativity."

"What you need is a dose of womanly modesty," he said, low and mean.

Niall started to speak, but she waved him back.

Looking the older gentleman over, she snorted. "Why? So I do not rouse your masculine insecurities? Should I ignore my gifts at *your* whim?" She gestured. "At theirs? No. Absolutely not." She eyed him up and down. "Perhaps you cannot understand, lacking such blessings yourself."

"Young lady—" he began to bluster.

She stepped closer to him. "I shall explain it so you can understand. I work hard and make good use of my abilities. I do not neglect or ignore them. It would be an insult to the giver and to myself. Just as it would be an insult for you to ignore the unmistakable hard work of your valet in procuring such expansive corsets and wrangling you into them."

Niall choked.

Lord Latham gaped.

Kara lifted her chin. "Good evening." She swept away and through the ballroom doors.

The gentleman struggled to marshal a response, but Niall didn't wait to hear it. "A pleasure," he said quietly, and, grinning, he sauntered on.

He found her pacing outside the refreshment alcove. As he approached, she stopped a footman and requested a glass of lemonade.

"I dare not have the champagne," she said wryly. "Imagine what I might say under its influence." She sighed. "I daresay this will be the last Society invitation I will receive."

"Wrong," he declared. "I predict they will pile up. They will all wish to hear what you will say next."

She laughed. "It is a possibility," she conceded. The footman returned with her lemonade, and she took it with gratitude.

"Come." She waved the glass. "Let's go find the cardroom."

"I asked earlier," Niall told her. "This way."

The cardroom had been set up in a spacious parlor. One of Lady Loudin's footmen admitted them, and Niall paused just past the threshold. The place was crowded, the air filled with chatter and smoke. Tables had been set up throughout, except in one corner, where another of the yellow-liveried footmen attended a lavish bar cart.

"There we are. That's him." Niall nodded toward a gentleman sitting alone at the table closest to the liquor cart. "He looks to be keeping the barman well occupied." He offered Kara his arm. "Allow me to begin, if you will. I'll speak with him."

They approached, and Niall requested a glass of champagne. He made a show of glancing toward the man sitting nearby, then looking back, after a moment, with a frown. "Lord Peter?" he said on a note of surprise.

The gentleman looked up, then lurched to his feet. His manners were intact, even if his legs did wobble.

Niall bowed. "You might not recall, but we were introduced once, at the Royal Academy."

Lord Peter frowned, looking him over. "Yes. I recall… You were with Stayme, wasn't that it?"

"Indeed. A pleasure to see you again." Niall hesitated. "I don't mean to presume, but are you quite all right?"

"No. Not at all." The young man started to sink back into his chair, but he caught sight of Kara lingering behind Niall's back, and he straightened again, though he had to reach out a hand to the wall to steady himself.

She stepped forward. "You must be distraught at the death of Mr. Forrester. We offer our condolences for the loss of your friend."

So much for Niall leading the conversation. He watched as Lord Peter started. "How did you—? I've only just been to make an identification of the body. I didn't even tell my family about it yet. Who are you?" He glared back and forth between them.

"You already know Mr. Kier," she said gently. "I am Miss Levett."

He gaped. "Levett? But that's… You…"

"I assure you, I did not kill your friend." She cocked her head. "Did *you*?"

Lord Peter's eyes nearly bugged out of his head. "*What?* No! Of course not!" His outrage was clearly growing. "Why would you ask such a thing?"

"Well, in case it might be true." She gave him a long, measuring look. "I see that it is not."

"Your reaction to the lady's name tells me that the police are still considering her as a suspect—and that we are wise in trying to discover who might truly have murdered Mr. Forrester." Niall downed the rest of his champagne and set the glass aside.

"You truly didn't kill him?" Lord Peter asked Kara. "The police intimated as much."

"I didn't. But I hope to find who did."

"Unfortunately, we did not know your friend, nor anything about why someone would wish to kill him. Do you, sir?" Niall watched the man closely.

"Do you suppose it was over his debts?" Kara asked.

Lord Peter's eyes narrowed. "I thought you didn't know him."

"I did not, but I did meet the mechanical surgeon who crafted his wooden arm. It's how I discovered Mr. Forrester's name." She paused. "The surgeon was quite upset about the money still owed him."

"Yes." Lord Peter had another long drink. "Forrester was always in debt, practically since the first day I knew him."

"Did he have other creditors? More dangerous ones, perhaps?"

"I don't know. I had begun to wonder if he might have owed a larger sum than I assumed. He'd changed, these last months, you see."

"Changed? How?" asked Niall.

Lord Peter sank a hand in his hair. "I'm not sure I can pinpoint it. It was a number of things, really. He seemed...troubled. His moods had grown darker. He was not available or about as much as usual, and he was secretive about what he was up to." He sighed. "And, of course, there was his utter fixation on the Great Exhibition."

"Fixation?" Kara asked.

"Yes. We went to the opening day. Everyone did. It was a lark. But Forrester was struck differently with it all. Enchanted, almost. He couldn't stay away. He dragged me back twice more. But then I balked. I refused to go again, but I know he went back."

"Do you know what it was that so entranced him?"

Lord Peter gave her a frank look. "You, for one thing. He went on about your metal marvel of a man."

"He did watch me from afar. More than once. It was a little unsettling." She frowned at the young man. "But he also disguised himself as a cleric and berated me for my work."

"What?" Lord Peter looked shocked.

"He did. More than once. He wore whiskers and a collar and caused a scene as he harangued me for trespassing on God's territory."

"That doesn't make any sense. He loved all the technical advancements on display. Suddenly he could speak of nothing but reaping machines and Jacquard looms, of image telegraphs and pistols that shoot six bullets without reloading. When he spoke of your work, Miss Levett, it bordered on worshipful."

"I don't know how to explain his behavior," she told him. "I hoped you would be able to help explain it."

"I wish I could. He thought the Exhibition was a doorway into the future. The last time I saw him, he was talking about how it was full of opportunity." He looked down into his drink. "I laughed and said it was full of everything neither of us could yet afford." He fell silent for a moment. "It was not well done of me. Forrester was never going to come into money. Perhaps if I had not..."

They let the silence linger for a moment, but then Niall pressed forward. "Where was Mr. Forrester lodging?"

"In Lambeth."

"Perhaps the police believed you, but I know the bailiffs ran him out of there," Kara said. "Where did he go?"

Lord Peter sighed. "To a miserable set of rooms near Hungerford Market."

Niall met his gaze directly. "You were his closest friend. He gave you a key, did he not?"

The young man bristled. "What if he did?"

"We are neither curiosity seekers nor money lenders," Niall said grimly. "We do not wish to take any of Forrester's possessions or rifle through his things without purpose. We want to look for a hint, any bit of information that might help us discover who killed him."

The young man sank down in his seat. "You only wish to clear her name." He sounded anguished.

"I do not wish to be accused of a crime I did not commit, it is true," Kara said. "But, Lord Peter, I also do not wish your friend's murderer to go free. His death should be avenged. He deserves that much. Something was clearly tormenting him in his last days. His strange behaviors and dark moods point to it. What was it? Who was behind it? His killer deserves to be punished."

Lord Peter sat up straighter. "Yes, by God, they do." He sounded almost savage.

"Then help us," Niall said. "Let us into his rooms. Preferably before the police find where he was lodging and get in there."

"Better yet, come with us," Kara urged. "You can give us more insight into his life than anyone, it seems."

"Fine, then," Lord Peter replied. "Yes, I'll do it. As long as I go with you."

Niall watched him expectantly, but he didn't move.

When Lord Peter looked up, he seemed surprised. "Well, I cannot do it tonight!" he exclaimed. "I've only just brought my mother and sister here. I cannot ask them to leave so soon."

Kara sighed. "When, then?"

"Tomorrow afternoon, at the earliest."

"Fine," she said shortly.

"Very well. I'll meet you at the Hungerford Market at noon."

Niall exchanged glances with Kara. "We'll be there."

"Thank you, Lord Peter," she said softly. "I hope that together, we can find justice for your friend."

"By God, I hope so too." With a wave, Lord Peter signaled for the footman's attention and motioned for another drink.

Niall led Kara away to the entry hall. "I assume we do not wish to linger?" he murmured.

"We do not," she agreed.

"Stay here, then. I'll go fetch our cloaks."

"Yes. I'll send someone to fetch Jenny and send for the carriage." They were not the only ones taking their leave. "There must be another event drawing them away," Kara said as they followed a group out of the house.

Servants and torches lined the street. Some sort of altercation had broken out amongst the drivers and grooms of the two town carriages right out front.

A footman in that sunshine livery stepped close. "There seems to be a mix-up here." He nodded toward the angry men. "If you don't care to wait, you can step down toward the corner and I'll see your carriage is sent around to you."

"Thank you." Niall followed as the servant led Kara and the maid on. The Loudins' townhouse was just a couple of houses away from the corner of Margaret Street. Kara and Jenny had their heads together as the footman stopped where the pavement neared the busier street.

Distracted by the squabbling groomsmen, Niall walked a few yards behind them. He saw the moment when something in the circular garden grabbed Kara's attention. Taking a few steps back, she peered across the wide street. Just then, Jenny gave a cry and fell to the pavement. Niall rushed forward to help her.

The maid scowled at the retreating footman as Niall assisted her up, but then her gaze went past his shoulder and her eyes widened in horror. "Miss!"

Niall whirled. Kara was still staring across into the garden. She took a step off the curb and onto the cobblestones—just as a decrepit, old-fashioned Stanhope buggy came by at a clip and swerved right toward her.

"Kara! Watch! To your right!"

Her reflexes were excellent, thanks be to the gods. She jumped back. The driver of the gig, who had leaned down with his arm outstretched, just missed sweeping her up.

But he was still coming. Niall and Jenny stumbled out of the way as he drove the horse and buggy right up and over the pavement before veering off into the traffic on Margaret Street.

Jenny was back down on her knees. "Are you all right?" Niall asked, even as he was turning to search Kara out—

He froze. Her still form was stretched out, her feet in the road, her eyes closed and her head lolling where it surely must have struck the pavement.

Chapter Eleven

KARA FOUGHT HER way to consciousness. The darkness was reluctant to let her go. It grabbed for her, pulling her down, but she pushed on, climbing higher and opening her eyes at last to the faint light of early morning.

Wait. She frowned, turning her head toward the window, but gasped at the pain. Good heavens. What was wrong with her head? How did she—Why did she not remember—

Fighting back panic, she sat up, moving slowly. She was back in the Woodland Chamber at the White Hart. She startled when she saw Niall in a chair next to the bed, but he was slumped down, asleep, his legs propped on the end of the mattress.

The shadow of his beard had sprung up overnight. He looked rumpled, still in his formal attire, but his coat hung over the back of the chair and his linen had wrinkled. He still wore his kilt. She learned forward for a better look. It had fallen back a bit, exposing a fascinating length of bare, muscular thigh. Her pulse quickened, and she winced as she felt the throbbing of it in her head.

Reaching back, she felt along her scalp until she came to the lump at the back of her head. No wonder it ached: she had a good, egg-sized bump back there. But how—

Suddenly, it came back. The ball. The gig. "Jenny," she gasped.

Niall jerked upright. "You're awake. Thanks be to the old gods." Rubbing the sleep from his eyes, he reached back, took the pillow from his back, and tucked it behind her. Fluffing and fussing, he eased her back until she could rest, but still sit semi-upright. "How are you feeling? Any dizziness? Blurred vision?"

"No."

"Nausea?"

"No. Just a clamor in my skull. Where's Jenny? Was she hurt?"

"She's fine. You were the only one affected. Are you sure you are well?"

She tried to lick her lips. "I need a drink."

"Of course." He poured a glass from a pitcher on the table. "Just a sip, at first." He left her, going through the parlor to open the door to the passageway and bellow for Jenny.

Kara took another sip, then looked down and realized she was in her shift. Awkwardly, she pulled the covers up with one hand as Niall came back.

"Any nausea now?" he asked.

"None."

"The doctor said to go slowly."

"Doctor?" she said, shocked. "When? How did I get back here?" She frowned and tried to recall how the evening had ended. "I don't remember."

"What *do* you remember?"

"Leaving the ball. The buggy coming toward me..." She stopped. Had she seen what she thought she had?

"Kara, you saw something, didn't you? Across the street, in the garden, perhaps? You were staring so intently, and then you stepped into the street."

She frowned again, casting back. "Yes." The image flashed in her brain. "It was a boy. I recognized him. He was one of the urchins out by the boiler room the other morning. He was watching us. He looked terrified. He was waving his hands..."

"Beckoning you into the street?"

"No. No. He looked frightened half to death. He was pointing farther into the square. I think he meant to warn me of the gig coming."

Niall sank down into the chair. "I don't understand what that driver was thinking. He reached for you as if he meant to grab you, but he never would have been able to haul you up."

"He did grasp at me. It all happened so fast, but his fingers scrabbled for a grip. I saw it in his face, the moment he realized he couldn't get one—and then he *pushed* me instead."

Niall jumped out of the seat. He paced to the hearth and looked back.

She took another sip of water. "What is it you are not telling me?"

He opened his mouth to answer, but at that moment, Jenny burst in.

"Oh, miss! Glad I am to see you awake and back to yourself!"

She set down a tray, but Kara was caught by her wording. "Back to myself?" She looked to Niall.

He shrugged. "You did mutter a bit as we brought you home, and we could not get you to wake. There's a doctor lodging here. Hywel asked him to look you over."

"Oh, gracious." Kara wondered what she had said while insensible. "Well, I'm fine now, Jenny." The maid draped a shawl over her shoulders. "Thank you." Kara pulled it close.

"Here now." Jenny handed over a steaming mug from the tray. "You drink all of this, miss. My sister sent it special. It's good willow-bark tea. It will ease your aching head. And she says you should take no laudanum, no matter what the doctor says."

"That's very thoughtful of all of you. Thank you." Kara took a sip and made a face.

"It's vile, I know, but it works wonders. Now, you finish that and I'll fetch you some proper tea and a bite of toast. Just a bit, mind you." Jenny looked to Niall. "I'll be right along back," she warned him as she left.

Kara grinned. "Still chaperoning, is she?"

"And taking her duty very seriously. She's been worried."

"Niall. Tell me."

He paced from the hearth to the door and back again. His expression grew serious. "What you said about being pushed only confirms my suspicions. It was planned, Kara. We found a yellow livery coat abandoned by the Loudins' doorway. The man who led us to the corner was not one of the countess's footmen; he only pretended to be. He was positioning us. He also, apparently, started the altercation between the carriages that blocked our exit. And he tripped Jenny deliberately to distract us as that carriage headed our way."

She drew a deep breath. "Well. I suppose I must add this to my number of attempted abductions."

"It was my first thought, too. But that's just it. I think this was something else. Kara, I think someone might be trying to harm you."

Her skepticism must have showed in her face.

"Think. We were positioned so that we were in a clear path to be run down by a rogue vehicle skipping over the corner of that pavement. But you stepped out of the correct angle. And so the driver altered his approach and reached for you instead. Why? He could never have lifted you into that high seat with him. The best he could have done was to drag you along with him into the busier Margaret Street."

"Where he could have dropped me into traffic?" She mulled it over. "I would likely have been killed."

Pressing his lips together, he said nothing as Jenny bustled back in.

"Tea and toast will be here soon," she announced. "Now, Mr. Kier, you need to go out for a bit while I see the young miss settled."

"I can breakfast here," he objected.

The maid sighed. "A lady needs her privacy in the morning, sir. And though our miss is a marvel, sitting up and discussing things all rational, just hours after being attacked by a monster, she needs a bit of time to herself."

"A monster?" Kara's eyes darted between them. "Then I didn't imagine it? I thought it might have been a trick of the torchlight."

Niall looked grim, but Jenny shuddered. "No, miss. You saw him right. A demon, he was, marked by the fires of hell."

"I thought it a mask," Niall said. "Meant to frighten any by-standers."

Kara's mind was back, reliving those terrifying few moments. "It wasn't a mask." She recalled the livid purplish-red marks across the man's face. They had crept out of his hairline from his temple, spreading over one eye and tapering across and down to his neck. And all of his face had been in perfect motion and symmetry when he grimaced at her. "I think it is a scar, perhaps."

"But who is he? Whose bidding is he doing?"

She thought back over the evening. "Lord Latham," she mused. "He called me ungodly. And Forrester used that word and a great many more." She looked up. "Do you suppose it could be religious fanatics? Upset over that nonsense about my challenging God, and defiling his creation with my own?"

Niall looked startled. "I hadn't considered that."

She pursed her lips. "I have another theory, but you will not care for it."

Jenny put down her foot. "You can tell him all about it after you've readied yourself for the day, miss." She made a shooing motion in Niall's direction. "And you could use a wash and a change yourself, sir."

"Fine, I'll go," he said with bad grace. "But I shall return."

"We'll be counting the minutes," Jenny said.

IN THE END, it was nearly two hours before Niall returned to Kara's room. He knocked but heard no answer. After a second knock went unanswered, he quietly eased the door open.

She was asleep in a chair pulled close to the window. A blanket lay over her lap and her head leaned against the high sides of the chair. She'd dressed for the day, and her hair was caught up loosely in a net that disappeared into her ebony locks.

It caught him off guard, how peaceful she looked. It was such a contrast to her usual busy, bright, spirited demeanor. He stood a moment, drinking it in, until he realized what he was doing and began to retreat.

A board squeaked under his feet, waking her. Turning her head his way, she smiled and beckoned. "Come in."

"You must need your rest."

"No. Jenny's sister says that I must not be allowed to sleep the day away. I am inclined to follow her advice, after her brew worked so well. The headache is nearly completely gone."

"Good news."

"Pull up the other chair," she invited. "It is nice here in the sun. The view is just of the kitchen garden, but it is tidy and comforting, and you can hear the birds."

"I wanted to be sure to speak to you before I left to meet Lord Peter."

Her eyes widened. "I'm going with you."

"Kara…" he began.

She sat up straight. "I'm going with you, Niall. You don't even have to leave for another two hours, and I tell you, that will be long past the time I will be happy sitting here, accomplishing nothing."

"Haven't we just put forth the notion that someone may be trying to harm you?"

"We did. And it may well have begun with the attempt to frame me for murder."

He scowled.

"Would you have me sit here, hiding away?"

"It would be safer."

"Perhaps. Or perhaps my supposed enemies would track me

here and move in once I am alone."

Damn it all, but he hated that she was right. He saw the set of her shoulders and the blazing determination in her gaze and sighed. "I admit, I would feel the very same way."

Her eyes widened.

"But at the very least, you should have another dose of the willow-bark tea before we go," he insisted.

"If that's your price, I'll pay it," she grumbled. "But the stuff is nasty."

She leaned back, and he did as well, crossing his legs and settling into the plush comfort of the chair.

"Jenny told me you sent word to Turner of my accident. Thank you."

"Of course."

"He is important to me." She sighed. "I know it is unusual. I've been told often enough, but I don't care. He's my closest friend. I rely upon him."

"You are lucky to have him. He seems just as devoted to you."

They sat quietly for a few moments. Her eyes had closed. He wondered if perhaps she'd fallen asleep again.

"Do you wish to hear my other theory about last night?" she asked.

Not asleep, then. "If you are ready to share it."

"It occurred to me that I am likely not responding in the way that Scotland Yard expected once they decided to pursue me as a suspect in Forrester's murder."

"If they expected you to cry and wring your hands and protest in vain, then yes, they are likely at a loss. But it is your inability to prove your whereabouts that night that likely drives them on."

"Someone there thought I would be an easy mark."

"Foolish," he said lightly. "But honestly, I don't think you can paint them all with the same brush. The inspector that I spoke with seemed a good man. I think he's truly interested in justice for Forrester."

"I hope you are right." She hesitated. "I admit, I may have a bias against the Metropolitan Police force. We have had differing opinions and butted heads in the past."

Niall frowned. "Over the abduction attempts?"

"They don't tend to take them seriously. They were never very helpful, even when my father was alive."

He thought about that for a moment. "But your first abduction, the only one, you said, in which the kidnappers were successful in taking you? Surely the police—"

"Rescued me?" she interrupted. "No. They did not. Turner did."

"Ah."

"Yes," she said sharply. "Quite."

He waited, giving her the choice.

"I've never told anyone about it," she said after a long, silent stretch.

Still, he waited. It could go either way. He spent the time trying to calculate the odds, but he would never, ever push her.

"I was eleven," she began quietly. "So young. Carefree. I had a busy schedule. There were so many things I wanted to learn and explore. I was bouncing on the seat of the carriage, on the way to my mathematics tutor. I had solved a difficult problem and couldn't wait to show him." She paused. "They knew my schedule. They shot the coachman and took me from the carriage."

He made an involuntary sound of protest. "You must have been terrified."

"Utterly. I was so afraid that I thought I would choke on it. I'd never been treated so roughly in my life." She shrugged. "A privilege to say such a thing, I know, but it didn't lessen the terror for me. They left me alone in the dark with only rats for company—rats that I had to fend off, with my arms and legs tied. Hungry. Thirsty. Lost and frightened. But at least they were not brutal. It could have been so much worse. I was lucky in that, at least."

"Who was it?"

"People who needed money and thought I would be an easy way to get it. My father said the police were convinced it was a footman who had recently been fired from Bluefield Park. They thought he was after revenge and money both, and refused to seriously consider anyone else."

"It wasn't him?"

"It was not. In fact, it was the man who had been hired to replace him. He and one of the kitchen maids had conspired to have the first footman fired. Once the new man was in the position, they were free to set it all up. Turner was also a footman at the time. He read the signs, saw them plotting, whispering. He had heard the new man boasting of the pub he and his brother were going to buy when their 'ship came in.'"

"Did Turner go to the police?"

"He did. They did not listen. Sent him on his way. He pursued it himself, and he was the one to find me, bound and gagged and left in a dark attic in the very pub the villains meant to purchase. He rescued me, and was nearly killed himself in the process."

"And he's been with you ever since."

"Yes. He's intelligent and intuitive. He knows me so well." She shook her head. "I can't tell you how many times I have come up with a question for him to investigate, about my work, my research, my life—only to find he's anticipated me and already knows the answer."

"A valuable friend, on many levels," Niall remarked.

"Yes," she said wryly. "The sort one keeps even when society disapproves."

"Oh, I understand." He gave her a lazy smile. "Try to imagine the furor that results when I introduce Gyda as my assistant."

"Oh!" Her eyes widened. "Yes. I had considered that she must have met resistance in her role, but I suppose you have as well."

"Resistance, innuendo, and a great deal of ribbing, but I have never regretted the decision for a moment."

"How did it come about?"

He hesitated. "That is more Gyda's story to tell than mine."

Her brow rose. "Understood. Perhaps the time will come when she feels comfortable sharing it with me."

"I hope so. Gyda is smart and so genuinely amusing and fiercely loyal. She is a great friend of mine and always will be."

"Yes," she said, smiling into his eyes.

They shared a moment of perfect accord, and Niall took a moment to marvel at it. Friends he'd had in his life, but never someone he felt such a rapport with on so many levels.

"I look forward to getting to know your Gyda better," she said.

"As I do Turner." He laughed. "If he will allow it."

"He is protective. I hope he hasn't insulted you."

"Not at all. I'm glad he's careful."

"He's had to be, I'm sad to say. Even with respect to the Metropolitan Police."

"You don't truly think they are behind last night's 'accident'?"

"It is unlikely, but not impossible. It would be far easier to pin me with a false murder charge if I were too dead to fight back."

He knew she was trying to lighten the mood, but he frowned. "Thinking further, though, they will not be pleased if we unmask the murderer before they do. We'd make them look even more foolish."

She lifted a shoulder. "Better they suffer embarrassment than I a false conviction." She sat a little straighter. "Speaking of which, pull the bell cord, won't you? I understand that the willow-bark tea must steep for a while, and I wish to be ready in time to meet Lord Peter."

Chapter Twelve

KARA AND NIALL left the Strand on foot and followed New Hungerford Street into the market. Shoppers wandered, assaulted by the cries of the vendors and an assortment of smells rising from the fish market on the lower level.

"Oh! Look there." Kara pointed. "There is Mr. Gatti's stand. Have you seen his chocolate-making machine at the Exhibition?"

"Seen it—and tasted the product," Niall confirmed. "I heard he's selling pastries and ice cream here." He gestured toward the long line waiting to be served. "Only a penny for a taste of real ice cream? I'd buy you one, if it were not for Lord Peter awaiting us."

"I would thank you and decline for today—and come back another time, prepared."

"Prepared?"

She nodded toward a young man happily spooning up the last of his treat. He licked the small glass shell clean, then walked back to hand it to an attendant at the stall. The attendant thanked him, scooped up another serving into the dish, and handed it over to the next person in line.

"Oh," Niall said faintly.

"Bring your own dish. Or better yet, come to Bluefield Park and I'll have my cook prepare you a selection of flavors."

They moved on past the footbridge leading to Lambeth and

past the Great Hall, a timber-roofed building housing aisles of fruit and vegetable vendors.

"There he is."

Lord Peter lounged on a set of granite stairs, next to a flower seller. His eyes were closed.

Kara stopped before him. "Good afternoon, my lord."

He cracked an eye open to peer up at her. "Oh, damn it. You're real."

"I'm afraid so."

"I was hoping you were a champagne-fueled dream." He sighed and pulled out his pocket watch. "And besides, it's only just noon. Not only are you real, but you are punctual." He groaned.

She rolled her eyes. "Very well. Good noon to you, my lord. And you were the one who arrived early."

"It was easier than going home." Heaving himself to his feet, he smiled at the flower girl, tossed her a coin, and helped himself to a lacy sprig of elderflower. Bowing, he presented it to Kara. "For you." He winced. "To brighten up that navy ensemble. And in hope you may live up to its promise."

"Zealousness?" She named the characteristic that the flower stood for, took the delicate spray, and tucked it into a buttonhole. "You may depend on it."

"Good. Let's go find the bastard who killed Walter."

He led them through the market, then north and east through an alley. After crossing the narrow lane of Charles Court, he stopped in front of a run-down building. The pavement leading up to it was cracked. The shutters listed. Paint on the door peeled away in strips. Trash lay everywhere, and several doors down, a woman slept, propped against a doorway and snoring loudly.

"Good heavens, what is that smell?" Kara asked. "It's worse than the fish market."

Lord Peter's skin had taken on a green hue. "I don't know, but it doesn't go away."

"Was London so important to Forrester?" Niall asked abruptly. "He comes from a family of solid gentry, I heard. Why live in a hovel like this? Why not go home?"

"He would never," Lord Peter declared. "There was no love lost between him and his family, I assure you. Walter was as disgusted with them as they were with him." He shook his head. "No. He only ever saw a couple of his cousins, and those infrequently. He would never bring them around or introduce us, though."

"Why not?"

Lord Peter looked uncomfortable. "Walter's family might have an ancient bloodline, but I do not believe they have any sense of morality or honor. Some of the things he's told me... Well, he got his penchant for scheming honestly. He's mentioned some greedy, reprehensible acts. But as for the cousins, something he said once made me think that at least one of them is in service." His voice lowered. "Walter was likely ashamed."

"So, he's a young man whose family and financial situations restrict him to the fringes of upper society, and then his accident and amputation likely shoved him even further out. But he didn't give up on his wish to belong? To run with you and your...fellows?"

The young nobleman looked grateful at Niall's mild choice of words. "No. He was determined to make his way inside."

"Nearly impossible," Kara declared. "To force your way into such circles, if you are not born to them." She raised her brow at the young lordling. "Why did he not go his own way? Did you encourage him? It would have been kinder to gently point out the realities of the situation."

"I did try," Lord Peter insisted. "But Walter was so determinedly optimistic. It's part of what made him such a good friend. I've never had anyone credit me for much so wholeheartedly. He was endlessly kind and supportive. It was dashed difficult not to return the favor. And he was determined to do it, to make his fortune and win acceptance—and to see the faces of those who ridiculed him once he'd done it."

"He must have known that if he made his fortune in trade, he would still not be entirely acceptable," Kara said with the conviction of experience.

Lord Peter gave her a sideways glance. "He knew it. It's been done, though. He meant to achieve it for himself, somehow. He was forever scheming over it."

"Well, then," Niall said. "Let's go in and see if we can discover anything about his latest plans, for they may be what got him killed."

The inside of the place was worse than the outside. The smell in here was unmistakably the ammonia odor of urine. Lord Peter had the key, and quickly led them to a set of rooms on the first floor, at the front of the house.

Dim and dusty, that was Kara's first impression. She strode across to throw open the curtains and then surveyed the result.

Had Mr. Forrester owned more possessions, the place would undoubtedly have been a mess. Instead, it was merely untidy, with his few clothes and personal items tossed about the single room, on and around the bed, a table, and a desk.

A stool beside the bed was cluttered with ointments, potions, and lotions. The desk and the table were both covered in papers. In unspoken consensus, Kara and Niall stepped toward the desk. Lord Peter went to root amongst the piles of newspapers on the table.

Side by side, they stared down at the tangle of tailor's bills, crumpled broadsheets, playbills, scribbled vowels, letters in several languages, and greasy papers that had once been wrapped around fish or meat pies.

"How many languages did Forrester speak?" Kara asked.

"At least four," Lord Peter replied absently. "He was most fluent in German. He thought it only prudent, given the queen's connections with the German nations."

"This whole stack is in German." Niall picked up a pile of letters. "Signed only by someone who goes by the letter W."

"What's this?" Kara retrieved a page that had been beneath the letters. It was divided into three columns. At the top of each column was a letter: F. B. W.

"Ten numbers in each column," Niall said, scanning it. "Numbers one through thirty, but not in order or any pattern that I can see."

"These numbers at the bottom are larger," Kara said. "One in each column. Twelve. Fifteen. Seventeen."

"They look as if they were added later," Niall added. "The ink is different."

"I know a fair bit of French, but not German." Kara turned toward Lord Peter. "By any chance, did you partake of German lessons with your friend?"

"A few," he replied.

"What can you tell us about these letters?"

He glanced through them. "They seem normal enough on the surface. Asking after Walter and acquaintances they have in common." He frowned. "There's something, though. The writer is reminiscing about times they shared in Berlin. I know for certain Walter never traveled outside of England." He looked up. "Do you suppose it's a code of some kind?"

"Perhaps. Can you tell me what this phrase says?" She showed him the words scribbled across the bottom of the columned sheet.

Lord Peter made a face. "I believe it says...Meet at *Kneipe* in Moabit on the thirty-first."

She frowned. "Moabit..."

"It's a small region outside of Berlin," Niall said as she circled back and handed him the page. "Industrial."

"And *Kneipe* translates to pub or tavern," Lord Peter offered. "That word I am familiar with."

"So, we assume the three columns are assigned to individuals? F for Forrester? And two more? They are to meet outside Berlin in either July or August, since both of those have thirty-one days and we are still in June." Kara snorted. "Why do I feel as if this is significant, even if I have no idea what it means?"

A low moan came from Lord Peter. "Oh, no. I'm afraid I have an idea of what it means."

Kara and Niall turned as he unrolled a coiled document he'd dug out. He held it up, and she saw it was a diagram. Plans for some sort of machine.

"I can't tell what it is meant to be," she said.

"I think I know." Lord Peter handed it over to Niall. "I think it's one of the objects that captivated Walter's attention."

"From the Exhibition?" Niall asked.

"Yes. That damned Jacquard loom."

"It doesn't look like a loom," Kara pointed out.

"I can't believe I know this, but it's a device that is fitted to a loom. Somehow it simplifies the process of creating complex textiles like damask or brocade. When you fit them together, it becomes a Jacquard loom. Walter did go on about it." Lord Peter's shoulders slumped. "A few weeks ago, he asked me if I knew a good draftsman who worked fast."

Kara stilled. "Did you give him a name?"

"Of course not! What use have I ever had for a draftsman? But surely this must be what he wanted it for. He must have had copies made."

"He was selling trade secrets? Plans? Designs?" Kara's eyes widened.

"Well, we know there are those who think such theft is worth a man's life," Niall said quietly.

"Who?" Lord Peter demanded. "Who equates material things with the life and soul of a man?"

"The Exhibition committees, the Crown, and the government," answered Niall. "As exhibitors we were all warned about honest and impeccable business practices. There are collaborations, vast dealings, many opportunities, and huge amounts of money coming from this event. Any thefts or disruptive practices would be seen as imperiling the nation—treason." He gestured toward the plans. "If Forrester had been caught with that, he likely would have been hanged."

"Good heavens." Lord Peter sank down into the chair at the table. Frowning, he gestured toward the columned page on the desk. "But what is that about?" He glared at Kara. "And why did he steal the arm of your automaton? Why not just take the plans?"

"Because I do not work from plans like that." She nodded toward the diagram. "I sometimes draw out a difficult mechanism, something small, part of a whole, that will be needed to accomplish a specific task or motion, but it's usually a rough drawing in my notebook. Plan a whole piece ahead?" She shook her head. "My process is different. I start with an idea, but I forge ahead one piece at a time, and the project grows and changes as I go."

"It's because you are an artist as much as an engineer." Approval colored Niall's tone and warmed her.

"I don't know." She spread her hands. "I can only work the way I work." She gave Lord Peter a stern glare. "And I will tell you the same as I told the magistrate—your friend had only to ask for my help. I would have created anything he wished, with no fees, no bills due, no bailiffs. Just to help him and to move the current methods forward." She waved the page. "Thirty numbers in mixed-up order. Three columns. Three initials. Perhaps they stand for pages of stolen designs and there are three accomplices, splitting them up to get them out of England and to Berlin, where they will be assembled again."

"It's possible," Niall mused.

"Perhaps they are something else altogether, but if these mean he was working with others to steal products, plans, or ideas, then I imagine some would indeed kill him over it."

They all jumped abruptly as a loud pounding started on the door. "Forrester! I hear you in there! I want my money!"

Kara looked between the young nobleman and Niall as the pounding resumed. Niall shrugged and started toward the door, but there came a rattling of keys, and it swung open with a flourish.

"Aha!"

They all exchanged shocked stares with the old woman in a yellowed cap who stood in the doorway.

"Who the devil are you?" Lord Peter demanded.

"Me?" came the outraged reply. "Me? I am the owner of these premises. Who the devil are you, sir? And where is Forrester? He owes me two months' rent!"

"Please, come in, Mrs....?" Kara said soothingly.

"Mrs. Armstrong," the woman answered, standing straighter.

"Would you care to come in and sit, Mrs. Armstrong?"

"And who are you, to be inviting me into rooms in my own house?" She stayed where she was. "Not that I'm not happy to hear you say it in English," Mrs. Armstrong muttered.

"Did you expect us to speak something other than English?" Niall asked.

"Why wouldn't I?" she demanded indignantly.

"Are there so many foreigners about here, then?"

"A regular parade of them through here, Forrester has led! And so I told that nosy cow, Mrs. Moore from down the street, when she quoted the papers at me. No sign of the troubles and riots they predicted, is there? No flood of foreigners invading the streets? Ha! All she must do is sit in my passage and she'll see!"

"What sort of foreigners have you seen, Mrs. Armstrong?" Niall asked.

"How should I tell them apart? All speaking in different tongues—and likely heathen, half of them!" She sniffed. "That's what comes of hosting such a thing, and in the middle of London, too. Too many people, too much talk of machines and manufactures and foreign goods."

"I take it you have not visited the Exhibition, ma'am?"

"I should say not! At a shilling a head? And in such crowds? But enough about that. I want my money, I do. Where are you hiding Forrester? Months of rent, he owes me."

"He's not in hiding," Kara said gently. "I'm afraid he's passed away."

"Dead? And without paying his shot? Isn't that just like him?" Lord Peter made a noise of objection.

The old woman glared around at each of them. "You can just take his things with you and go. Else I'll be selling them to get a bit of what I'm owed."

"I will pay Forrester's debts to you, madam." Lord Peter stood. "My men will come to remove his things."

"Not before the police see them," Kara said. "They should know." She waved a hand toward the documents.

"Why? Because they provide alternate motives?" he asked sourly. "You might have convinced me with the description of your creative process, but Scotland Yard is going to think you don't have any plans because Walter stole them. They'll weigh you, already in hand and now accompanied by a ready motive. And in the other hand, they'll look at a sheet of random letters and numbers that they might somehow use to find a killer. Which do you think they will be more likely to embrace?"

"Scotland Yard? A killer?" Mrs. Armstrong repeated, aghast.

Lord Peter turned to the old woman. He peeled a couple of bank notes from his purse and crossed over to hand them to the landlady. "Everything will be gone tomorrow." Turning, he nodded at Kara and Niall. "Good day."

"I knew that boy was trouble," she muttered, counting her money.

"Should we take the documents?" Kara asked Niall.

He considered. "They'll be boxed up and shoved in Lord Peter's attics if we do not. And we could always decide to show them to Wooten and his men when the time is right."

She nodded. Gathering up the plans, letters, and the strange columned page, she let Niall deal with the landlady.

"We'll all be tidied up and gone by tomorrow." He held out a coin. "And this is for you, ma'am. I invite you to come and see the Great Exhibition for yourself, before you judge it so harshly. There are a great many wonders and works of art to be seen.

Perhaps we might all begin to look for the good in our fellow man and what he can offer, instead of expecting the worst." He looked to Kara. "Do you have it? Let's go, then."

She nodded and took his arm, only looking back once at the sad relics of Walter Forrester's life.

Chapter Thirteen

"**A**RE YOU SURE this is a good idea?" Niall asked the next morning. He and Kara were just entering the park on their way to the Exhibition.

"Turner says that my attendance at the Loudin ball is all the tittle-tattle in Society. Scotland Yard will hear it and know I am still in Town. Until we have a chance to follow up on our theory of Forrester stealing industrial secrets, I think I should try to resume a schedule as normal as possible."

"I mean to try to make an acquaintance in the French delegation," Niall told her. "It might be useful to know if they realize that the plans for the Jacquard machine have been copied."

"Turner also has contacts within the Metropolitan Police," Kara said, eyeing him askance.

Niall raised a brow in surprise.

"He earned the respect of some of the officers who know what he did to save me during that first abduction. They know how he was treated then, and how our reports of threats have been treated since." Kara lifted a shoulder. "And in any case, they do say you should know your enemy."

"Your enemy?" Now he was surprised. "Is that truly how you see them?"

"They have never acted as my friends or allies," she pointed out. "And now they seem to be acting against me."

He supposed she was right. But he didn't like it.

"His friend told Turner that someone from Scotland Yard was sniffing around the Zollverein displays and the men who accompanied them."

Now he was surprised. The Zollverein was the economic coalition of German states that had sent goods to display at the Exhibition. "Do you think they've got wind of Forrester's activities?"

"Why else? Those letters were in German. That document mentioned a meeting in Prussia. One of those other accomplices might be representing the interests of one or more of the German states. It would be good to know if any of the delegates has a name that begins with a B or a W."

"We should find out, if we can."

They entered the Crystal Palace through the main doors. As they approached the barrel vault, a figure stood up from the edge of the Crystal Fountain.

"Inspector Wooten," Niall murmured as he approached.

"Good morning, Mr. Kier," the inspector called out. He gave Kara a courteous nod. "Miss Levett. I am happy to make your acquaintance at last."

Niall formalized the introductions, and she inclined her head. "Inspector."

"It's glad I am to see you returning to the Exhibition, miss. Your continued absence may not have been well looked upon."

"It has been a difficult couple of days, sir. I am looking forward to getting back to a normal, uneventful pace of life."

"I heard there was some sort of accident," Wooten said, watching her closely. "I hope you are well?"

"I will be, once the bump on my head finally subsides."

"Good. Good. Mr. Towland speaks highly of you. I am inclined to agree with his stance on your innocence."

"Thank you, sir."

"There are others, however, who still hold reservations about you, miss. And about your involvement in Mr. Forrester's death."

"You tracked down his identity, then," Niall said.

"We have, although we discovered Miss Levett had been there before us." Wooten inclined his head. "You recognized the significance of that maker's mark before our boys did. I congratulate you on your quick thinking."

"Thank you," Kara replied. "The gentleman spent days watching me, quite unnervingly. And other days he donned a disguise to harass me in front of a large audience." She gestured around them. "I wished to know what drove this strange behavior. I still wish to know. His mechanical surgeon was unable to help me. If you discover any explanation, I hope you will share it, sir."

"And so I will," the inspector assured her.

"Miss Levett discovered his name and the fact that he owed outstanding debts," Niall said. "Have you found anything else that might account for the man's murder?"

"We don't know much more than that, alas." The inspector looked sharply between them. "I hope you will also share anything of import, if it comes your way."

Niall was impressed when she agreed without a flicker of hesitation.

"Very well, then." Inspector Wooten breathed deeply of the perfumed air. "I will take my leave of you and allow you to begin your busy day, but for one thing more. Please stick close, Miss Levett. If you disappear again, it will make it harder for me to bring your doubters around to the right side."

She nodded. "I will be right here, sir. Good day."

"Good day to you." With a bow and a nod, the inspector strode outside.

"Well," Niall said as they turned into the British nave. "I shall have to remember that."

"What?"

"How casually you told that lie."

She stopped walking. The Canadian canoe hung silently

overhead. "Inspector Wooten lied first. He did not tell us everything he knows, even as he asked us to do so." She met his gaze directly. "I want you to understand that I do not lie, not in the natural course of things. But I will absolutely do so to protect myself from someone who means me harm, or to protect someone I care for. It's another…technique I've learned. Another weapon I arm myself with. And I refuse to feel bad about it."

Something inside him eased a little. "I don't wish you to feel bad about it. I'm only sorry you've had to learn such things and work so hard to protect yourself."

"I certainly never thought to put those skills to such use as this, but I suppose they will come in handy." She glanced up at him as they resumed their progress. "I suspect you have a few useful skills I haven't seen, as well."

"Time will tell," he said with a grin.

They arrived at Kara's exhibit first. Turner had done his best to repair the automaton, but Niall could see the dismay she felt as she realized how much damage had truly been done.

"So much work, gone in an instant," she said mournfully. "And yet it is as nothing compared to Mr. Forrester's death."

"And nothing compared to the mischief he might have caused you," Niall reminded her.

She sighed. "I suppose I will begin to restore him, but I confess, my heart is not in it."

"Just stick close to your exhibit. You should be safe here, and you should rest when you can. I'll stroll over to the Zollverein exhibit and see if I can strike up a conversation."

She bade him a good day easily enough, but she was still standing in front of her automaton, staring silently, as he headed back the way they'd come.

Chapter Fourteen

I T TURNED OUT that the men from the Zollverein were running late that morning. They appeared to be in a frantic mood, as well. When Niall tried to strike up a conversation, one of them brushed him off, stating they were short-handed and busy today.

Niall bowed and nodded, then headed back, as the gates were about to open to ticket holders. But it wasn't a complete waste, as he'd passed through the French display on the way to the private refreshment room set up for the exhibitors. He began a casual conversation with the Frenchman lurking near the Jacquard loom. Hopefully, he would be able to follow up and draw the man into a more pointed discussion.

Now he was back at his own display, however, and greeting those who stopped to admire his work or ask questions. He glanced now and then toward Kara's spot, worried that she might tire or suffer another headache. She looked her usual serene self, though. He was relieved—that was, until he looked down to see her laughing with Mrs. Braddock. Not that he objected to Kara's widowed friend, but he stared in horror at the tiny older woman standing next to her.

The Marchioness of Abbington. Her hair was white, her face set in stern lines. She used a cane, but the ramrod-straight line of her spine made him suspect it was an affectation.

"Odin's *arse*," he whispered.

Gyda, who had only just arrived a moment ago, looked over at him, startled. "Good heavens, what is it, Niall?"

"It is a first-class level of emergency, that's what it is," he said. Ducking behind the tall frame of his Scottish-themed gates, he resisted taking a peek down the nave. "I have to disappear for a little while. I know you came to consult with a prospective customer, but please, cover for me?"

"Of course." Gyda might not know all the reasons behind his odd fits and starts, but she was used to them. She didn't question them, either. It was a courtesy he appreciated more than he could say.

"I'll return," he assured her. "When it is safe."

Niall ducked behind the textile exhibit next door and made his way down to one of the side doors leading outside. Trying to appear nonchalant, he strolled along a path outside, passed the barrel vault, and entered again, into the nave housing the foreign exhibits. Getting his bearings, he headed toward the French showing. He might as well put the time to good use.

His acquaintance from this morning hailed him as he strolled past, just as he'd hoped. They spent a few minutes in friendly conversation. The Frenchman had a lot to say about the food he'd encountered in England—all of it disparaging. Niall convinced the man to accompany him to dinner later, after the closing hour.

"I promise," he said, "it's not all slabs of rare beef and brown bread."

His new friend readily agreed. Niall took his leave after dawdling as long as he dared. Moving stealthily through the crowd, he kept an eye out for Mrs. Braddock and her grandmother. He ducked into the furniture display just before Kara's, hid behind a massive chair shaped like a shell, and surveyed the field.

He let loose a sigh of relief. No sign of the ladies at either her exhibit or his. He stepped out and headed back, but nearly jumped out of his skin when Kara came out from behind her long-case clock.

"Niall! There you are. We were looking for you."

"We?" he asked.

"Yes. Eleanor stopped by. She brought along her grandmother. Lady Abbington has indeed agreed to let it be known that she approves of my participation here."

"That is good news."

"Perhaps I shouldn't let it bother me, as you said, but the marchioness is influential, and it is a relief to know there will be less nasty talk about me."

"As long as we can keep you from being accused of murder," he said with resignation.

"Yes." She deflated a little, but recovered a smile quickly. "And about that...more good news. Lady Abbington is hosting a dinner this evening. We are invited."

"Ah—" he began.

"That is not the best part." She gave a little hop of excitement. "I convinced Eleanor to invite her German acquaintances. You recall the exhibitors from Berlin, who crossed the channel with her?"

"Oh, yes."

She reached out and squeezed his arm. "We will dine with them this evening. It will be an excellent chance to steer the conversation toward opportunity and sharing of knowledge and fear of losing trade secrets. We could possibly learn something useful. And we can discover if any of their surnames begin with a W or a B!"

"Oh, yes. Very good work, indeed. But..." He made a face.

"But?"

"But I have only just agreed to take one of the French exhibitors out to a decent dinner this evening."

"Oh." Her face fell. "We truly cannot just show up with an extra guest in tow."

"No, of course not. But it's no matter. We shall just divide and conquer. You should be safe enough with Eleanor. I will try to discover if the French are aware that their plans have been stolen and copied, and you can find out all you can from the Germans. Perhaps we shall get to the bottom of all this that much quicker."

"Yes, perhaps."

He tried to hide the relief he felt at having escaped an encounter with the knowing old marchioness. "We'll have your name cleared in no time, I hope."

>>>><<<<

ELEANOR VERY KINDLY sent her carriage to fetch Kara and to ensure that she came early, before the rest of the dinner guests were expected.

"Oh, heavens," her friend said, kissing her cheeks in the European manner. "Don't you look lovely tonight? No one ever shines in jewel tones like you do, my dear."

"I could certainly never pull off that color," Kara replied, admiring the light sea-foam silk of Eleanor's gown. "But you are divine in it."

"Thank you, one does try! And how fitting that you should use the word *divine*." She gave Kara a sly smile. "However, it is not my gown that I want to show you."

"You mentioned your latest painting?"

"Yes. I want to show it to everyone, but I am glad you will be the first."

She led the way toward a large and inviting parlor. "Grandmama will be down shortly. But first...I was working on this while I was in Dusseldorf." She brought them to a stop before a large painting mounted over the mantel. "I call it *The Artist as Peitho*."

"Peitho?" Kara frowned. "One of the minor Greek goddesses, isn't she?"

"Indeed. She is the goddess of persuasion." Eleanor's color

was high, her eyes bright. "You know what they said about me, after my marriage. About William, as well. He was an old fool. I was a young adventuress. Impossible that I might care for him. I was an opportunist only after his money. I heard them—so many jokes, innuendoes, and sly barbs. I took every terrible comment and put them into this."

Kara stared. It was a vivid, colorful self-portrait. Eleanor wore classical robes, but in scarlet hues. Her hair was escaping its elaborate coiffure. Her defiant gaze met the viewer's with a smirk. Behind her, an image of her husband, looking older than when Kara had last seen him. He reclined on a chaise surrounded by greenery. He wore a look of fatigue, and his hand extended out toward Eleanor's back. From his fingers flowed a river of gold coins that piled at her feet.

"Persuasion. Temptation. Seduction. His family are the worst culprits, of course, but there are plenty of others, in every part of Society, who speak of me with scorn and derision." Eleanor grinned fiercely. "Now I've given them an image to go along with their nasty little whispers, a picture to bring their words to life." Her chin lifted as she looked to Kara. "What do you think?"

Kara burst into tears.

Eleanor was as surprised as Kara was. "Oh, my dear! What is it? Have I shocked you?"

"Yes!" Kara said on a sob. "I was worried for you at first, when you announced your betrothal. It didn't seem to be your idea."

"It was Grandmama's idea. But it was a good one."

"Yes, that's what I thought. I thought you were content. Happy, even."

"Dare I say it? I *was* happy. As was William."

The tears started again.

"Kara! What is it?"

"I thought it was enough. For you. And for your husband. I thought you were both happy, and you had each other and the good friends who knew the truth of it—and I thought that was enough. You said it at the Loudins' ball. *What does it matter what they all think?*" She fluttered her hand, indicating London, Society, the rest of the world. "But clearly it does matter. It all burrowed inside of you, rankled in your soul, caused you so much resentment that you were forced to create this...to paint yourself in their image."

Eleanor stared at her. "Well. Yes."

"I thought you were strong. That you let all that scorn slide off you. But it *wounded* you."

Eleanor drew her to a settee. They sat down, and she wiped a tear from Kara's cheek. "You are right. They did wound me. They made me doubt myself, and that made me miserable. And then I grew angry. At them and at myself. I started creating this painting, and do you know, it has helped me to heal. As their image took shape beneath my brush, I realized it's *not me*. I had to paint it to show myself that I was right all along and that their opinions do not matter. I won't let them change me. I understand myself now. But I am compelled to show them the painting. They need to see it, to see how ridiculous their words are. That I understand them and their scorn, and that now, at last, they don't matter."

"Yet their talk caused you so much angst and anger and sorrow...and you didn't even kill a man!" Kara started to cry once more.

"Kill a man? Kara? What on earth are you talking about? Tell me, right now!"

She did. She told Eleanor everything. About how she'd finagled her way into the Exhibition, about the murder and how her name got mixed up in it, even about her unusual response to Niall Kier.

"Oh, goodness. You have had a time of it." Eleanor rang for a servant and requested a couple of handkerchiefs. "And a bowl of cool water," she called after the retreating butler, rising.

She raised her brows at Kara. "We need to be rid of those red eyes before the other guests arrive." She sat back down and looked intently into Kara's face. "Tell me. Truly. Have you been this upset all along, as this little adventure has played out?"

"No. I have been determined to clear my name and relentless in pursuing any avenue of investigation. It was seeing your pain that upset me, not only for your sake, but because I realized how bad it might go for me if we do not succeed."

"We?"

"Yes. We. I haven't been alone in this. Not for scarcely a moment." Kara sighed. "To tell the truth, I've felt alive in a way I never have before. I've actually enjoyed myself a bit."

It sounded like a confession, because it was one.

"Because of Niall Kier," Eleanor said.

"I've never had anyone treat me so kindly, or go to so much trouble to come to my aid."

"If it was anyone but him, I would suspect this was all an elaborate plot to get close to you."

Kara blanched, dismayed at both the notion and the fact that it had never occurred to her. "It isn't."

"You are ridiculously rich and notoriously hard to approach," her friend reminded her. "I see I've shocked you once more. Well, hold on, for I'm about to do it again." She breathed deeply. "I tried to seduce Niall Kier when I met him in Rotterdam."

Any remaining color in Kara's face drained away. She *felt* it go.

"Do not fret. He did not take me up on my offer. In fact, he adroitly turned me down without making me feel bad about it. Still, as nice as he was, it did sting a bit. It led me to ask around about him."

"What did you find?"

"Not much. He is a respected artist and businessman. He is fiercely independent. One lady described him as a lone wolf. It's rumored that he never mixes business with his personal life, so the fact that he's thrown that aside for you...it must mean something."

Kara could not suppress the shiver that Eleanor's statement

gave her.

"He's not a fortune hunter. That much we don't need to worry about. Everyone I spoke to agreed that he has money enough. His business is successful. He travels for it, and he stays at the right places and associates with the people who can further his career, but he never fawns or seeks favor. He's known as a good man."

"I already know that much," Kara said with conviction.

"Good. Well, now that we have him sorted out, we must go about clearing your name. You were right about one thing. As bad as it was for me, it would be infinitely worse for you, should you actually be accused of murder."

"I thought I could bear it," Kara whispered. But her eyes moved to the painting once more, and she shivered.

"No. We must avoid it. You are already different from all of those Society girls. You would only be proving them right, that anyone not exactly like them is not to be trusted. It would be incredibly ugly and haunt you forever, even if you were absolved. No, don't tear up again!" Eleanor rose. "Here is Fields and the cold water. Sit back and soak your eyes for a few moments. The other guests will be arriving soon."

Kara soaked a kerchief and wrung it out, then leaned back and draped it over her eyes. Beside her, she felt Eleanor jiggling her knee as she thought out loud.

"Well, at least I understand why you wished me to invite the German gentlemen this evening," she said. "We will ask them if they are worried about losing the secrets of their industries and watch to see if any of them grow wary at the discussion."

"And we must discover if any of the Zollverein exhibitors have surnames that begin with a W or a B," Kara said. "We have a theory that Forrester had two accomplices and that they meant to divide up either parts or plans to get them out of England. We think they mean to meet up near Berlin soon."

"Our task is clear, then. It should be easy enough for the two of us," Eleanor declared. "What group of gentlemen could resist us?"

Kara laughed.

"Whoops. Take that cloth away and dry your face," Eleanor said. "I hear the first carriage pulling up outside."

Chapter Fifteen

NIALL'S HEAD FELT as if had grown two sizes overnight. And surely there was a gremlin in there now, pounding on his skull from the inside, trying to stretch it further. The morning light was not helping. He pulled his hat lower and leaned against the stone of Kara's building on Adams Street, where she had spent the night after her dinner last evening.

"Oh dear."

He opened his eyes to see Kara watching him with amused sympathy.

"You didn't try to keep pace drinking with a Frenchman, did you?"

He only groaned in answer.

"Hold there a moment." She disappeared inside the coffee shop and came out with a small cup. "Drink that. It will help. It's French, and I have no doubt your friend is having one this morning as well."

He tossed back the dark brew and shuddered, but by the time she came back from returning the cup, he had to admit that the throbbing in his temple was lessening. "Thank you."

"You are welcome." They set out, moving at a slower pace than usual, thanks be to all the old gods. "Well, I can see that you enjoyed yourself. Did you learn anything useful?"

"Other than *Monsieur* Masson's capacity for spirits? Not much, unfortunately. I broached the subject a couple of times, but honestly, it seems as if he is entirely unaware that at least one of his displays has had its design plans copied. And if he is unaware, surely the rest of the French exhibitors are as well."

"How on earth did Forrester manage to pull that off?" she asked.

"I have no idea. But what of you? Did you learn anything from Mrs. Braddock's German friends?"

"Indeed. I learned that Germans are quite accomplished at flirting, that they are entirely confident in themselves and their own excellence, and that they seem completely unconcerned with the idea of their secrets being stolen."

"Because, having determined to steal others, they've taken steps to protect their own?" he asked sourly.

"Perhaps. There is a certain fascination to their unflagging sense of assurance. Certainly Eleanor seems to respond to it." She'd been a little surprised at how blithely her friend went along with her guests' imperious belief in their own prominence. "In any case, there is no way to prove it, but it seems unlikely they would show such confidence without reason. Eleanor believes it is likely at least some of them are involved. She's spent some time in the region, and she says there is a great deal of political maneuvering going on. The court in Berlin squabbles among themselves, and they square off with Austria over the idea of unifying the German states. She says there is a great deal of anti-English sentiment in Prussia."

"But there is a Prussian delegation spending time with the royal family even now. There are rumors of Prince Albert jockeying to wed his eldest daughter to the Prussian heir."

"And she's so young," Kara said. "She's a mere child."

"I'm sure, after some of the disasters in the royal family in the last generations, they think it wise to arrange her marriage early."

"Well, based on what Eleanor says, I'm sure there will be opposition. There is a significant faction that believes England weak and our way of government too liberal. They hope to tighten alliances with Russia instead."

He groaned. "Those are problems too grand for me to contemplate, especially this morning. But what of their surnames? Did any of them have the right initial?"

"None of the men attending did, but I did manage to discover that one of the men being sent home is called Wernher."

Niall stopped walking. "We must find him. Before he leaves England."

"Indeed. Eleanor means to help. She made an appointment to meet one of last evening's guests today for ices at Gunter's. She will find out all she can."

He frowned as they started walking again and entered the park. "You told her—"

"Everything," she replied. "I trust her. She will help, if she can."

Carefully, he nodded. His head didn't fall off, which greatly improved his mood. "At this point, we need all the help we can get." He looked her over. "By the way, how do you feel? You had a long day yesterday when you likely should have been resting."

"I'm a little tired, but mostly I'm just growing anxious."

"I understand. It feels like a dark cloud hovering just overhead."

"Yes."

He almost felt the light touch of her gaze as she glanced askance at him.

"It hasn't been entirely horrible, though. All of this," she said gingerly.

That look, her tone—they were a breeze brushing against his customary alarms, setting them to chiming a little. He knew what that meant. It was time for him to retreat, to withdraw, to slow whatever intimacy might be growing and put up a wall against expectations.

He knew how to do it. He was skilled at it.

"No," he said instead. "There have been bright spots, haven't there?" He tried for a grin. "Amongst the false accusations, death, and assorted assaults."

She didn't laugh, and he didn't pursue the topic any further. They continued on in silence into the Crystal Palace.

She brightened, however, as they stepped around her glorious case clock and found a brightly beribboned box left on her worktable.

She hesitated, though, as she took it up. Niall both approved of her caution and deplored the course of her life that led her to have such a reaction.

The look she gave him had a question in it.

"No," he said, startled. "It's not a gift from me." He pursed his lips. "Do you think Inspector Wooten might have left it?"

"Perhaps." She untied the ribbon and opened it to find a selection of honeyed candies. "Or one of the Prussian gentlemen?" She gave a slight shake of her head. "I admit, after everything, I am hesitant to trust even such a small kindness." She didn't look happy about the admission.

He was about to agree, but was distracted by a tug on his coat. He looked down into the wide eyes of the boy who had spoken with him days ago.

"Don't let 'er eat it," the urchin said earnestly. "The monster left it."

Niall looked quickly back to Kara, but she had heard. She replaced the lid and knotted it up tightly with the ribbon. Then she smiled at the boy. "Thank you," she said softly. "You were trying to warn me the other night as well, weren't you?"

The boy nodded mutely, staring at her, transfixed.

Niall couldn't blame him. She was likely the loveliest creature the child had ever seen.

Kara rested her elbows on the table, leaning in the urchin's direction. "Thank you."

The boy kept on nodding. "Ye're welcome, miss."

"My name is Kara," she told him. "What's yours?"

"They all call me Pip, miss. But me mam named me 'arold."

"Harold," she said warmly. "I like it. It fits a boy as brave as you have shown yourself to be."

"Brave?" he squeaked. "Shut yer saucebox! Me? Brave?"

"What else, when you have stepped forward, twice now, to warn me of danger? And Mr. Kier said you also defended me against the accusation of harming Mr. Forrester, that you would tell the police that you knew I was not involved."

He stood taller. "And so I will, should those blue-bellies try to say ye 'ad a 'and in it," he vowed.

"Thank you, Harold. I am going to ask you to be brave once more and answer my question." She paused to regard him solemnly. "Did you see Mr. Forrester's murder?"

He shrank back into himself and darted a glance from side to side.

Niall braced himself, ready to reach for the boy, should he run.

"Harold, it is your decision." Kara kept her tone level. "But it could be a great help to us in clearing my name if you tell us what you saw."

The boy visibly wavered, but he rose to the occasion. Lifting his head, he met her gaze. "I'll tell ye, miss."

She smiled at him.

He gulped. It took him a moment to begin. "I was sleepin' in the boiler room. It stays warm in there even after the sun goes down, after it's all shut off," he explained. "I was jest drowsin' off when I heard 'em arguing. I snuck a look out in the courtyard and saw two o' 'em, standing by the tall stone, tellin' each other off." He hesitated a moment. "I couldn't see 'em, but I knew there was more out there, 'idin' in the dark."

He stopped, and Niall and Kara exchanged a look and waited.

"The nob that was killed, 'e was 'olding the arm from yer metal man. The other one grabbed it off him."

"What did the other one look like?" asked Kara.

"Couldn't tell. 'e were wrapped in a dark cloak, with the 'ood up over 'is face. 'e talked low and mean. I didn't 'ear it all, but then they started fightin' over the arm, and I thought the nob might win, but then the monster stepped out o' the shadows and grabbed 'im. 'e was big, bigger 'an the other two. Strong."

"Is that why you call him a monster, Harold?"

"No. It's because I saw 'is face. 'ood fell back and I saw it. 'e must o' come straight from the devil, 'cause his skin was still boilin' red and bubbled up from the flames."

Niall raised a brow at Kara. "Did he stab Mr. Forrester?" he asked the boy.

"No. The monster held him tight, but 'twas the first one who stabbed 'im. Tore somethin' long and sharp from inside the arm and drove it right into his neck. I 'id then, 'cause they dragged the body into the boiler room, but I saw them duck out through the loose boards behind the 'edges, jest like we do."

We being the flood of street urchins, Niall supposed.

"They tossed the metal arm deep into the bushes, but I wiggled in and fetched it out." The boy looked up at Kara with large eyes. "I woulda brung it to ye, miss, but Tom Ratter snatched it away that morning."

"I'm sure you would have," she reassured him. "You did fine. Thank you for telling us what you saw. You've been very helpful."

"Ye must be careful, miss. The monster is after ye now. 'e tried to run ye down with that carriage, and now 'e's left ye yon wee box." He gazed fearfully at it. "Don't trust it, miss. Not fer a moment. Leave it fer the rats."

"I will take care and be sure those candies do not harm anyone," she promised, then frowned. "Harold, have you or the other boys ever seen this monster before?"

"No, miss. Nor 'eard of any like 'im." He shivered but then rubbed his hands together, watching her closely. "I'll talk to the blue-bellies fer ye, miss, but do ye think ye can get them to promise not to send me to the 'ulks?"

"The hulks?"

"Fer trespassin' in 'ere? Without payin' my shilling?"

She grew serious. "Harold, I will be sure that no harm comes to you."

Niall thought that sounded like more than a temporary promise.

"Do you perhaps know the layout of the city well, Harold?"

The boy straightened. "Like the back o' me 'and, miss!"

"Excellent. If I write a note, could you deliver it to a gentleman on Welbeck Street? And wait to bring back a reply?"

"Yes, miss. Fer certain, miss."

Kara looked to Niall. "I'll ask Dr. Balgate if he can test the candies, or perhaps find a chemist's shop to do so." Her gaze unfocused for a moment. "There is something else I'd like to ask him as well."

"Fine, then." Niall nodded.

"We'll report back later," she said with a grin. "Come, Harold—you can examine my sailing ship while I write a note."

Niall turned and headed toward the exhibitors' refreshment room. Something told him he was going to need more coffee.

➤➤➤◄◄◄

THE BOY'S WORDS echoed in Niall's head all morning. The "monster" was after her now. He kept his eye on her, but at least from this distance, she appeared to be her usual self, if perhaps a bit subdued.

Sometime during the morning, though, Turner joined her. She looked more relaxed then, smiling and laughing with the servant who was her right-hand man and good friend, and engaging the people who flocked to marvel at her creations. Feeling better knowing she wasn't alone, Niall turned back to his own guests.

It was sometime in the early afternoon that a gentleman approached him with a friendly smile. "Mr. Kier, I presume?"

The man held out a hand, and Niall took it. His grip was firm, his handsome face alight with pleasure.

"I simply had to meet you, sir, and, of course, I must thank you for coming to the aid of my cousin."

"Your cousin?" Niall said. "I'm afraid you have me at a loss, sir."

"Oh, do forgive me. I am Lord Camhurst. Miss Levett is my cousin. I have heard how you hastened her from harm's way after that nasty business here and made sure she gave a statement about it to a man of the courts. Exactly what she should have done, but I won't be surprised to hear if it took a bit of persuading."

Niall grinned. "I did have to work at it. But I am glad indeed to meet you, sir. It was a relief to hear that Miss Levett has a close male relative whom she also counts as a friend. She seems to be alone so often."

"Friend? Did she say so, by Jove?" The baron flushed with pleasure. "I'm sure I've always thought us good friends, but she can occasionally make a chap feel...superfluous."

"She does seem to have an independent spirit."

"Heavens, yes. And always has done so. But so many talents, as well. I say, have you seen her case clock?" His eyes brightened. "So very clever, the way she's fashioned it to resemble a tree— and that squirrel! I'm sure I don't know how she contrived to have it dart amongst the branches like that, and to disappear into the tree itself! It's a wonder, I vow."

"I am partial to her sailing ship, myself." It would always remind Niall of the first time he met her. "My jaw nearly dropped when I first saw it wound up. So many intricacies. Your cousin truly is a marvel, sir."

"Indeed, she is." The baron's smile broadened as a young lady wandered to his side from the jewelry display. "And here is another. Mr. Kier, my fiancée, Miss Bailey."

Niall bowed. "A pleasure, Miss Bailey."

The girl was pretty, with fine features and hair just a shade too dark to be blonde. She gave him half a smile. "Good day, sir.

Some of your jewelry looks to be very fine."

"I offer my thanks."

"Mr. Kier is the brave soul who convinced Kara to speak with a magistrate," the baron added.

"Ah, then we do owe you a debt of gratitude." The girl looked down the nave toward Kara's exhibit as she said it. Her gaze lingered.

Niall looked too, but saw only Kara smiling as she and Turner interacted easily with the hovering crowds.

"Not at all. I was happy to come to Miss Levett's aid."

"Ah, but we are grateful," Lord Camhurst insisted. "We would love to get to know you better. Why do you not come to dinner? You and Kara both? My cook does a leg of lamb with spiced apples that Kara is quite fond of. Let us make an evening of it."

"Thank you. That sounds delightful."

"Miss Bailey will help to set it all up, won't you, my dear?"

"What's that? Oh, yes. Of course." Her attention was still fixed on Kara. "Darling," she said to the baron as she laid a hand on his arm. "Who is that gentleman with your cousin? They seem quite friendly with each other."

"To whom are you referring, my dear?" Lord Camhurst strained to look through the crowd.

"The gentleman in black. He looks to be slightly older than she, but that is of no consequence, is it? Is he someone who shares her interests, assisting in her projects, perhaps? Dare we hope that her affections might be engaged at last?"

The baron looked again, then let out a sudden laugh. "Yes, I should say he works with her, my dear! That is Turner, her butler."

The girl reared back, shocked and entirely disapproving. "The butler? Oh dear. It is no wonder people talk of her, then! Come, darling. You simply must have a word with her. It is not at all the thing to be so easy with one's servants!"

Her betrothed laughed again. "Kara doesn't give a fig about

people talking about her. You'll just have to reconcile yourself to her ways, my dear. She's a good girl. A smart girl. She might push the line, but she never goes beyond the pale."

"Nevertheless, you are the head of the family. It is your duty to voice your objection," Miss Bailey insisted.

Lord Camhurst looked skeptical. "Kara's got her own opinions on things. I'm not sure she'll care to hear mine." As Miss Bailey's expression continued to be mulish, he sighed. "Very well. I will speak with her."

A light dawned in the girl's eyes. "Did you mention a dinner party, my dear? Yes, that would be just the thing. Surely we can find an eligible young man or two to invite? Your cousin just needs to meet the right sort of man. Once she's married, we won't have to worry about her...eccentricities."

"We can certainly try, my dear. Generous of you to think of it," he said fondly. "But don't be disappointed if it doesn't go your way. You must begin to understand, my dear." He sent a resigned gaze down the nave. "Kara is a law unto herself."

The baron patted his fiancée's hand and gathered her close. After bidding Niall a good day, he took her off to see the rest of the Exhibition.

Niall watched them go. Kara's cousin did seem fond of her, but there was no doubt the family arrangements were odd. If he had to guess, he would surmise that Lord Camhurst had taken a good deal of ribbing about his pretty, intelligent, rich, and independent cousin. And though his betrothed might be a bit of a prig, she was right about one thing: Kara's oddities would reflect on them, and on their growing family, as the years went on.

Ah well. Families. Hers would have to go a long way to approach the flaws and instabilities of his own.

FEELING A LITTLE fatigued, Kara left Turner to handle the masses and retreated to her worktable at the back of the exhibition space. She felt a pang every time she looked at her poor, ruined *Gambler*. She'd thought to start in on his repairs, but she just could not summon up any sort of enthusiasm for the idea. She found her mind drifting instead to the Scottish glen she'd promised to re-create for Mr. Grant.

Her fingers drifted amongst the smallest of her supplies while she imagined sheep grazing on the hills in a Highland scene. They had plenty of sheep there, did they not? The clockwork would have to be tiny, and perhaps she could manipulate some fine brush wire for wool...

She startled as someone close by cleared their throat. Loudly.

"Oh! Mrs. Armstrong." She blinked up at the elderly woman. "You did come to see the Exhibition after all. I'm so glad. Have you been through it all? What do you think?"

"I think there is a good deal too much naked marble flesh about," the older woman said. "The machines are infernally noisy. And who would consider a set of teeth carved from a hippopotamus? But the furniture is very fine," she said begrudgingly. "And the stained glass is quite well done."

"And have you seen Mr. Kier's fine work?" Kara asked with a glance toward his space. It was crowded, as usual. And there were a great many young women lurking about. As usual.

"I have, and I admit, it is grand. If I still had a garden, I would commission him to make me a set of gates for it." Mrs. Armstrong gazed around. "But your work, young lady? The mantel clocks are nice, I admit, but the rest of it is too fanciful for my tastes."

Kara grinned. "You are not the first to say so, Mrs. Armstrong, but they are just fanciful enough for me."

The woman sniffed and changed the subject. "Your fine friend, his lordship—his men finished cleaning out Forrester's rooms this morning."

Kara nodded. It all seemed such a sad end to a sad life.

"They were gone before the sun had a chance to rise over the city, almost, but they left too soon. Just before I set out, there was a package delivered, and addressed to Mr. Forrester. I don't know how to reach his lordship, but perhaps you do. Can you direct him to send one of his men back to fetch it? I'd rather it all done and taken care of before he departs."

Kara blinked. "Departs?"

"Well, I did hear the servants gossiping amongst themselves. One lorded it over the rest, as he was meant to go abroad with their master."

"Oh, I see." Kara's mind was spinning. Lord Peter had not mentioned a trip abroad to her, or to Niall, that she knew of. "Thank you for alerting us. I think the easiest thing would be for Mr. Kier and me to come along this evening. We'll take the package and drop it off at Lord Peter's, so it can be stored along with the rest of Mr. Forrester's things."

"Very well, then." Mrs. Armstrong nodded. "Now, then, I'm off to sample this famous new mineral water in the refreshment center. Bubbles, indeed," she scoffed, and she was off.

The afternoon wore on, and eventually the time came for the last of the attendees to pass through the doors. Kara had sent Turner home to Bluefield Park earlier. She thought he'd looked tired lately, and she wanted him to rest. Now, she hurried over to find Niall and tell him about the package and Lord Peter's plans to go abroad.

He made a face at the news. "It could be entirely innocent," he mused. "The man did just lose his best friend. He might just be looking for a change of scenery and company."

"True," she said. "Or perhaps he's traveling to an industrial town outside of Berlin. Either way, I'd like to hear what he has to say about it. The package gives us the perfect excuse to bring it up."

"It does." He finished settling his exhibit for the night, and they headed out through the park.

"I met your cousin, by the way," he told her. "Both Lord Camhurst and his intended bride, actually."

"I told him to stop by and introduce himself. I couldn't get away." Kara glanced askance at him. "What did you think of Joseph?"

"I quite liked him, actually."

She noted the faint note of surprise in his tone. "His conversation does tend to wander, but Joseph has a good heart."

"He has a real fondness for you, I believe, which must be a point in his favor." He smiled. "He wishes the two of us to dine with him and Miss Bailey."

She bit back a laugh. "I'll wager he mentioned the lamb with spiced apples."

"He did."

She shook her head. "I paid the dish one compliment, and now I am doomed to be served nothing else at his table forever."

"It could be worse, I suppose. A good thing you did not compliment fish pudding or something equally horrendous."

"Fish pudding? Not a favorite?" she asked with a grin.

"Not of mine." He shuddered. "Gyda is more than passing fond of it, though. A memory from her childhood, I gather."

"I promise never to serve you fish pudding, then."

"Thank you. If it's to be a pudding, I prefer a solid old beefsteak and suet, myself."

"Duly noted." She cocked her head at him. "But what did you think of Miss Bailey?"

He hesitated. "I think your assessment was correct. The less time you spend together, the better you will get along."

She laughed. "Also noted. She did tell me that I must make an effort to be more like other young ladies." She rolled her eyes. "But as long as she makes Joseph happy, I will not quarrel with her."

She let a few quiet moments pass before she changed the subject.

"I should tell you, though, that young Harold performed admirably today," Kara informed him. "He came back this afternoon with an answer from Dr. Balgate. He informs me that the candies were laced with opium."

Niall stopped dead in his tracks, and she was forced to stop and look back. "What the devil did the oaf mean to do?" he demanded. "Let you eat the drugged candy, wait until you were falling off your feet, then abduct you in full view of thousands of witnesses?"

"I'm sure I don't know what's in a madman's mind. None of it makes any sense to me." She kept to his side as he resumed walking. "There is something else, though."

Looking resigned, he waited for her to continue.

"I've seen quite a few injuries, working with Dr. Balgate," she explained. "I've examined both fresh wounds and those long healed. In none of them, however, have I seen scarring like our 'monster' carries. It made me wonder if it is scarring at all. So I described it to the doctor in my note. He wrote back, and he says it sounds like it could be a certain type of birthmark—a skin discoloration that can grow and change over time. It shows up early and is often smooth, but it can grow in size with a child and can also thicken, or bubble up like stones have formed under the skin."

Niall frowned. "I only caught the quickest glimpse of him. You saw him better. What do you think?"

"It sounds like what I saw that night. The doctor said it could be a family trait, or just random, but that the afflicted sometimes suffer from fits or difficulty learning or speaking."

"How reassuring," he said wryly.

She sighed. "Well, young Harold did put the notion in my head that our 'monster' is taking orders from someone and is not the mastermind behind the plot. I suppose this could reinforce it."

"Perhaps." Niall waved toward the intersection ahead. "Let's jump aboard the omnibus. It will make its way around to and down the Strand."

She was happy to agree and take a seat on the crowded plank, if only to give her feet a rest. Her mind wandered as the bus moved on. It had been a busy few days' work.

She had the vague realization that she should be distraught over it all. She'd lived so long with the pall of attempted abduction hanging over her head like a dark cloud, and all of this—false accusations and physical threats against her—should feel bleaker and more alarming. Yet it did not.

It was as she'd told Eleanor: the lack of it was due to the man sitting beside her. Mr. Niall Kier had proven himself stalwart and true. He was intelligent and quick and possessed of a dry wit that complemented her own sense of humor. He had somehow easily done what no man in her life had managed—he both viewed and treated her as an equal. Like a person with her own brain, wits, and will—and the ability to use them to make decisions about her own life. Only her father had come close, but he'd held a set of dictates that she never could get around.

Niall Kier stood back while she dictated the course of her own life. He had disagreed with her—notably about speaking with the magistrate—but he had explained rather than persuaded and allowed her to decide. And he'd been right, she was forced to admit.

These last days had been harrowing, but she felt challenged and exhilarated instead of oppressed and disheartened, and it was all due to him and his bolstering presence.

"The next stop is the market," he said, leaning down. "It won't be far to walk from there."

Nodding, she looked up to meet his gaze directly. "Thank you."

He caught the solemn weight behind the simple words. "For what?"

"For everything."

He searched her face, then gave her a grin. "Do not worry. We are not there yet, but we'll get there. We'll find them."

They would. And she would feel vindicated and free—and also quite a deep sense of loss.

"We will." She stood as the bus began to slow. "Let's go see who sent a package to a dead man."

Chapter Sixteen

"**W**ELL, I GIVE you this much, you stick to your word."
Mrs. Armstrong held open the door to her apartments
and beckoned them in.

Niall was grateful. Even more so when she shut the door and
blocked out the ammonia smell of the passageway. Blinking, he
looked around at the surprisingly fine parlor. The furniture was
old-fashioned, light and delicate—and had once been expensive,
he would bargain. The carpet was very worn but looked Persian.
The drapery was heavy velvet, and the room smelled of camphor
and cooked eggs, which was a sight better than urine. There was
more to Mrs. Armstrong than a cranky demeanor and a dingy
cap, he surmised.

"Here's the package." The landlady took up a square parcel
from a side table. "Small, so it's likely not much, but I wouldn't
feel right about keeping it, not after his nibs paid all of Forrester's
debts and a bit besides."

"Thank you, ma'am." Niall held it in his hands. It was perhaps
eight inches square, and he thought he felt something clanking
together inside as he took it.

Kara frowned at the package. "It didn't come in the post?"

"No. Delivered by hand, it was."

"Who delivered it?" Kara asked.

"I don't know. Never saw him before. A deliveryman." Mrs. Armstrong thought a moment. "Young, he was, but not a boy."

"Did he wear livery?"

"No. He was just a young lad, doing the odd job."

"Did he speak with you?"

"Only to ask if I would take the package, as no one answered Forrester's door. I didn't bother to tell him the man had died."

"No foreign accent?"

"No. Not this one. Just a normal delivery lad."

The woman's patience was wearing, it was clear.

"Thank you, Mrs. Armstrong," Niall interjected. "It was good of you to take the delivery and to tell us of it. Forgive our questions, but we are looking for any information which might help us find who killed the young man."

She nodded. "It's good of you, but Forrester owed money all over London. He likely borrowed from the wrong sort, if you know what I mean."

"I do. It's a distinct possibility. But there are other theories, as well. If you happen to remember anything that might help us, I hope you will let us know?"

"Aye. I'll do so."

"Thank you." He smiled at her. "Now, I understand you visited the Exhibition today? I hope you found it to your liking?"

"I found it a mixed bag," she answered. "But I do take your point. Mayhap mankind does have more to offer other than strife and corruption." She sent Kara a sharp glance. "I noticed, too, that you were the only woman with her own exhibition space, young lady, and not just a bit of fancy work hanging on a wall."

"Not the only one," Kara corrected her. "Surely you saw Madame Caplin's corsetry?"

The old lady looked scandalized. "I did, but the less said about a lady's underthings on display, the better!"

Kara fought back a laugh.

"Well, I had a good think over it on the way home," said Mrs. Armstrong. "And good on you, I say. You show them a woman can have a brain as good as any man's. Although I'm guessing that there's more than a few men who don't want to hear it."

"Quite a few more than a few," Kara said with a little sigh.

"Well, you keep at it. You've inspired me, in fact." Mrs. Armstrong raised her chin. "There's no reason a woman can't manage a building as good as any man. I'm going to start fixing things up around here. Going to stop that fusty old bugger Holmes from pissing in the passage, fix up the shutters, and paint the door. I'm giving Forrester's rooms a deep clean and a bit of a patch before I rent it next. Also, when old Boskins next door finally gives up the ghost, I might just buy his place and fix it up, too."

Kara's eyes had widened and her color deepened. She looked flummoxed, so Niall stepped into the breach.

"Good for you, Mrs. Armstrong. Such ambition is to be lauded, and I am convinced you will make a success of it. And, of course, I wholeheartedly agree that Miss Levett is a fine inspiration."

The landlady flushed herself. "Yes, well. I should get on with it."

"Indeed, we will leave you to your work," Kara said. "I wish you the best of luck, ma'am."

They said their goodbyes, and had just stepped from the walkway into the dark and narrow way of Charles Court when the door opened behind them again.

"Hold a moment! I did recall something." Mrs. Armstrong followed them out to the street. "The boy—the delivery lad. He gave me a tradesman's card as he left. He said he'd been instructed to hand out as many as he could before he returned. I'd just tucked it in a drawer, but here 'tis."

Niall took it. "Thank you, ma'am. Good evening to you."

"Can you see it?" Kara asked as the woman returned inside. "It's so dark here."

"No." He tucked it in his pocket.

"Where are we bound?" she asked. "I think I would like to see what's inside that package before we see Lord Peter."

"I had the same thought."

"I hate to go all the way back to the White Hart and then out again. Shall we find a coffee shop?"

"No. Your presence will be frowned upon, and we won't be safe from prying eyes in any case." They came out onto the Strand. "I know a spot. It's on the way to Portman Square, too."

He led her across the busy street and through a few back ways until they came to the church at St. Martin's. They headed north on St. Martin's Lane until New Street, where he turned in and stopped before a narrow townhouse.

"Just do me a favor? You will have questions. Comments. Just hold on to them until we are done and on our way again. We need a bit of privacy, and that we can get here."

She agreed, although she looked mystified.

"Thank you." He took a breath and knocked on the door. When there was no answer, he knocked again.

Abruptly, the door was thrown open. "Yes, yes! What is it?" A very pretty woman wrapped in a gauzy robe frowned at them. Her face changed, broadening into a grin when she recognized him. "Niall, *tesoro!* It is you! Whatever are you doing here?"

"I wish to leave something for Gyda, if you don't mind." He paused. "She's not here, is she?" he asked hopefully.

"No, no. She is out, with nearly all the rest. A party in someone's garden somewhere. But me? I am not feeling like a celebration. My heart is broken."

"Again?" he asked.

"*Amore,* she is a harsh mistress, no?" She beckoned. "Come, come in. Your friend must wait here in the antechamber, though. You know the rules—" She stopped suddenly and reached out to take Kara's hands. "Wait!" she breathed. "It is her? This is she?"

Niall bit back a smile. "Indeed. Miss Levett, may I present Miss Emilia Nardonne."

"How do you do?" said Kara.

"I do very well, now that you have come to Lake Nemi. We are great admirers of you here."

"Lake Nemi?" Kara asked. "As in, the one near Rome? Diana's mirror? Where the temple to the Goddess Diana sat? That lake?"

Emilia pulled her inside and into the main entry hall. "Oh, thank heavens. She has a mind for more than metal and clockwork." Smiling, she nodded. "Yes, Miss Levett. We style ourselves after the temple to Diana." She led them into a parlor that ran the length of the house, all done up in varying shades of greens, browns, and creams. It looked entirely respectable, if one did not pay too close attention to the art and bric-a-brac placed around the room.

Kara, of course, was not so inattentive. She stared, eyes widening further with each discovery.

Niall warmed a little. The art was very fine, very explicit, and very much themed to suit the original intent of the place.

She gasped a little at the sight of the marble sculpture in the place of honor above the hearth, as so many did, once they mentally untangled the coil of limbs and realized what they were looking at.

"Good heavens." She rounded on Niall. "Have you brought me to a brothel?"

He dropped his head. "That's one of the questions I meant for you to wait to ask."

Emilia reached out and smacked him on the shoulder. "You didn't tell her before you brought her here?"

"I'm sorry, but I do not know where *here* is," Kara said.

Emilia's chin rose a notch. "We are not a brothel. We are a social club. For women."

Kara stared at the large painting on one wall, a graphic rendition of the goddess Diana sporting with her ladies.

Emelia sighed. "We are the maidens of Lake Nemi. We began as a place for women to freely explore their Sapphic curiosities, but we have grown into much more."

"More?" Kara repeated.

"Yes. Out of necessity. We have expanded our intentions. Now all women are welcome, regardless of their proclivities, age, or status. This is our sanctuary, the home of our hearts. Here we can rest, and also put aside all of the restrictions that society seeks to force upon us."

Kara's alarm visibly lessened. She began to look interested.

"We have been hoping to tempt you here for a visit." Emilia glared at Niall. "You might have prepared her or brought her when the others were around." She looked down. "And I was dressed."

"I shall bring her back with due notice," he promised, before turning to Kara. "These are women after your own heart. Some are interested in the sciences, but they don't have the means, permission, or approval to explore their interests. Here, they can do that."

"We have set up a lab upstairs. Perhaps you would come back for a tour and give us some suggestions for it?" Emilia asked with a smile.

"Oh. Of course," Kara replied.

"We have artists and scholars as well," Emilia said with enthusiasm. "We have a studio and a library for their work. Some of our members like to travel, and they plan trips together from here. And some of our members just need the freedom to relax and be themselves. This is the place for a woman to pursue all of her interests."

"How wonderful," Kara said, her enthusiasm growing. "It is a fascinating idea."

"I am one of only two gentlemen who have been offered membership," Niall told her.

"That sounds a true honor. Who is the other?"

He grimaced. "I don't know. They won't tell me, and I've yet to encounter him."

"You don't spend enough time here, *caro*," Emilia complained.

"Nor can I this evening. We just need a few minutes to leave this for Gyda and to have a private conversation."

Emilia raised her brows. "Like that, is it?"

"No," he said sternly. "Miss Levett is a *lady*. We will act in a perfectly respectable fashion, but we need to do it away from prying eyes."

"How dull." The Italian beauty sighed. She led them back to the middle of the house and down a passage to open a door at the back of the house. "Here you are." She leaned in toward Kara. "I will leave you alone in case you wish to convince him to act disrespectfully."

"Alas, we've no time tonight," Kara said with a laugh. "But we do appreciate your accommodation."

"Bah! You may repay me by returning to spend the day with us sometime."

"I would love that." She sounded as if she meant it.

Emilia departed, and Kara leaned against the door. "Out of necessity," she whispered.

"I'm sorry," Niall said as he went to root in Gyda's desk. "I hoped I could squire you through to here without going into the details."

"I was shocked at first," she admitted. "But I am glad to know the details. I hope Emilia was not insulted."

"She would have been had you become judgmental, but as you did not, she will be even more impressed with you."

As was he. He liked her. He liked her more the more time he spent with her. But he had to admit, he'd been nervous about how she would react as she got to know Gyda. It warmed him to know his best friend needn't fear insult or rejection before Kara even got to know her.

"The education of women—or more specifically, the lack of it—is a travesty. A blight upon the nation. I support anyone who seeks to address the notion." She glanced at him, eyes alight. "My brain is abuzz with possibilities."

"Good. Let's get you safe and clear of murder charges, and then we'll address them all." He gave a grunt of triumph and pulled a knife from the drawer. After setting the package on the desk, he cut the string and unwrapped it.

Only to find another parcel inside. Tucked beneath its strings was a note.

Now what do we do?

It wasn't signed.

He handed the note to Kara and repeated the process on the second parcel. He found a smaller wooden box inside. Something rattled inside as he lifted it out of the paper.

Carefully, he opened it. It was stuffed with straw and several smallish, different-shaped bits of metal. Tucked in with it was another note.

I can't do it. Find someone else. I'm being watched.

Niall sat down at the desk and pulled out each of the metal bits. "Ten of them," he said, looking at her.

"As in ten numbers in each of those columns?" she suggested.

He took up the second note. "We have to compare this to those German letters. I think the writing is similar."

But she had picked up one of the metal parts and was running a finger over the odd, branched shape of it. Her expression had gone very still. "Niall," she said in a strangely flat tone. "That card that Mrs. Armstrong gave you?"

He pulled it from his pocket and stared down at it.

Kara was across the desk and unable to see it, but she held up the bit of metal. "Mr. Harry Boggs. Bootmaker. Tool repair. Surgical mechanic."

Niall stilled, too. He laid down the tradesman's card. It was on thick paper, elaborately decorated and inscribed with exactly those words.

Chapter Seventeen

"I SHOULD HAVE known," Kara said again as she stalked into Portman Square. "Boggs sent that package. He's in on the whole thing. Those were parts he was filing. Not tools he was repairing. In pairs! He must have been copying them." She shook her head. "But all I had on my mind at the time was the chance to see the artificial limbs he'd designed."

"Are you sure you want to do this tonight?" Niall asked. "It's growing late. You've had a long couple of days, and you need rest after your injury."

"I cannot rest," she growled. "Boggs's shop is closed. I have no idea where he lives. Eleanor sent word that her German friend doesn't know where Wernher has gone. I have to do *something*. So Lord Peter it is."

She marched right up to the door and knocked. The same young footman they'd spoken with last time answered. He looked at Kara, his eyes widened, and he hurriedly stepped outside and closed the door behind him.

"It's you, miss!"

She stepped back a bit. "Yes."

"If you mean to track down Lord Peter again, you must be careful! The countess has got wind of it. Someone told her they'd seen you with him, out and about. She's got herself in a tizzy, she has, and she don't know whether to tear her hair or start counting your money."

Kara had no idea what to say to this—again. This night just seemed to be full of moments that knocked her askew.

"Where is Lord Peter tonight?" Niall asked roughly.

The footman looked about, uneasy. "He's at Wellberg's. I heard him say something to his valet." He shook his head. "You must take care. That place wears a nice front, but it's particularly unsavory."

"I know it."

The young man leaned in. "It's a den full of tricksters, thieves, and liars. Lord Peter is a sharp one, but there's been plenty of green 'uns that have found themselves taken in and deceived. It's no place for a lady."

"We'll be careful." Niall tossed him a coin. "Thank you."

"Aye, guv," the lad said with resignation. He smiled at Kara. "I'm rooting for you, miss."

"Thank you," she said faintly. "Good heavens," she muttered as she turned back toward the street. Niall hurried behind her, and she turned to give him a glare meant to shrivel his innards. "Well. Now I know how you got him to talk last time."

"It worked," he said, unrepentant.

"Tear her hair," she muttered. "As if I would look twice at her man-child of a son."

"He's looked more than twice at you," he assured her. "But that's normal behavior for any man with red blood in his veins."

She snorted. "Is that supposed to be flattery? Even if it was, it wouldn't get you out of this one." She stopped and glared up at him again. "You may be sure I will return the favor, if the need arises."

"I give you full leave to injure my reputation in the course of our investigation." His grin brightened his dark eyes. "And I look forward to the flattery afterward."

"Don't hold your breath waiting," she scolded, continuing on. But she couldn't hold back a grin of her own. "You'll get neither an apology nor any bit of flattery, just the reminder that what's good for the goose works just as well for the gander."

"Honk, honk," he said happily, and raised his arm to hail a cab as they emerged from the square.

"You said you knew the place," she said as a hack pulled up before them.

"I do, although I've never been inside. It's quite infamous. Exeter Street," he told the driver. She let him hand her in. "You'll want to put your hood up," he warned.

It took two coins to get them both in the door of Wellberg's. A porter led them through the crowded rooms. Lord Peter's footman had been correct, she thought. The place looked solid, traditional, respectable. But passing through, she detected the scent of desperation and deceit mingling with the clouds of smoke and the press of bodies.

The porter stopped at a door that he said led to a private room. He gave a patterned knock, and after a moment, the door was thrown open.

"Yes? We've got this room for the entire night," the young gentleman inside said. He'd discarded his coat somewhere and held a pair of dice in one hand. Behind him, the room was full of crowded tables, smoke, and the loud, swaggering talk of men at play.

"Visitors have arrived, requesting to see Lord Peter, sir. They say it's urgent."

The young man looked Kara up and down. He didn't bother to turn around, just threw his head back and shouted, "Wallflower! There's a skirt here to see you!"

Kara stiffened. Not in indignation, but in shock. *Wallflower?*

Niall's brows had risen high. All the sharp angles of his face hardened. *W?* he mouthed.

"Wallflower!" the young man shouted again.

A chorus of grumbles answered him, along with one order to shut his trap.

"He don't want to see no one!" someone shouted back.

"Stuff it, Harlot!" the man before them snarled. "I was talking to Wallflower!"

"Damn it all to hell!" Lord Peter rose from a low sofa at the back of the room. He saw who awaited him, groaned, and sat back down again.

"Thank you," Niall said stiffly. "I'll fetch him myself."

NIALL MARCHED LORD Peter out and asked the porter to show them to a spot where they could speak privately and without interruption. The servant met his gaze, looked over at the thunder gathering in Kara's expression, and gave a quick nod. He led them to a small study, showed them in, and then departed, shutting the door behind him.

"Good evening, *Wallflower*," Kara said, her tone laced with indignation.

Lord Peter had the intelligence to look worried.

"Forrester, Wallflower, and Boggs," she recited clearly.

The lordling groaned. "No. It's not me." He frowned. "Wait. Who is Boggs?"

"Walter Forrester's mechanical surgeon," Niall said tersely.

The confusion did not clear from Lord Peter's expression.

"You recall," Kara said. "The man who crafted your friend's artificial arm and hand."

The young nobleman's eyes widened. "Oooh. That makes a certain amount of sense, I suppose."

Kara took the small wooden box from her cloak's pocket and slammed it on the desk in the center of the room. "Where are your ten bits, my lord? Shall we find them at your home? Or are these yours? Sent to Mrs. Armstrong because you thought she would keep them—or sell them to settle Forrester's debts? Either way, you wouldn't be caught out with them, would you?"

Niall watched closely while Lord Peter stared in confusion,

his gaze darting between the box and Kara's fierce countenance, and then to Niall, with a clear but silent call for help.

"Three columns, if you recall," Niall told him. "Ten mixed-up numbers in each. Thirty in all. And the initials B, F, W."

Lord Peter groaned. He sank into a chair and hung his head in his hands. "It's not me," he repeated. "I admit, I was struck by the initials after I left you the other evening. Because of our nicknames."

"Nicknames?" Kara asked icily.

"Yes. They come from a stupid skit we put together in school long ago. A performance for our housemates. We each played a woman's role. I was Wallflower. Forrester was Fishwife. At first, I nearly turned back to mention it, but I thought you might make too much of it. Especially since we don't even have anyone who starts with a B." He gestured toward the door. "You saw Charles—he is Harlot. We also have Chaperone, Abbess, and Milliner. But that is all of us. No B!"

Niall and Kara exchanged glances. He shrugged. He was inclined to believe the young man.

"I swear!" Lord Peter continued. "On a Bible, on my father's title, on my mother's life, anything! I know Fish"—he paused— "*Walter* was up to something. But I am in no way involved."

"Then why did we hear that you are leaving the country?" Kara demanded.

The lordling looked stricken. "I'm just...tired. Oh, I didn't even think! It does sound bad, doesn't it? But honestly, it's just wearing on me. I keep waiting on him to walk in. I hear the door open and I think it must be Walter, come to sponge a meal or regale me with the latest gossip."

Kara did not look convinced. "You don't have your own box hidden away? Filled with ten metal pieces of...something that doesn't belong to you—or to Forrester either?" She overturned the box, and the straw and metal bits spread out on the desk.

"Of course not! I—" He stopped, staring at the parts while the color drained away from his face.

"What?" Kara had stopped breathing.

"Oh, no. No, no."

"What is it?" Niall demanded.

"He wouldn't have been so stupid!" Lord Peter stood up and backed away from the desk. "Oh, Walter. You *idiot!*"

"Are you saying you know what these are?" asked Kara.

"Yes. Or at least, I think so."

"Well? Speak, man!" Niall urged.

Lord Peter groaned again and wiped a hand down his face. "They look like pieces from that damned Colt percussion revolver."

Niall stilled. "The six-shooter? Six rounds shot before you reload?"

"Yes. Walter dragged me back to the Exhibition one day to see Mr. Colt's demonstration." Lord Peter looked at him. "Have you seen it?"

Niall shook his head and gestured toward Kara. "We hear things, but we are largely kept busy at our own exhibits."

"Walter was caught up with the idea. For good reason—a great many other people are as well." Lord Peter shook his head. "Colt is an American. Large, loud, and brash. He draws a crowd when he does one of his events. We watched him take ten of the revolvers, disassemble each one, right in front of everyone, then put one together again, with pieces from all the others, or from storage bins. *Thirty* pieces," he said weakly. "All made by machines."

Niall grasped the significance of it at once. "Uniform pieces? Interchangeable? Not the work of an individual gunsmith?"

Lord Peter nodded. "Walter marveled over it. He kept wondering what a man could do with those parts." He sank down into the chair again. "Like an idiot, I said that it was the plans for the machines that make the parts that would make a man a fortune."

"But surely Mr. Colt would not travel with those," Kara said. "Not when his factory is back in America."

Niall made a face. "He may be right. There are rumors. Colt

presented engraved revolvers to the master general of the ordnance. There are whispers of a contract with the British military and of a factory to be built in South London."

"You said it before," Lord Peter whispered. "It would be next to treason."

The enormity of it was dawning on Niall. "Any of them might have murdered him. His accomplices. The men he sought to steal from. The countries or manufacturers who must have agreed to pay him for stolen plans or parts."

"The government," Kara said darkly.

"Surely not," Niall objected.

"It doesn't matter," Lord Peter said. "He got involved in something foolish and dangerous." He straightened. "We must not tell anyone, though."

"Oh, yes. We must," Niall countered.

"No! Walter is dead. Murdered. No good comes of shredding his reputation now. God, how he would hate that."

"Wrong." Niall kept his tone flat. "Scotland Yard is pointing their collective finger at Miss Levett because she is an easy target and they don't have anything more concrete. Now we do. We have to tell them what is going on here. They will need to guard against any of the others succeeding in this scheming."

Kara reached over to take the lordling's hand. Niall supposed it meant she believed him, at last.

"I'm sorry," she said. "You can take solace in the fact that none of the people involved will wish for word of this to spread."

"Especially not the Crown or the government," Niall added.

"Yes. I suppose it is something." The young nobleman could not quite hide the rise of tears in his eyes. "I'm sorry. I know he did wrong, but he was my friend. He had a difficult time of it, too, you see." He sucked in a breath. "His family…they are hard people. Vicious and self-serving. Walter was more tender-hearted, and they were rough on him. Once he got away to school and made friends, he saw how things were different outside their sphere, and he did his best to change. He wanted to be better."

"And then he had his accident—at school, wasn't it? Lost his arm?" Niall asked. "It must have been devastating."

"It nearly broke him. His family were terrible at that time, as well. Told him he was finished. Useless. But his friends rallied around him, and Walter began to come back to himself eventually. He became fixated, though, on the idea of proving himself, to be better than they said he could be. To be better than them, even."

"None of it easy." Niall sighed.

"No. At times he feared it was impossible. He had dark periods. His spirits would sink so low and he would be full of despair. I would try to jolly him out of it. The others, too. And he would rally, finally. He would always say he might have lost an arm, but at least he escaped the family curse. When he could make the joke, that's when we knew he'd turned the corner and was on the way back. We would laugh and say the true curse of his family was a heart of stone—and *that*, he would never have."

Kara pulled her hand away. She glanced up at Niall, then stared intently at Lord Peter. "What did he mean, though? When he spoke of the family curse? What was it, if not a heart of stone?"

Lord Peter raised a hand and traced a circle in the air over his face. "Markings. Great red or purple blemishes on the face and neck. He said someone of every generation was afflicted. He was always so grateful that it hadn't been him."

Kara's grip tightened on the arms of her chair until her knuckles whitened. "His own family," she whispered, meeting Niall's gaze. "Surely not?"

Niall had to unclench his jaw to answer her. "It must be. The coincidence is too great."

"What?" Lord Peter looked between them. "What are you talking about?"

"I don't understand." Kara looked suddenly, heartbreakingly vulnerable. "Why on earth would they kill him? And why are they trying to kill *me*?"

Chapter Eighteen

W HEN LORD PETER heard everything they'd learned, especially young Harold's account of his friend's death, the young nobleman railed furiously. He was ready to set out for Shropshire to confront Forrester's family at that moment.

"It won't do you a bit of good," Kara reminded him. "The man who killed him, if he is indeed Forrester's family, is in London. As we said, he tried to run us down with a carriage just the night before last. And he left drugged candies for me at the Crystal Palace this morning."

He raged on again for a bit. After a while, Kara calmly informed him that they were going to handle this her way.

"We need to go to Scotland Yard," Niall told her, almost reluctantly.

"No. I will not place myself in their clutches. But we do need to inform them. We need to present everything we've discovered." She thought a moment. "Here's what we'll do."

She sat down. A rummage of the study produced a pen and paper, and she began to list tasks and recruits. They split off, working through the night, gathering and organizing, and pledged to meet at the appointed hour.

As the early-morning light moved over the city, she and Niall were standing on Catherine Street, waiting for Mr. Boggs to open his shop.

They waited. And waited. Eventually, Niall pulled his pocket watch out. "We're going to have to go. We cannot be late."

The door to the upholsterer's next door swung open with the jingle of a bell. The shopkeeper came outside, wiping his hands on his apron. "The pair of you waiting for Boggs?"

"Indeed." Kara smiled. "Do you know if he has usually opened up by now?"

"Aye, but it won't do you any good to wait today, nor anytime for the next few weeks. He's closed up the shop. Taking his wife abroad, on a trip about the Continent."

"Thank you for informing us, so we don't waste any more time." With a nod, she turned away. "Too late," she said to Niall as they headed for the carriage awaiting them in the Strand.

"Hurry," he urged. "We want to get there before the inspector does."

"Maybe he can send men after Boggs," she said, stepping up her pace.

In the end, they reached the apartments on Adams Street before Inspector Wooten. All was in readiness. They were in the blue rooms, Kara had insisted, as Scotland Yard already knew of these, and she hoped they still had not reasoned out the particulars of the building.

Lord Peter sat brooding, looking out over the balcony. Jenny, the maid from the White Hart, fluttered about, sneaking glimpses of the nobleman when she could. Rachel, from the coffee shop downstairs, had set up a sideboard with coffee, tea, muffins, scones, and assorted butter, cream, and jams. Turner hovered over the food and Kara herself while young Harold sat nearby, methodically eating his way through one of everything before starting over.

Kara patted Turner's arm. "Are you well?" she asked, concerned over the stoop of his shoulders. "You look fatigued. Are you sleeping?"

"How can I? Here you are in danger once again, and I can do

nothing but arrange the breakfast board," he said with a sigh.

"That's not true. I've kept you running between Bluefield and the White Hart. You've been my relief and such a big help with the Exhibition. But mostly, just knowing you are there for me to turn to is the greatest reason I have not yet run mad."

He looked gratified. "You know I cannot like bringing Scotland Yard into this. There are still plenty of men there who want to pin that murder on you."

"The situation is larger than me now. We have to be responsible. But I intend to look out for myself as well."

"You must. We know no one else will."

"Except you," she said with a smile.

He patted her arm as she had his and gave her a fleeting smile. "I am still concerned. We don't know why this creature killed the young man, nor why he appears to be targeting you."

"No. We don't."

Niall approached. He nodded to Turner before addressing her. "I had a thought. Do you recall Lord Peter mentioning the cousins that Walter Forrester kept in touch with? He thought Walter was ashamed that one of them was in service. But what if he was also ashamed because of the man's affliction? Could our 'monster' be this cousin? Might he be in service—perhaps employed by someone involved in the thefts?"

"It seems unlikely," she replied. "But it would explain much—except the fact that I would expect him to side with his cousin instead of his employer."

A knock sounded on the door. Kara waited while Niall went to admit Inspector Wooten. The gentleman entered, looking around with growing curiosity. "Goodness. The summons was unexpected, but all of this is even more surprising."

"Come in, Inspector. Help yourself to coffee, tea, whatever you like." Kara indicated the table of food and drink. "And please, make yourself comfortable. We have discovered quite a bit of information about Mr. Forrester's activities, and about his murder. We think it is time to share it with you."

The inspector accepted a cup of coffee from Turner and gave her a nod. "That does sound promising."

She smiled at him. "We also think it is time for you to share what you know."

His face fell. "I'm not sure I—"

"I did not kill Mr. Forrester," she interrupted him. "Nor do I have anything to do with the nefarious activities he was up to. But I now find myself targeted by the same people who murdered him."

"You know who killed him?" he asked, shocked.

"We will tell you what we know once you agree to our terms."

Still, he hesitated.

Her ire grew. "What I deserve is protection, sir. But past experience has showed me not to expect fair treatment from the Metropolitan Police. And so I insist on repayment with information, which may help me to protect myself." She narrowed her eyes. "It is the very least you can do."

He gazed at her, clearly weighing her words and his options, then he ran his eye over their motley crew of allies. "Very well, then."

Kara let loose the breath she'd been holding.

The inspector took out a notebook and pencil, then looked back up suddenly. "Will you also tell me how you escaped the men who came here looking for you?"

"No," she said flatly.

He bent a little. "I had to try."

She invited him to take a seat. Once he was settled, she began to talk, telling the tale from the beginning. She asked the others to break in, to speak of their own parts in the story.

Wooten listened carefully, making notes. He asked only an occasional question until they reached the end, when he flipped his notebook back to the beginning and began to ask for clarification here and there.

He closed the book at last, though, and looked around at each of them, shaking his head. "I must say, you've done some very good work here. This is going to cause an uproar back at the Yard, but I am not afraid to say I'm impressed."

Lord Peter snapped his fingers. "Yes, yes. All very well. But now it is your turn to impress us. Tell us what you know."

The inspector nodded to where young Harold had slumped asleep, his mouth hanging open. "Could you?" he asked. "I would rather keep this to a minimum number of witnesses."

"Jenny, would you mind putting him down for a rest in the bed and keeping an eye on him?" asked Kara.

The maid bobbed a curtsy. "Of course, miss."

After she'd roused the boy and shuffled him off to the bedroom, Wooten cast an eye toward her butler.

"Turner stays," Kara insisted.

Wooten's expression lightened. "Ah, you are Mr. Turner?" He gave her friend a nod. "It's glad I am to meet you, and to know you are still at Miss Levett's side."

Turner bowed and kept silent.

"Very well, then." The inspector went to look out over the balcony, then turned back to face them. "We are aware of the espionage Mr. Forrester was engaged in."

"Espionage?" Lord Peter repeated.

"That is exactly what it is—the theft of secrets that could affect the Exhibition, the national economy, the military, even the statecraft between nations."

The young nobleman groaned.

The inspector gave a sheepish shrug. "I am embarrassed to admit, you have uncovered more detail than we have done so far."

"How did you discover the scheme?" asked Niall.

"One of the ladies of the court was visiting the Exhibition. She was enjoying the displays from the Zollverein when she overheard a conversation. A conversation in German." Wooten raised his brows. "I suppose the men thought themselves safe, speaking in front of an English lady, but they forgot, or perhaps did not realize, that many of the courtiers do speak German now. The lady found them suspicious, as she thought they were speaking about stealing from some of the displays. One mentioned a buyer that insisted on both parts and plans. She heard Walter Forrester's name mentioned."

"She came to Scotland Yard about it?" Niall asked.

"No. Worse. She went to Prince Albert."

Kara's eyes widened.

"Yes. You may imagine his reaction. They have been hosting a delegation from Prussia since the start of the Exhibition. Any such trouble might upset delicate plans. Special Branch was involved, of course. And all of us were to look out for this man, Forrester. The very next morning, I was notified of the murder of a one-armed man at the Crystal Palace. It took too long to realize they were the same man and to positively identify him as Walter Forrester."

"You suspect someone from the Zollverein exhibit was involved?" asked Niall.

"Yes."

"Does his name happen to be Wernher?"

Wooten looked grim. "You figured that out as well?"

"We discovered his name. But we have been unable to find anything further."

"Well, neither have we. He was one of the men the lady overheard. And he appears to have gone missing."

"As has Mr. Boggs," Kara reminded him.

"Perhaps one of them killed Walter on their way out of the country, to cut him out of his share of the profits," Lord Peter said darkly.

"Perhaps you might send men looking for them at the railway stations and ports," Kara suggested. "Or even as far as Moabit."

"I'll do both," Wooten said.

"After all," Lord Peter sneered, "how many taverns could there be in an industrial town outside of Berlin?"

The inspector did not take offense. "We will do our best."

Turner cleared his throat. "Excuse me, but this Wernher, did he happen to have markings on his face, such as we have heard described?"

The inspector shook his head. "No. Blond and blue-eyed is the description I have. Today is the first time I have heard of this marked man."

Lord Peter snorted.

Wooten went to look out the window again. Kara had the idea that he wasn't seeing the street outside.

"It's entirely possible that Forrester's murder was not related to his thievery," he mused. "We should at least consider it."

Niall straightened from his spot leaning on the mantel. "Is Forrester's family particularly religious?" he asked Lord Peter.

"No. They particularly are not. It's entirely more likely that his family got Walter involved in this nasty business," the gentleman proclaimed. "It sounds exactly like something they would involve themselves in."

That had Inspector Wooten pulling out his notebook again. "Shropshire, you said? We will look into it right away." He gave Kara a kind look. "Perhaps, while we do, it might be best if you stick behind the scenes? Spend more time at your lovely home at Bluefield Park?"

She stiffened. "Thank you for the suggestion, sir. I know it was kindly meant. But I believe I will be safe enough amongst the hundreds of visitors we see every day." She looked to Niall. "I will be careful, though, after hours."

Wooten sighed. "Please do. Keep alert."

She bristled.

"I know," he said. "Don't go anywhere alone. I don't mean to insult you, Miss Levett. I just don't want to see anything happen to you."

"Anything further," Niall corrected him sternly.

"Exactly." The inspector tucked his book away and approached her. Bending over her hand, he gave her a smile. "I have a great deal of work to do now, thanks to you."

Kara glanced first at Niall, then at Turner. "As do we all. Good day, Inspector."

"Good morning."

As he left, Kara crumpled into a chair. "It is disheartening, and more than a little frustrating, to think we are now supposed to just sit back and allow it all to go on without our involvement."

"The hell you say," Lord Peter responded. "Let them run out to Shropshire. I'm going to see if I can track down this member of Walter's family in Town—this marked man."

"If you have an idea how to find him, I'd like to hear it," Niall told him.

"I don't. Not as of yet. But I shall go through Walter's papers and ask Harlot and all the others if they have any idea where he went to meet his cousins, or if there is anything else they might know."

"Send word if you find anything. I hate and despise the thought of just sitting and waiting for him to strike at Miss Levett again." Frustration sounded clear in Niall's tone.

"I will. Good day." Lord Peter looked to Kara, and his face softened. "Thank you for including me in all of this. And do be careful."

"I will. You be careful too."

As he left, Jenny slipped out of the bedroom. "Still sleeping," she said of Harold. "Perhaps you should stay here and rest today, my lady."

Kara shook her head. "I don't want to miss the entire day, but I admit, I could use a short nap before I head to the Crystal Palace." She eyed Niall for his reaction. "You?"

"It wouldn't come amiss."

"You can take the room next to Harold's. I'll go next door." She stood and went to Turner, who had started clearing cups and plates. "Leave this. One of Rachel's girls will see to it." She took his hand. "I want you to go back to Bluefield, put up your feet, wrap yourself in your grandmother's wool blanket, and have a day of rest."

"But, Miss Kara, there is so much—"

"Rest," she insisted.

He smiled. "Very well, then. It does sound…a novel idea. But you'll be careful? You won't leave the Exhibition alone?"

"She will not." Niall stepped forward. "I promise you."

The men exchanged a long look.

"Very well, sir." Turner inclined his head. "Thank you."

She had the feeling there had been more exchanged here than those simple words.

Chapter Nineteen

NIALL SLEPT FOR two hours and woke still feeling tired and out of sorts. Kara looked similarly frazzled as they set out on the short walk to the park. They held their silence, and it was a relief to know they could just do what was needed without feeling uncomfortable, ill at ease, or as if they needed to fill the quiet.

It was a lovely, mild day for once, with a nice breeze. A refreshing break from the heat they'd been enduring, which meant that the crowds were out in force. Together, they battled their way into the Crystal Palace, and Niall stayed close as they made their way toward Kara's exhibit.

Turner had sent a footman from Bluefield to watch over things. Kara smiled her thanks at him. She drifted toward the case clock. It was about to strike the hour, and a group of young girls waited breathlessly in front of it, their families and nursemaids watching indulgently.

The chimes sounded, and the girls gasped with delight. They clapped their hands as the squirrel emerged from the foot of the "tree" and scampered his way up, darting in and out of the case among the limbs and branches and leaves.

"How do you get him to climb up so fast? Is there a track inside the case?"

She turned to Niall in surprise. "Oh, it's not all the same squirrel," she whispered. "It's several. It's all in the timing. They are timed to appear in order, with clockwork."

"Fascinating," he whispered back.

Once the little fellow was tucked up into the top with his nut, Kara invited the girls to come further into the space, to her workbench. Niall drifted after the families as they followed.

Kara reached for a box beneath the bench and drew out a brightly painted clockwork bird. She wound it up as the girls pressed close, then set it loose on the tabletop.

The smallest girl tried to push in to see, but the bigger girls were too entranced by the hopping, pecking bird to give an inch. The little one gave up and went around to the side, laughing in delight as the bird stopped, warbled a quick song, then wound down.

Kara scooped it up and offered it to the smallest girl. "I should like to give him to you, for I can see you are kind and careful and will take excellent care of him."

"Me?" the girl whispered while the others watched in awe.

"Yes. He needs a friend who is thoughtful and kind, as do we all." Kara looked over the girl's head and into Niall's eyes as she said it.

He held her gaze as something shifted inside of him. He'd tried. He'd tried to be cautious, to remember the limits and rules he lived with. But now he found himself helpless to do anything but smile at her—and then turn to retreat to his own exhibit.

He came back to the same spot, hours later, after a particularly busy afternoon. He'd sneaked glances at her down the nave all afternoon. She'd seemed...subdued. He found her now slumped over her workbench.

He suffered a moment's panic, recalling the tainted candies, but she breathed naturally and just seemed to have fallen asleep. By her hand he found a tiny metal sheep with a long black face, floppy ears, and bristly wired wool.

Smiling, he touched her shoulder. "Kara? Shall we get you to your rooms?"

She sat up, blinking. "Do forgive me," she said, her voice gone husky in a way that sent a shiver through him. She picked up the small sheep. "I was making this for Mr. Grant's Scottish glen, but I dreamed of a clock where the sheep chase the shepherd around every hour." She blinked again. "I think that now I must make it."

"You are tired," he said gently. "Let's get you home."

"I am. I am tired." She frowned. "But sleep is not what I need."

"What do you need?" he whispered.

"Balance," she declared. Reaching out, she grasped his arm. "I need to go somewhere. Will you come with me?"

"Need you ask?"

"No." She sighed in satisfaction. "Good. Let's go."

⤜⤜⤜×⤛⤛⤛

"WE DO SEEM to spend an inordinate amount of time in this part of Town," he said as they left the Strand and headed north toward Covent Garden.

"It's a fascinating area. So full of life."

"All kinds of life," he said wryly as a rat streaked across the narrow cobblestones, and he steered her away from a couple embracing in the shadow of a doorway.

"Exactly," she said, moving forward eagerly.

She was in the lead this time, and he let her drag him along with her until she stopped in front of a decrepit pie shop.

"It's closed," he said as she peered in the window.

"I see them inside." She pressed her nose to the glass and waved.

The door opened. On alert, Niall stepped forward as a woman reached out and grabbed Kara, pulling her to her ample bosom.

"My dear young miss!" she cried. "It's been too long since we seen ye!"

Kara saw him relax as she leaned into the embrace. "It's good to see you too, Maisie."

"Come in, then! Gracious saints, look at ye! Skin and bones, ye are. Are they runnin' ye ragged at that Exhibition?"

"They are, among other difficulties. I'm sorry to show up so late."

"Nay bother! Ye know ye're welcome anytime." She eyed Niall closely. "And who's this, then?"

"This is my good friend, Mr. Kier. Niall, meet Maisie Dobbs, who bakes the very best pies in all of London."

"And then some," the woman asserted. "Come in, sir. If ye've made a friend of my young lady, then ye can count us as well."

"Thank you." He gave Maisie the slowly spreading smile that always tempted Kara to stop and bask in it.

It gave Maisie pause as well. "Saints be praised," she whispered, before she turned around to lead them inside. "Ah, a good day to come in," she assured Kara. "Rosco's brought in the first blackberries of the season, and I made the pies this afternoon."

"Ooh," said Kara. "Hand pies?"

"Aye. We'll take them around to the pubs and taverns tomorrow."

"We'll share one," Kara told her. "But I was also hoping you'd have one of those chicken and leek pies left?"

"And so I do—and the gravy is spot on today, if I do say it meself."

"We'll share one of those too," she said happily. "Come and sit," she invited Niall.

They took a seat near the empty hearth, and she wondered what he thought of the place. It was small and cramped, with room for only a few small tables, but it was clean, and for Kara, it breathed the warm acceptance she always felt when she spent time here.

"How are things, Maisie?"

"Aye, well enough, though it's gettin' harder to get good flour. Ah, the things they think to put in to stretch it further!" Maisie shook her head. "Miller tried to sell me a batch that was more full o' plaster than my kitchen wall."

That set Kara to thinking. "Is Davey around?" she asked as Maisie served them plates with both savory and sweet pies. She sniffed appreciatively and took a bite of a savory one. It was delicious, thick with steaming gravy and seasoned with sage and rosemary.

"Aye," Maisie answered. "Davey!" she shouted suddenly, and Kara grinned when Niall jumped.

An answering shout came from a back room.

"Our good young miss is here!" Maisie called.

The youth emerged, and she couldn't help but exclaim over him. "How tall you've grown! How are you, Davey?"

"Well and good, ma'am. Well and good."

"Well enough for a trip out to Bluefield Park?"

The boy—almost a young man, truly, she realized—looked to his mother.

"If you will deliver an eel pie and one of these sublime berry creations to Turner at Bluefield this evening, then I will have my man of business deliver ten sacks of flour here in the morning. The good flour," she clarified. "Unadulterated. No plaster, chalk, or anything else."

Their eyes lit up. Maisie nodded at the boy.

"I'll make it fifteen sacks if you get it to Turner while it's still warm."

The boy laughed. "Easily done, my lady. We have a cart now," he said proudly. "I'll barter the use of it for a trip with a trap and pony."

"Well done, Davey. And thank you. Mr. Turner could use a treat."

"He does love my eel pie," Maisie said with satisfaction as Kara rolled her eyes at the taste of the berries, like sweet sunshine on her tongue. "And I'll throw in an apple, as well. He can save it for tomorrow and rub it in the face of that fancy cook of yours."

Kara laughed, and Niall smiled.

"Maisie," she said, struck by a sudden thought, "if Davey will be going farther afield with a cart, might it be that you could use another hand around here? In the shop or perhaps taking a basket out and around to the local areas? I happen to know a lad. He's lived rough, but he's of good character, quick as a whip, and knows the city."

The older woman shot her a fond look. "Taking in another stray, are you, young miss?"

"Well..."

Maisie laughed. "You've a good heart, my girl. Bring him around to me and let me get a look at him."

"I will." Kara beamed. "And, of course, I'd be happy to contribute toward his room and board."

"Not necessary, not as long as he's pulling his weight around here. But if it means we see more of you, I'm happy to do it."

"Thank you, Maisie."

"It's always a good day when we see you, young miss. And a good thing, indeed, that ye come today. Seein' as it's a Thursday."

Kara straightened, excited. "Is it? Oh! It is!" She looked out to see the dark rolling like fog over the city. She stood and gave Maisie another quick, hard hug. "Thank you. You know seeing you lightens my spirits."

"Just as ye've always been a bright spot fer us, dear girl." Maisie patted her back. "Now, go on with ye. Ye don't want to miss it."

"You're right." Kara let her go and backed toward the door. "Thank you!" She beckoned Niall and whirled to head outside.

"How?" he asked, following. "How did that friendship come about?"

"Come. Hurry. It's not far, but it will start as soon as it turns fully dark. I'll tell you once we're there."

She led him through the maze of alleys and side streets on the fringe of the market. When they reached the Screaming Eagle, it was doing a booming business. She pushed her way through the crowded taproom, Niall on her heels. She waved at the barman before scooting down a narrow passage and out into the courtyard.

One corner of the bare dirt yard had been covered. Beneath the rickety roof of mismatched wood, a dais had been made of pallets trussed together. The rest of the space was covered with seating made from a variety of leftovers and spare bits.

"There are still a couple of good seats in the front." She pulled Niall along a fence to a corner of the makeshift stage. She sat down on an overturned bucket and waved for him to take the dilapidated folding chair next to it.

"Questions." He was looking around at the growing audience, wildly mixed by gender, status, and cleanliness. "So many of them."

"Go ahead. They've just started lighting the lanterns." She shrugged. "I looked into putting in a couple of stage lights, but the risk of fire was deemed too great, so lanterns it is. I did get a grand tour from the theater manager I consulted, though, and climbed like a monkey from the taproom to the catwalks."

"Of course you did," he said on a laugh.

"We have a few minutes." She waved a hand. "Ask away."

He looked eager, as if he was mentally rubbing his hands together. "First, why does the Screaming Eagle not have a sign out front? I saw the name painted over the door, but if ever there was a pub that er...screamed for a dashing sign, it's this one."

"They have one," she told him. "Only it must have been stolen again."

"Again." He looked as if he might pursue the subject, but he controlled himself and gave her a warm look. "More about that later. But for now, tell me about Maisie Dobbs."

"I did promise." She drew a deep breath. "I met her when I was thirteen. I had a tutor who was meant to teach me how to get about the city. My father thought I should be able to handle myself in the streets without being frightened or making myself a target."

His expression stilled. "You know, I myself had quite an...interesting childhood. But your upbringing? It beats anything I've ever heard of."

She laughed. "Yes, but it's turned me into the many-faceted woman I am today."

"I won't argue with that."

"You took me to a Sapphic brothel. You have no leg to stand on here."

"I cannot argue with that, either."

"You showed me one of your secret places in the city. I felt compelled to do the same."

"Now you've shown me two," he reminded her. "I owe you another." She brightened at the thought, but he said, "Another time. Go on with your story."

"Fine, then. I was tested by being let loose in assorted less-than-fashionable parts of Town, and I was supposed to make my way back to an assigned point. My tutor was meant to follow me, but to let me handle myself unless he needed to step in."

He closed his eyes and shook his head.

"It wasn't that bad."

"Until it was, I'll wager."

"Well, yes. It wasn't too far from here, actually. A street bully got my scent. He tailed me. At first it was only words, and I held my own with him there."

"That, I can well believe."

"I made a wrong turn and ended up in a dead end. He knew he had me. A group gathered to see my comeuppance."

"I'll bet you held your own then, too."

"For a bit. But I grew tired, and he only grew angrier. I was down, and he was poised above me, foot raised, ready to give me a walloping kick. I thought my tutor would step in."

"He didn't?"

"No. Instead the bully got hit right in his sneering face by a steak and kidney pie. It unbalanced him, and he went over backward. Such a sight! He was blinking gravy out of his eyes and dripping meat and pastry. He jumped back to his feet, roaring, and a chicken and mushroom followed the first. The little ones moved in then, a swarm of them, snatching bits of meat and pie, and stuffing it in as fast as they could. They pressed in on him, and it was enough to slow him down."

"It was Maisie Dobbs."

"Yes, with her basket of pies as her cache of weapons. She threatened to hit him with every one, and the basket next, if he didn't leave me alone."

Niall chuckled. "I would have backed down, too."

"The bully didn't, but she told him I'd proven myself, and if he looked close, he'd see I was Quality, besides. And did he want more of my sort coming after him in kind?"

"And that did the trick?"

"It did. She took me back to her shop, fed me, and cleaned me up, and we've been friends ever since."

He looked gratified. "That is a damned good story."

"And every bit true."

"And this place?" he asked, looking around at the full crowd settling in.

She nodded toward the dais. "Listen. You'll see."

A pretty young woman had climbed up onto the dais. She wore a costume as cobbled together as the makeshift stage, with short skirts, a laced corset, a pirate's hat, and a red sash.

"I need a comedy bit for my auditions," she told the crowd. Drawing a deep breath, she launched into an amusing ditty about the life of a pirate's wench—weeks of drunken revelry followed by months of boredom, and the mischief she concocted to liven it up. Her voice was fine and suited to the song, and she was as lively as the lyrics. The audience was smitten, laughing at all the right spots and applauding enthusiastically at the end.

"Give us a swing of your hips at the chorus," someone called out.

"Hold your note longer at the bird of paradise bit!" yelled

another helpful audience member.

"I'll take you on at the Empire!" a gentleman called. He stood out in the audience, dressed in a flashy suit and a purple ascot.

A chorus of catcalls took aim at him.

"Don't you do it, dearie!" a woman called. "You're good enough to hold out for a big production in one of the real theaters!"

Niall turned to Kara, brow raised.

"It's a local tradition," she explained. "Up-and-coming young performers come on a Thursday night to practice their bits. They get experience, comments, advice, sometimes an opportunity."

"Like purple ascot offered?"

"Sometimes. That's Henry Platt. He owns the Empire, a music hall. He comes looking for acts for his shows. But not everyone is a professional performer. Some come because they like to sing, dance, make people laugh, or to share their poetry. Sometimes it's a traveling acrobat troupe. You never know what you will see."

She spotted someone over his shoulder. "Oh! There! That is Glass of Port Pauly. He is my very favorite."

"Glass of Port Pauly?"

The man, dressed in fine clothes and carrying a violin, approached the stage.

"He comes often," Kara said. "Sometimes he'll turn up at a different pub or tavern during the week. Platt would love to get him at the Empire. He plays only one tune per evening, and the only payment he will accept is a glass of the finest port the establishment offers." She hitched her thumb back toward the pub. "Here at the Eagle, we take turns paying for his drink and have him covered for months in advance." She nodded toward the stage. "Just listen."

The crowd had quieted. They knew what was coming.

Pauly lifted his violin and bow and began to play. As one, the audience sighed. It was a plaintive piece tonight. Pauly bent and swayed, and the music poured off the stage. It lifted Kara right out of the worry, tension, and dread she'd been carrying. It tugged her along on a journey through so many emotions. Hope and longing, desire and despair, and a long, sweet, rolling surrender. When it was done, she hung there for a moment, suspended in the last notes of the music.

Silence held for a long moment.

Then the audience erupted into applause, and she glanced at Niall.

His eyes were still closed, his expression rapt.

Relief, excitement, and joy brimmed inside her. He heard it. Felt it. He understood.

His eyes opened, and he looked at her. His pupils were large and dark. Connection sparked between them.

"Let's go," she whispered. "When it is like this, I want it to last."

They made their way out. Silent, but full of music and portent.

She led the way back to the Strand, where they caught a hack. He gave her a questioning look when the driver asked for their destination.

"The White Hart, please," she said. "It's too late to go back to Bluefield, and it's begun to feel more like home there than the empty rooms on Adams Street."

Niall gave the address and bundled her in. The coach moved into traffic, and she allowed herself to relax.

"Thank you for coming with me. I get so wrapped up in what I'm working on, sometimes I forget everything else. I feel like I've done the same with these investigations."

"Balance," he said. "You mentioned it earlier."

"Yes. We've been so caught up with chasing lies, theft, danger, and death. I needed a bit of laughter and *life*."

"And soul-stirring music," he added.

"Yes." The light was dim. She hoped he heard the grin in her voice. "I'm glad to know we are compatible in the light as well as the dark." She also hoped he understood what she meant.

"Yes," he rasped.

Silence stretched out again. She laid her head back and let it sway with the motion of the carriage.

"I'm afraid," she said. It was easier to say it into the darkness.

"That man won't get anywhere near you again." It sounded like a vow.

"No. I'm afraid because Turner seems suddenly...frail. Tired. Older."

"Oh. I'm sorry."

She sat up. "I don't know what I would do if anything happened to him. He's the one who usually reminds me to keep balanced, you know. He's always been there. Since the night he found me in that attic, he's been by my side. *On* my side."

"He still is."

"But he won't always be. I'm beginning to see it now. It frightens me more than the thought of that scarred murderer."

He sighed. "I've made massive mistakes in some of my own relationships," he confessed. "But I will share one thing I've learned. Treasure your friends while you have them. You are a good friend. Those pies will warm Turner's heart as well as his belly, because you thought to send them. Just remain that friend. Keep him close for as long as you have him."

"Yes. I will." It was her own vow.

"And one thing more. Don't forget balance in that area of your life as well. Keep your ties strong with the other people who are important to you. Don't forget the rest because you feel you must concentrate on one. Let them help. Let them know how you value them. They'll be there for you if something does happen."

She sighed and leaned back again. "You are a wise man, Mr. Niall Kier."

"And you are a surprising woman, Miss Kara Levett."

She liked the sound of that. She let it echo in her brain, and she might have dozed a bit as the carriage rocked on its way. She sat up suddenly, though, struck by a thought. "Will Mr. Hywel be able to provide a nice picnic basket if I request it?"

"If you request it, I rather think he'd contrive a picnic with the queen."

She was caught, for a moment, by the possibilities his statement dredged up, but she eventually brushed them off. "Nothing so difficult is required. But I think I shall take your advice. I will leave the Exhibition a bit early tomorrow and invite my cousin to picnic with me in the park."

"And his betrothed?"

She sighed. "Yes, her too. You see how you are reforming me?"

He scoffed.

"No. I am serious. I've been too long alone and unopposed. It might be uncomfortable to have my faults illuminated, but you do it so gently that I cannot complain."

"I don't recall doing any such thing."

"Perhaps you merely lead by shining example," she suggested with a grin.

This time he audibly snorted.

"Well, perhaps it is just that I have needed someone to challenge me. In any case, I believe I shall invite Turner as well. That should rile Miss Bailey. But perhaps *she* needs to be challenged. In any case, she must learn how things stand."

"Turner will likely insist on serving, won't he?"

"Yes, but I will insist that he also sit with us to eat." She rolled her head toward him. "Should you care to join us?"

"I should like nothing better."

"Good." She smiled into the dark. "Good."

Chapter Twenty

THE NEXT AFTERNOON, Kara looked from the sight of Niall, approaching down the nave, to the massive picnic basket Hywel had sent, then up to the deluge of rain striking the glass panels of the Crystal Palace.

"Well, they were hardly the best laid plans," she said to Niall. "Still, they have managed to go awry. I doubt we will see Joseph this afternoon. The streets must be a muddy tangle."

"You'd be wrong," he answered with a lift of his chin.

She looked to where he'd indicated and saw her cousin bearing down on them, covered in a still-dripping greatcoat, his trousers wet to his knees.

"Joseph! You are soaking!" she cried. "I'm surprised you left the house."

"Said I would come, didn't I?" he said cheerfully. "What's a bit of rain when I can spend the afternoon with you? And you too, Kier, of course."

"Miss Bailey is not with you?" She tried not to allow her relief to show.

"No, no. She had something urgent to attend to. A family matter, I surmise." He waved a hand. "She left early, long before the rain began. Before your invitation even arrived."

"Shall I go and save us a table in the exhibitors' refreshment room?" asked Niall. "No use wasting good company and a large picnic basket."

Kara hesitated. "Not yet. Turner has yet to arrive."

"He may be late," Niall said. "The mud may be bad enough to delay him until closing time."

"It's not like him," Kara fretted. "He would have set out early. I sent a note asking him to bring along a footman as well, to watch over the space while we are away from it. I honestly don't like to leave it unattended." She thought a moment. "I know. I'll clear off my workbench and we can eat there. If you will scrounge up a couple of extra chairs?" she asked Niall.

"Of course."

"Capital idea!" Joseph said, gazing around at the crowd. "I can see why you like it here, Kara. It's quite an energizing environment, isn't it?"

She cleaned off the bench top, keeping everything tidy and organized, despite Joseph's help. Together, they spread out the luncheon and sat down to roast beef sandwiches with pickle and horseradish, a great hunk of cheese, fruit, and slices of cake.

"It's quite cozy in here, isn't it? With the rain coming down?" Joseph bit into an apple.

"It is rather," Kara said. She asked after his parliamentary work and listened with satisfaction as he spoke eloquently about the work he was doing helping to modernize supplies and provisions for the military.

"And the wedding plans?" she asked.

"Oh, Audrey is charging ahead. It will all come off splendidly, I know." He grew more serious. "She was disappointed, though, when you missed the shopping expedition with her mother."

"I am sorry I had to disappoint her."

"Oh, she's over it now," he assured her. "Though she does wish you were more like other girls, I believe she's quite looking forward to our visit to Bluefield. She spent the whole of last evening quizzing me about the place. What it's like, how many bedrooms, how big is the ballroom? She wanted to know about the gardens and the art, even the kitchens." He nudged Kara. "I told her she must petition you for the details about the origin and value of the paintings and sculpture, but I could indeed tell her about the kitchens." He grinned. "Do you recall the days we spent there? Rainy days, like this one. Your cook would stuff us full of toast and hot chocolate."

"I do indeed remember. Almost as well as the grand games of hide-and-seek we got up to. We would play on the grounds when the weather was fine," she told Niall. "But our longest, most challenging games were inside on the rainy days."

"So many nooks and crannies to hide in," Joseph said. "I told Audrey about that too. She found it ever so droll and had an amazing number of questions about where and how the servants lived, too."

"Miss Levett?" someone said.

She perked up, listening.

"I believe someone is calling your name," Niall said.

The call came again. "Has anyone seen Miss Levett?"

"Oh, do excuse me for a moment, gentlemen," Kara said.

Joseph took a slice of cake and waved her on. She went out to see who'd called her and felt Niall close on her heels.

"I am Miss Levett."

It was a young man in livery. He bowed. "A message for you, miss." He handed over the sealed letter and slid away into the crowd. Likely, he meant to see as much of the Exhibition as he could get away with before he had to return, she mused, turning to go back to the picnic. Niall had gone on before her.

"I wonder if he had to pay his shilling to get in?" she said as she followed him. "If they let him in with a message, word will spread and we'll be overrun, as every servant in livery will try their luck." She frowned down at the unfamiliar seal, then realized. "It must be from Lord Peter." She glanced at Niall, then clutched the letter close while she turned to her cousin. "Joseph, one of the reasons I wished to see you today was to inform you of a…situation. To tell you of all that has happened since the night the police interrupted your dinner, looking for me."

Joseph bristled. "They are not back to accusing you of having something to do with that murder, are they? I'll tell them a thing or two myself! I do have friends in Parliament, you know, Kara. I'll speak to them as well."

"No," she interrupted hastily. "They no longer believe I had anything to do with killing Mr. Forrester."

"Good."

"Unfortunately, we do have reason to believe that the people who killed him may be attempting to harm me."

"What?" he asked, aghast. "No. No. Why on earth—Is it another ransom attempt?"

"We do not think so, but we don't know." Kara looked to Niall for help. He began to explain while she broke the seal of Lord Peter's letter.

The second cousin is a woman. All I've discovered so far. Any idea who it might be?

"Good heavens," Joseph said. "A marked man? Do you mean he is tattooed? Like the sailors you see at the docks?"

Niall explained while Kara's brain whirled. A woman?

For one long, horrible moment, her brain dredged up Eleanor's fascination with the German gentlemen's unrelenting confidence.

No. No, that could not be.

She looked up just as Joseph spoke again.

"Oh, yes. I have heard of that sort of thing. Funny, even Audrey's mama has a similar affliction. Great red marks on her neck, I understand. It's why she always wears high collars on her gowns. And why Audrey is so careful about her own complexion."

Blood pounded in her head. A mixture of relief and horrid certainty threatened to choke her. She struggled to even out her breathing.

She met Niall's startled gaze and passed him the note. "I have yet to meet Miss Bailey's mother," she said to her cousin. "What was her family name? Do you recall, Joseph?"

He frowned, thinking. "Stone? No. Oak. Tree. Forest! Yes, that's it. Forrester!" His eyes widened, and he frowned again. "Yes. That is it. I swear, I saw it on some of the legal papers we shuffled through, hammering out the bridal settlements." He looked from one of them to the other. "But wait—that's the dead bloke's name, isn't it? Why wouldn't they have said something that evening, when the police came looking for you?"

"The police did not yet know the victim's name at that point, did they?"

"Oh, yes," he breathed in relief. "They said only that it was a one-armed man. Still, it's a damned strange coincidence, isn't it?"

"No, Joseph. I don't think it is," she said gently.

The look she exchanged with Niall was silent, yet still held oceans of understanding.

"Where did Miss Bailey go this morning?" Niall asked.

"I don't know." Joseph sounded bewildered. "I don't think she mentioned her destination. She only told me, when I left her last night, that there was some family business left to her to finish. Why?"

"Where would she go if she needed to hide something?" Kara asked, a dark thought dawning.

"What would she need to hide? And where would she go, in any case? Her family is from the country."

"You said she asked about the servants at Bluefield. About their quarters and where they lived?"

"Miss Bailey and her family didn't take a townhouse for the Season? They are staying with you?" Niall asked.

Joseph began to look panicked. "Why do you ask?"

"She wouldn't be at Joseph's house." Kara's mind was whirling fast.

Her cousin looked wildly back and forth between them. "You don't think she—" He slumped down into his chair.

Kara thought back to that run-in with Miss Bailey at the

Loudins' ball. "Her father has property here. Somewhere…in Greenwich, she said. Parkland along the river."

"Should we go there?" Niall was on his feet. "Should we tell Inspector Wooten to send his men?"

"No." Dread was coalescing in her chest, weighing her down. "Turner is still not here. I think we need to go to Bluefield. Now."

Chapter Twenty-One

I T TOOK WELL over an hour longer than it should have to get home. She insisted they take the railway for part of the way, but they still needed a carriage to get to Bluefield from Hammersmith Station. When they finally arrived, Kara leapt out without waiting for the groom and rushed into the house. Both Niall and Joseph followed.

The servants were clearly not expecting her. The footman at the door stammered in confusion as she strode past him.

"Where is everyone?"

"I...uh... In the kitchens, miss."

She rushed through the green baize door and down the stairs. Most of the servants were gathered around the long oak table in the kitchen. Tea had been passed around, and one of the kitchen maids was making her way around, pouring a dollop of good brandy into those cups held out for the stiffener. She looked up from her pouring, spotted Kara, and nearly dropped the bottle. "Miss! You are here already!"

Chairs scraped all around as they all stood.

"Yes, I am here," she answered. "Where is Turner?"

One of the maids burst into tears. Mrs. Bolt, the housekeeper, set down her teacup and came closer, obviously distraught. "Did you not get my note, miss? We sent it around noon."

"We likely passed the messenger," Kara said. "What did it say?"

Silence.

"Where is Turner?"

Mrs. Bolt squared her shoulders. "He's gone missing, Miss Levett. I'm so sorry. He arrived yesterday afternoon and said he meant to spend the rest of the evening in his rooms. I saw him when your delivery arrived for him." She paused. "He was very pleased, indeed. But he seemed tired. I didn't worry too much when he didn't come down for breakfast. We sent a tray to his room later, but the cook's girl found his room empty."

"Had his bed been slept in?"

"If it was, he had made it up. He's been going in to help you so often lately, I didn't think too much of it. Until late this morning." She turned and indicated the tearful maid. "Elsie went to your rooms, miss. To air them out. She found a note left there."

"By Turner?"

"We don't believe so." The housekeeper's gaze dropped.

"Where is the note?"

"We sent it with the messenger."

Kara closed her eyes. "What did it say?"

She was met with silence again.

Niall and Joseph clambered in behind her. The gathered servants stared, then began to stir. The cook stood to put on another kettle. The footmen started to move forward, ready to take their coats.

"No. Wait," she ordered them. "I promise, no one will be in trouble. I need to know what the note said. It's important. Someone has obviously read it. Tell me, now."

Mrs. Bolt pressed her lips together. She crooked a finger at the tearful maid.

The girl's eyes widened, and she stepped away from the table, coming a few steps nearer. "I'm so sorry, miss. I didn't mean to read it. It wasn't sealed like a letter, just folded over."

"It's fine, Elsie. What did the note say?"

The girl drew a shuddering breath. "It said, *If you want to see your precious Turner again, you'll do exactly as I say.*"

A great, raw swell of anger, fear, and loathing rose in Kara's chest. She held herself stiffly to keep from staggering. Next came a tightening, a press of obstinacy, and an iron resolve.

"Nothing else? No directions?"

"No, miss," the maid whispered.

"No demands?" asked Niall from behind her.

The girl shook her head.

The housekeeper raised her chin. "Elsie came to me in a tizzy. I scarcely believed her, so I read the note as well. Truly, miss. That was all that it said."

Kara breathed deeply and forced her fists to unclench.

Turner had not failed her. She would not fail him.

"All of those questions," Joseph whispered. "Where the servants sleep. How long do they work. This was why she wished to know?"

Kara did not have time to comfort Joseph. "Robert," she snapped at the footman who had admitted her. "Find dry clothes and hot drinks for our gentlemen guests. Mrs. Bolt, please come with me."

She wheeled about and squeezed past the men, heading upstairs. All the way upstairs, to her rooms, with the housekeeper trotting behind. She entered, marched to her desk, and began scribbling notes. "Give this to Mr. Kier." She handed off the first one. "In ten minutes." Writing fast, she handed over another. "Hold this one for thirty minutes longer, then give it to my cousin." A third. "Send this to the stables straightaway."

She had already begun unbuttoning her bodice when Mrs. Bolt spoke up. "He's been taken, then? It's true?"

"He has," Kara answered grimly. "But do not fear. I will get him back."

Come to my rooms.

That was what the note had said. Niall had drained a cup of coffee, pulled his damp boots back on, and headed out. He knocked softly on the door and started in surprise when Kara yanked it open and pulled him in.

"Don't say anything about it," she warned. "I won't change and I don't want to hear it. I need to be ready for anything."

He raised his hands. "I said not a word." There were no words for the sight of her—that curvy form clad in formfitting dark trousers and a long-sleeved black shirt. There was only an instant, hot rush of appreciation, mixed with a healthy dose of fear.

She coiled her long locks and pinned them up tight under a dark knitted cap. "I might need to climb something. I cannot do it in skirts."

"Climb?" He gave her a dark look, then slapped a hand to his forehead. "Let me guess. You had a tutor?"

Her chin lifted. "I did some training with a parlor jumper."

He just eyed her and waited.

"A thief who breaks into houses, getting in through the windows. He taught me to shimmy up a drainpipe, climb a stone wall or trellis, and how to break glass without making a sound."

"I should have expected as much. Skills every young lady needs to know."

"Skills every kidnapped young heiress could put to use," she snapped.

He conceded. "I suppose we are going through the tunnel and leaving Joseph behind?"

"Yes. He cannot come." She buckled on her black waist pouch, then picked up a dark cloak and wrapped it around her.

"No," he agreed. "It wouldn't be fair. His loyalties will be tested enough without involving him in the action."

"Not to mention, he is constitutionally unable to remain silent for long. Those games of hide-and-seek? All I had to do was wait…and listen."

He laughed, but even he heard the darkness in it. "Let's go."

"One thing more."

He waited expectantly.

"I didn't wish to say anything in front of Joseph, but I am woman enough to say it to you now. You were right."

"There's no need," he began.

"There is. You asked me, more than once, if all of this might be more about me than about industrial secrets and spies and things of that nature. And you were right. There's no evidence that Audrey Bailey knew anything about Walter's activities in that arena. It would seem she just wanted the estate, the paintings, the art."

"The money," he said.

"Indeed. And with me out of the way, Joseph will inherit both the title and the businesses, not to mention the fortune that goes with it. Granted, she would not have enjoyed discovering how much I've willed to charitable institutions, but there would have been more than enough to redo Camhurst Place, take society by storm, or whatever else she hopes to do with it."

"Well, she won't get the chance now," he said fiercely.

"No. We will make sure of that." She headed for the hidden panel.

"We'll make better time with horses in this mud, rather than a carriage."

"I've already notified the stables. And if we hurry, we can ride to catch the last train out of Hammersmith. Once we are in the city, we can take the railway all the way out to Greenwich."

"Let's go."

KARA, AFTER STUDYING the railway schedule, insisted that they disembark in Deptford, and Niall agreed it was likely safer. The sun had begun to set as she dragged him straight down to the dockyard, marching along until they came across a line of smaller boats docked near a busy pub. She took a pouch of coins from her ever-present waist pouch and handed it to him.

"We need a boat." She pointed toward the pub, from which spilled the sounds of early-evening revelry. "Information, too. You should do the talking."

She was right about that. He shuddered at the thought of a room full of sailors and dockworkers discovering she was a woman in such a getup. He tossed the bag to get a feel for the heft of it but turned his back on the pub and went instead toward a narrow bench at the edge of the dock. A weathered old man sat there, smoking a pipe. He nodded as Niall approached but didn't speak.

"Which is the sturdiest wherry?" Niall asked.

The old man pointed toward one of the larger crafts, its trim shining in the last of the sun and the light coming from the pub's lanterns.

"Steam, though?" Niall made a face. "We'd like something quieter. Which is yours?"

With his pipe, the man indicated a shabby skiff right before them.

"Most importantly, we need a waterman that knows the river best between here and Greenwich."

At last he spoke. "That would be me, sir." His voice was gravelly. With disuse, perhaps.

Niall hefted the bag of coins again. "Ah, but we require a man with discretion."

The old man gave a sage nod. "I'm yer man. Ain't no one here surprised not to hear a word outta me fer a week at a time."

"Ah, but would you be willing to talk to us, should we have questions?"

The waterman nodded toward the purse. "That has the

sound of a month's wages, guv. For that, I'll answer all yer questions and ignore anyone else's."

Niall tossed him the bag. "Very well." He looked back and jerked his head at Kara. "Let's go."

The waterman's name was Doggett. Night had fallen as they made their way out onto the river, but it didn't seem to trouble him. The tide was going out. He pulled strongly until they reached the currents, and then he just banked his oars and watched the water as they were pulled along. Niall waited until they were well away before he asked about the abandoned parkland.

"Aye, everyone knows of it. The land stretches out, narrow, all along the river. Abandoned for years, but lately, a toff bought it. He had some grand plan for it, but the gossips say it all fell through."

Niall exchanged glances with Kara. It fit what she had been told about Mr. Bailey's bid to host the Exhibition.

"For sale again, is it?" Kara asked.

"No, no. The gentleman had the idea to make it into a real pleasure garden again, like the ones he visited in his youth. He means to keep the prices high, though, to keep the riffraff out." Doggett shrugged. "No skin off my nose, if it brings folks with coin who might not wish to stick to a railway's schedule. Good for business."

"Has he started work on it?"

"Oh, aye. This gent has *ideas*. He brought in plans and hired some of our local lads. First thing they started on was a fancy outdoor theater. He's planning on plays and concerts and complicated reenactments of famous battles. A grand thing it is, too, with a pit for the orchestra and all the riggings of a real, fancy theater. He's got other ideas for the rest of the grounds. A circus. Dance platform. Balloon rides. A water grotto for stealing a kiss. But though the theater is close to being finished, it's not like to be done anytime soon."

"Why not?" asked Kara.

"Our boys have stalled it. They've yet to be paid for the work they've done, and they won't do more until the blunt is paid up. They had to bust up a few heads of workers the gent tried to bring in, too. It's all ground to a halt now."

"He needs money," Niall mused.

"Age-old dilemma." Doggett spat over the side of the boat. "So do we all. Were you wanting to put in at the stairs of the water entrance?"

"No. We would prefer a more...private entrance, if you could manage it."

The old man gave a creaky laugh. "Ain't no part of these waters or shores I don't know intimate-like. I'll put you down safe, right in the middle of the park."

He was as good as his word, landing them on a narrow, rocky shore with an easy climb up a bank into the garden proper.

"Best if I wait?" Doggett asked as they went over.

"Would you?" Niall asked.

The waterman shrugged. "I can smoke my pipe and enjoy the stars from here."

"Thank you, then."

After climbing up, they crouched in the meadow grass in the dim light of the climbing moon, getting their bearings. As the frogs and night insects sang around them, Kara made a noise of her own and dropped her head to her knees.

"Kara?"

"I didn't even ask."

"For the layout of the park? We'll figure it out."

"No. I didn't ask if you would come with me tonight. And yet here you are, by my side. Unhesitating." She gripped his arm. "I want you to know how much it means to me."

He made a disparaging noise.

"No," she insisted. "I have to tell you. I've never had a...companion like you. We've only known each other a short time, and yet—"

"I know." He placed his hand over hers. "It's the same with

me."

She ducked her head. "Perhaps I've done this wrong. Perhaps we should have waited for Scotland Yard." She shot him an agonized glance. "What if we cannot do this and I've put you at risk—"

"Don't be absurd. The die is cast. We go on. Together." He raised a brow. "Do you truly think the two of us, united, cannot handle this woman and her minions? Do you think there's anything we couldn't get done between the two of us?"

She straightened and tried for a grin. "No. Of course not. But just in case…" She turned around and crept back down the bank. In a moment she came up, and he waited, expectant.

"I offered Doggett another purse to go and fetch the authorities. It will take him a while to convince them, but I told him to mention a kidnapped heiress and a woman wanted by Scotland Yard. They'll be here eventually." She sank down next to him again. "You know, I have to give the shrew credit. Even with all of her talk about how I should be more like other girls, she understood me more than any of the others who targeted me."

"How is that?"

"She knew what she was about, taking Turner. I will do anything to get him back. She figured out he's always been my staunchest ally—and he would be my weakness." She sighed. "Things are different now, though. I have two people in my life who make me feel strong. If she had taken you, it would be the same," she said softly. "I would be barreling in here just as bullheadedly."

"Likewise." He grinned at her. "I think you are wrong, though."

"Me?"

He laughed. "Yes. I think if young Harold was at risk, you'd be right here. Or Mrs. Braddock. Maisie Dobbs. And what about Jenny?"

She looked surprised—and a little worried.

"You'd best be careful," he warned. "Before long you'll be

just like every other young lady, with more than a handful of people to care about."

"Oh, shut your saucebox," she said with a laugh.

"Never mind, I think you've been spending too much time with Harold."

They exchanged a smile, and together, they moved toward a structure not far away.

"A puppet theater," she whispered, her hands curling around the carved edge as she peered inside. "Empty."

"There were no signs of light or life as we passed those parts of the grounds." Niall waved behind them. "Let's go on in the same direction until we find something or reach a fence or hedge."

"Then go on around and down the other side?"

He nodded, and they crept on, encountering two poles with platforms facing each other.

"Wire walker?" she asked.

He shrugged.

They crossed a circular dance floor, then passed a grove of statues and a Chinese pagoda.

"There's a light ahead," she whispered. "There. Look."

"Keep low. Let's check it out."

It was the open theater.

"Good heavens," Kara whispered.

It was large and beautifully done. The ceiling was high, ornately carved and supported by rows of pillars. It was a huge covered space, open to the air on three sides and including a vast, empty, sloping auditorium. No seating had yet been installed. The stage was wide. Elaborate backstage spaces were still visible, as the framing had not been finished around the stage to hide it all.

The light came from the wings off stage right. He could see lanterns, a table, and at least one figure moving.

"More than one? I can't tell."

"Let's get closer," she breathed. "We'll move together. Pillar to pillar."

Crouching low, they made their way slowly down the outside of the seatless auditorium.

"It's her!" Kara peered intently around the curve of their hiding spot. "Alone, it appears. Where's Turner?"

"Where's the marked cousin?" he muttered.

"She surely didn't come alone. Do you think? Where could Turner be?" She strained to see. "Perhaps in the other wing?"

"No." Niall reached out to keep her from moving. "On the stage. Look carefully. It's dark, but look mid-stage, toward the back."

He felt the moment she found the faint outline of the man. The tension in her shoulders increased.

"He's tied to the chair!"

"That means he's still alive. Asleep, perhaps?" Niall glanced around uneasily. "But where is our 'monster'? On patrol?"

Kara breathed deeply. "Let's think about this." She glared at Audrey Bailey's figure as the woman took a seat at a table. "She's relaxed. She expects this to be a long game. She left Joseph's home before the picnic invitation arrived, which means she expects I would have stayed at the Exhibition until it closed, perhaps worried about Turner not coming in, but certainly not frantic."

"She thinks you don't know yet," he added.

"She likely thinks that the earliest I could learn about the note would be about now, or later tonight or even in the morning." She thought a moment. "*And* she doesn't know we know about her family. She probably thinks we'll go on mucking about in Forrester's espionage activities, looking for clues leading to the kidnapper." She paused. "I wonder if she knew her cousin was involved in all of that? Or if she discovered it later, as we did?"

Niall brushed aside the question. "She wants you good and panicked." His anger hardened further at the thought. "That note deliberately gave no information. It was just meant to work you into a lather. Doubtless, she's arranged for another to be delivered tomorrow. That one might be more nonsense, or it might have actual instructions. Either way, you can bet that it won't lead you here. They will likely move out to a more neutral location."

"All of that means she isn't expecting us tonight. It gives us at least a small advantage." She huffed out a breath. "But it doesn't tell me what we should do! Should we wait for the local constable? Should we go in and cut Turner loose now? Should we wait for morning and catch them unaware?"

"I don't think we should wait until morning. Let's do it tonight, when they are not expecting it. But perhaps we should wait a bit, at least until we find out who else is with her."

"Yes. If the 'monster' is on patrol, he will likely come back around, won't he?"

They both jumped as a shout rang out, and from not far away.

"Audrey! There's someone here!" The large, marked Bailey cousin came stomping down the middle of the seatless auditorium. "I found the spot where they climbed up from the shore. At least two of them. And not long ago."

Audrey moved forward onto the stage. "No other sign of them?"

"No. But one is definitely smaller. A woman or a boy."

"Damn her!" This news incensed the Bailey chit. "Horrid, insufferable creature! How could she possibly find us so quickly?"

"There are only two of them," her cousin said.

"Are there? Or did she bring others, who might have landed elsewhere?"

He had no answer for that.

"Not once!" Audrey stamped her foot. "Not once can that girl do what she's expected. First, she somehow charmed Walter. So much so that he defied *me*, for *her*! Still, it could have been over that night she showed up unexpectedly at the Loudins', but she wouldn't stand where she was told to. She wouldn't even eat the damned candies! She would have been foggy and easily led, and I could have had her out of there and into our hands with a few words. But no! Infuriating girl! And these men, they all prance about, acting like her oddities are a virtue!"

Niall squeezed Kara's shoulder in silent support.

The Forrester cousin stood silently.

"Go on, then!" Audrey shouted. "Find them! And watch out for any others."

"What do you want done with them?"

"Kill them, you fool! Both of them. And anyone else they might have dragged into this. We will row them out and let the currents take their bodies out to sea."

Her cousin turned and lumbered back out into the darkness.

Audrey went back to her spot in the wings and took up a candle. She carried it to where Turner sat. He was awake now. Gagged, Niall could see in the better light, but his eyes glittered defiantly as the girl circled him, checking his bonds.

"Don't look so smug, old man," Audrey said nastily. "She's only hastened her own end." She set the candle down several feet in front of him. "You'll go soon after them."

She went back to her table, and Niall pulled Kara close. "Let's go get him now."

"No," she whispered. "Look at her. She's still so calm. Why? She doesn't feel threatened. You know what that must mean."

"She's unhinged?"

"She's likely armed. And she would not hesitate to shoot you." Her whispered tone grew more urgent. "I cannot have that. Think! We need you to deal with her cousin." She looked up toward the stage, to the catwalks above it. "You heard what Doggett said. This is rigged out like a premier theater. That means pulleys, gears, weights, counterweights, and rope. I'm familiar with them. I've worked with all of them, setting up some of my bigger pieces." He could hear the excitement climbing in her. "I can use what's here to distract her, even to subdue her, if I can maneuver everything just right."

"Kara—" he began.

"I can do this. I will neutralize Audrey. You must do the same with her cousin. I can do it, Niall. It's all in the timing and the precision. It's like clockwork."

Every instinct told him to refuse her, to handle both villains himself. But this was Kara Levett. If anyone could pull this off, it was her. And if he had any hope for their friendship to continue after all of this…he had to show he trusted her. "Very well," he said. "But be careful. She won't hesitate to shoot you, either. In fact, I'm afraid she'll relish it."

"I'll be careful."

"And Kara?"

Though already crouched and ready to move, she paused and stood up. "Yes?"

"I had no idea you have done larger pieces. When this is over, I will insist on seeing them."

He could hear the grin in her voice. "It's a deal." She squeezed his hand and, crouching again, moved to the next pillar.

He turned to go, trying like hell to put her part of this out of his mind. He needed all of his faculties focused and on point. He was going monster hunting.

Chapter Twenty-Two

K ARA HID IN the shadows at the base of the wall separating the audience area from the orchestra pit. She followed the wall across the wide stage, to the area in the wings, stage left, that would eventually be covered by the framing of the stage but now stood exposed. She eased herself up and found a shadowed spot. Holding still as she could, she stared about and above, taking stock.

She liked what she saw. Doggett had been right: Audrey's father had spared no expense. This stage was fitted with all the gadgets a director—or a woman on a mission—could hope for.

She moved carefully to the ladder that would get her up to the catwalks, seeing more with every step up. Everything needed for grand, mystical stagecraft creations lay in wait—but she was going to put them all to a much more practical use.

Once up top, she took stock and began to map out what she wished to happen. Really, it wasn't that different from planning the timing and movement of an automaton—but with one big difference. She would have to predict Audrey's actions and reactions. But she would have some control over the timing, and that would make up for it. She hoped.

She started in then. She scrambled silently about, setting up loft blocks and weights, loosening ties, adding knots and counterweights, plotting it all out in her head. A couple of times she made a small noise. She would freeze—and she thought she saw Turner flinch a time or two. Audrey never noticed, although she did rise a couple of times to stand upstage, peer out, and come circling back around Turner.

Kara was sweating by the time she had everything tied off, ready, and rigged to one spot so that she could time it all perfectly. She sat a moment, catching her breath. Climbing to her feet, she picked up the wooden ball she'd fetched from the thunder run. She would toss it upstage and let it roll back, and hopefully bring Audrey right where she needed her.

But right then, she heard it: a masculine shout. It sounded like it came from the darkness just beyond the auditorium. They all froze. She above, Turner and Audrey below.

NIALL FROZE. HE'D followed the dark shadow of the Forrester cousin away from the theater. The fellow had not gone back the way Niall and Kara came. Niall had to watch his step as he tried to creep nearer without letting the man know he was behind him. He stumbled once, and when he looked up, the dim form he'd been following had disappeared.

He slipped into the shadow of a tree and scanned around him. Nothing moved. Off to the left he could see a denser grove of trees. There must be a pond or stream there, judging by the incredibly enthusiastic frog chorus that emanated from that direction.

He waited, utterly still. Nothing moved.

And then the frogs stopped singing.

His head snapped in that direction, and yes, there it was. A large shadow moving in the grove.

Crouching low, he kept to the shadows as best he could as he headed in that direction. The silence echoed as loudly as the frog song had before.

Slowly, slowly. No further sign of movement. When he'd nearly reached the first tree in the grove, his foot struck something. It moved and gave a faint metallic rattle. He bent down to inspect it.

The motion saved him. At that same moment, something whistled past, ruffling his hair. It was a great plank. It moved right past where his head would have been and struck the tree. He would be knocked out, right in this moment, had it hit him. Or dead.

He clutched the object he'd struck. A chain. Rusty, but sturdy. He popped up and whipped it toward the shadowed form. It struck high, and a muffled grunt told him the villain had felt it.

The man still had a firm grip on his board, though. He tried again, swinging back in the other direction. Niall ducked again but stood quickly and kicked out, striking the bigger man in his middle and knocking him backward. Stumbling, the man lost his grip on his plank and went down on one knee.

The board lay between them now. Niall saw it had a chain attached to one end. Even as his opponent reached for it, he grabbed the chain and yanked it away. As the Forrester cousin rose to his feet, Niall realized what he held: a chain in one hand and a board and chain in the other. Parts of a swing. Sized for an adult, and one of several that must have hung in the secluded grove.

His turn now. He swung the plank, just as the man had done to him, but the villain was taller. He took a half step forward and took the blow on his shoulder. It was one strike too many for the old, damaged wood. The plank fell apart.

Niall tossed the wreckage behind him and was struck suddenly by a fast blow he didn't even see coming. His head rocked back, and he stepped one foot back to keep his balance. He still had the first chain, though. Quickly shifting his weight again, he cracked it, hitting the Forrester man at the top of his ear.

Another grunt of pain. And another punch came flying at

him. Niall avoided this one and struck back, hitting the man square on the jaw. Again. The big man stepped back. Again, Niall hit him. Another retreat, and this time his opponent got tangled in the remains of another dilapidated swing.

Off balance and trying to stay on the offensive, the marked man tried to emulate Niall and strike out with the dangling end of the chain he was tangled in.

Instinctively, Niall swung his own chain to block it. It did, but now the two chains were suddenly entwined and useless.

Forrester wrenched free. Niall stopped tugging and moved to face him, fists raised and ready. That mad, scarred face grinned evilly at him before he turned and sprinted back toward the theater—and the women.

Cursing, Niall chased him. He took a great leap and knocked the man off his feet. They rolled, each throwing punches as they went.

>>><<<

KARA COCKED HER head as the sounds of fighting drifted nearer. Cursing, Audrey pulled out a handgun. She ran lightly upstage, peering out. They all saw the two men stumble into the empty auditorium, locked in combat.

Audrey swore again and walked back toward Turner, her gun pointed at his chest.

"Show yourself, Kara Levett! I know you didn't send your lapdog alone. I know you are here. Answer me!"

Kara froze. She couldn't give away her current position. It would ruin everything.

"Oh, you think you are so very clever, don't you?" her nemesis called. "I am so *tired* of hearing how intelligent and creative you are. I give you credit, though! You should have been dead ages ago, your murder blamed on religious zealots disgusted with your mockery of God Himself. But you charmed my stupid cousin Walter, somehow. And he could not bring himself to go through with it."

Audrey walked the stage, peering into the darkness. Niall and his opponent had disappeared into the heavy darkness beyond the auditorium again, but the sounds of their fight could still be heard. Audrey crossed to pad quietly through the stage's left wing. Kara held still as a mouse in the catwalks. When Audrey still didn't find her quarry, she hurried back upstage, turning about, and shouted again.

"Contrary to some opinions, there are other intelligent women in the world. It is a fact that will be clear when I am done with you and your bumbling Joseph has the title, the estate, *and* the money—as it should have been all along! It will have to be my private triumph, of course, but I will gleefully remind myself of it, day after day, while I spend your fortune as I see fit." Sarcasm turned suddenly to fury. She peered into the darkness again. "*Now*, Kara! Or I will finish off your precious Turner and be done with it!"

Cursing under her breath, Kara cast about her. Her eye fell on the narrow wooden chute of the thunder run—and she knew. She grabbed up a length of leather hanging over a rigging rail and jumped up into the chute. The thing ran all along the length of the ceiling, all the way out over the auditorium to the end of the high ceiling on the other side. Normally, it would carry a series of wooden balls back and forth across the space, creating a grand imitation of rolling thunder right above the audience, but now it would help her save Turner.

Crawling as quickly and quietly as she could, she made her way to the small platform tucked into the pediment of the outer ceiling. Here, a stagehand would be positioned, rolling the balls back and forth to his partner on the other side as needed, but Kara stood there, curled the leather into a makeshift cone, and pointed it out toward the meadows beyond the theater.

She could hear the grim sounds of Niall fighting for his life below, but she could not see the men. Putting her mouth to the narrow end of the leather, she shouted into it, as loud as she could, "Leave him be, Audrey Bailey!"

The combat sounds below paused a moment, but Kara was already scrambling back to the spot she'd set up.

Audrey, drawn away from Turner by Kara's shout and confused by the distorted sound of it, paced back and forth along the stage, staring out. Kara needed her to move slightly back toward Turner...almost...

There!

She unknotted a rope, and a weighted sandbag plummeted to the stage, landing just to the side of the woman below.

"Ha!" Audrey peered up into the catwalks. She raised her gun. "You missed me!" she cried. "Who is clever now?"

Another knot was released, and another sandbag came swinging toward her from the side. Audrey caught sight of it and danced aside, but was still off balance when Kara let two knots go at once.

"Turner! Down!" she shrieked.

The blessed man threw himself to the floor, chair and all, as a painted wooden cloud came swinging from upstage, toward the back. Audrey was too unstable to duck, and it struck her hard, sending her sprawling, just far enough...

The last knot slipped, and a backdrop canvas dropped down, pulled slightly forward by the tackle and counterweights Kara had added. It landed heavily atop Audrey's prone, still form.

Kara raced down the ladder. While Audrey lay still unmoving, she dragged heavy set pieces over to weigh down the canvas around her. Breathing heavily when she was done, Kara looked in satisfaction at the bump of her adversary beneath the canvas, framed by a galleon, a mermaid, a rock, and several long rows of curved and pointed wooden waves.

Finally, then, she raced to Turner, who was still lying on the stage floor. Yanking the gag out of his mouth, she looked him over, anxious. "Are you all right?" She pulled a small knife from her waist pouch and started on the ropes around his right hand.

Turner gazed upon her with a proud smile. "I'm fine. I knew you would come for me."

"I should think so." Tears filled her eyes. "You came for me, didn't you?"

His hand came free, and he clasped one of hers. "I always will."

She squeezed it. "As will I. But we are not done." Kara gave him the knife and bade him free himself as she whirled away to the edge of the wings, where she jumped down into the auditorium. Silence lay heavy over the space, and she had no idea what it meant. "Niall!" she called. She started running. "Niall!"

"Here!" He came limping from the dark edge of the space.

Her heart stopped. A great stain of blood spread over his thigh. She ran to him and reached to support him. "Where is he?" She looked fearfully over her shoulder.

"Knocked out. Villain had a knife. Surprised me with it. He nearly got me," he admitted, leaning on her shoulder. "The bounder can fight. But your unexpected shout from above spooked him—and let me get back on my feet."

"Miss Kara?"

They looked up, seeing Turner coming upstage, dragging the chair, which was still tied to one foot. He pointed back toward the canvas. "She's awake and struggling."

Muffled yelling confirmed it.

"Should we cut her an air hole?" Turner asked.

They all jumped as a gunshot sounded and the screeching became slightly louder.

"It appears she's taken care of it herself," Niall muttered.

"Stay back, Turner," Kara called. "There might be more shots."

Another roared.

"Two pistols?" Kara asked. "Or a Colt revolver?"

"Can she tear free, starting at the holes from the bullets?" Turner asked, worried.

"No. That's thick canvas. She won't get out before the authorities get here."

"No further shots? She must not have a six-shooter." Niall sounded flippant, but she felt him sink a little lower against her.

"We've got to deal with that leg. Sit down. Right here." He protested, but she insisted. "Wait. Where is your neckcloth?" she asked.

"I used it to truss up our monster. And my stockings for good measure," he said, pointing his chin toward his feet.

"I need to stop the bleeding. Stay here while I go find something."

He grabbed her hand and grinned at her. "If only you were like other girls, you'd have a petticoat to tear into strips."

She yanked away, relieved that he had reserves enough to poke at her. "Oh, do shut your saucebox," she said with a laugh.

Chapter Twenty-Three

AUDREY CONTINUED TO threaten, curse, and moan, but Kara ignored her and had a good rummage in the portmanteau the girl had brought with her. She found a blanket to drape around Niall's shoulders, a jug of cold tea to pour down him, and a flask of good brandy to pour over his wound before she bound it with Audrey's petticoat.

"You don't want me to act like *that* girl, do you?" she asked him as she pulled it tight.

He shook his head. The color had drained from his face, but he willingly shifted himself onto a pallet she'd made of another backdrop canvas.

The two of them and Turner argued for a while about who should go to hurry the authorities along and how they would go about it, before deciding they would wait a while to make a decision. Kara had settled in and almost dozed off when voices sounded from the direction of the river and Doggett emerged with a couple of local constables and a magistrate.

It took a long time and a great deal of talking for explanations to be made, the two miscreants taken into custody, and Scotland Yard summoned.

Kara did not care to wait for them. It was a long way back through London to Bluefield. Going by water would be the easiest and smoothest way to transport Niall. With Doggett's help, she hired a wherry with a good-sized steam engine to take them back by river.

Once home, she set everyone in motion. Niall and Turner were both bathed, fed, and seen to by Dr. Balgate. She apologized to Joseph, apprised him of everything, and consoled him through an honest spell of grief, guilt, and misery.

At last, all was calm. Everyone was safe. And Kara collapsed into bed and slept through to the next afternoon.

Finally awake, she hurried to find Niall's wound healing cleanly and his brow cool.

That was when she truly allowed herself to believe it was over.

Joseph was waiting when she emerged from Niall's room.

"I didn't know, Kara. I had not a clue about any of it." He still looked distraught, but not as...broken as when she'd left him the day before. "You must believe me," he said quietly.

"I do. Of course I do." She rolled her shoulder, still feeling stiff and tired. "Let's go and sit down together. I'll have Cook send up some chocolate."

He nodded gratefully, and they sat together in her parlor silent until the tray arrived. She poured for them both.

Joseph took a long sip and sat back in his chair. "I liked her," he said sadly. "I feel like a fool now, of course, but I quite liked her. She was always so sure of herself." He saluted her with his cup. "Quite like you in that regard. It was comforting to think she always knew just the thing to do or say."

"I am sorry, Joseph."

"No. No. Certainly, you have nothing to apologize for. I am only regretful that I never saw what lay beneath that confident surface." He took another long drink. "I went to see her, you understand. While you were sleeping."

"And?" Kara asked in surprise.

"Now I know what lies beneath, and it is not a pretty sight. They've kept her separate, you know. Away from the other women prisoners, for fear of what they might do to her."

"For fear of the trouble she'll stir up, is more likely," Kara muttered.

"That was my thought exactly, after speaking with her." He sighed. "It's clear now. It was all a lie, her regard for me. Any feelings she professed. She wanted only the title and the estate and an idiot who would allow her to rule both, as well as him."

"You are not an idiot, Joseph," she told him firmly. "You are a man brave enough to open yourself to real feelings. Brave enough to know yourself and understand what sort of woman will make you happy and comfortable. It is not your fault that she only pretended to be that lady."

"She had me utterly fooled," he lamented. "She killed her cousin, her own flesh, because he thwarted her. She knew he was desperate. She charged him with killing you, you know. Offered to pay off his debts. She cooked up the scheme to disguise him as a righteous, offended clergyman to send the police chasing after religious fanatics as the culprits. But he didn't see it through. I don't think she knew about his other activities. He thought to use them to escape before she could suspect his feelings had changed."

"And paid with his life," she said quietly. "I owe him mine."

"She didn't want to go through with marrying me until it was clear she would get her hands on the money and the manufactories." He shook his head. "I don't doubt my time would have come eventually."

"Oh, Joseph," she breathed.

"It's true. I would have proven too slow or too unambitious to properly chase her dreams, and my turn would have come."

"We are fortunate to be rid of her," Kara said. "Far more fortunate than poor Walter Forrester."

"No. We were fortunate to have you, Kara. I've always been fortunate to have you, and I know it. I am happy with our family arrangement and always have been. The next time, I will be sure any young lady whom I am interested in understands this." He smiled at her. "Thank you, Kara. You saved me as well as yourself, and Turner and Mr. Kier."

"Mr. Kier had quite a bit to do with it," she said. "One person would never have been able to handle both Miss Bailey and her henchman."

"I've already given him my thanks, you may be sure." He set down his cup and stood. "Now, though, I must go. I've told Audrey's family that they must be gone from the townhouse directly." He wrinkled his nose. "The mother. Good heavens. It is clear from where Audrey's unpleasant qualities came. I must be sure they are removed. But I did wish to thank you."

She stood and embraced him. "I am fortunate in you, as well."

He straightened a little and tugged on his waistcoat, then set off. She watched her cousin go, and knew him for a sadder and wiser man.

NIALL INSISTED ON getting out of bed, but they were all still feeling the effects of their adventure. Kara invited him and Turner both to her parlor, where they spent a lazy afternoon resting, talking, reading the newspapers, and eating their way through the contents of a large basket that had been delivered to Niall.

"Whoever would know to send it here?" she asked.

He tucked away the card that had come with it. "A good friend," he told her. "One with eyes and ears everywhere."

The next day, he would not hear of staying away from the Exhibition. Kara was more than ready to go back with him. She took Turner aside and gave him some instructions, and they set out.

As they entered through the main entrance into the barrel vault, they found, once again, Inspector Wooten awaiting them at the fountain.

"This is an unofficial visit," he began.

"Of course it is," she said sourly.

"I am exceedingly glad you are both safe." The glance he directed at Niall made it clear that he knew about his injury. "I am not alone in that sentiment. There are others who feel a degree of gratitude toward you both."

"Please, do not damn us with faint praise! A degree of gratitude," she said tartly. "How fine. And all we had to do was solve a murder and a kidnapping and uncover an international espionage scheme."

"Yes, well." The inspector had the grace to look abashed. "It has earned you a friend or two. Myself included."

"We welcome your friendship," Niall broke in. "And we require nothing further."

"Yes, well, I rather thought you might feel that way, sir."

Niall looked surprised at his words, and not pleasantly. But Wooten continued.

"I thought you would like to know that we have apprehended Mr. Boggs."

"In a tavern outside of Berlin?" Niall asked.

"Indeed, and with a case full of stolen blueprints."

"What will happen to him?"

"He will be dealt with. Quietly."

"You should inform Lord Peter."

"I have. That gentleman asked me to bid you *adieu*, as he means to take a trip abroad."

"And Miss Bailey?" Niall asked. "And her henchman?"

"He will hang for Mr. Forrester's murder."

"But she is the one who stabbed him!" Kara protested.

"It's her word against that of a street rat. And her henchman, who is indeed her cousin, will not speak against her."

"What will become of her?" Niall asked.

"It has not been decided, but it will likely be prison."

"Good," Niall said.

"But what of Mr. Forrester?" Kara broke in quietly. "Has his family claimed his body? Made arrangements for services?"

"No. Indeed, they have not." The inspector frowned. "A nasty lot, they are. They refuse to claim him at all. They say they washed their hands of him long ago and fail to see a reason why they should bear the expense."

Kara looked shocked. "But what will happen to him?"

"He won't even rate a pauper's grave, since he was never in the poorhouse. It will be a poor hole for him, I imagine."

Niall looked between them. One looked more disturbed than another. "What is a poor hole?"

"A nasty great pit opened and not covered over until it is filled with the bodies of men and women who have no one to cover the cost for a decent burial," Kara said, whitening.

"More than a few of them are grabbed out—easy pickings for the resurrection men," Wooten added.

Kara was shaking her head. "No. I won't have it. I shall cover the cost."

Wooten stared. "But Miss Levett, he stole from you. He was hired to kill you! His family—"

"He was hired to kill me, but he decided not to do it, and that, in turn, cost him his life."

Niall stilled when Kara threw him a complex, layered glance.

"I would like to think I've learned something through all of this," she said softly. Reaching out, she laid a hand on Wooten's arm. "Would you make the arrangements for me, sir? I will pay the expenses, and I would like to attend the services. I owe the man that much, at least."

The inspector nodded. "I will. It is a kind gesture." He patted her hand. "You are a fine young woman, Miss Levett."

"Not yet, perhaps." She was still holding Niall's gaze. "But I would like to be."

"Very well. I shall get word to you." Wooten straightened his hat.

"And we will go back to the Exhibition in peace." Niall took her arm.

"I will let you get to it." Inspector Wooten bowed. "Good day. And thank you."

"Well, that's that," she said with satisfaction as they strolled toward the British nave.

"Thank goodness," Niall agreed.

WHEN THE DAY was done, Niall sank down into a chair with a groan and let Gyda finish readying the exhibit for the next day. She had been hovering over him all afternoon, driving him mad.

"You know I don't like it when you go adventuring without me," she scolded.

"It all happened so fast, I didn't have much choice."

"Yes. She does seem a force of nature," Gyda said with a smile. "You know Emilia is half in love with her."

"Emilia is half in love with a great many women," he said with a scowl that made her laugh.

"I will warn her off. Safer for you both." She nodded down the nave. "Speaking of the devil, here she comes. I'll go now. I'm sure you have things to discuss." Gyda grasped his chin and kissed his forehead. "You know I cannot do without you. Be more careful."

He watched her greet Kara on her way out, and then Kara was standing before him, looking him over carefully. He suffered the sudden urge to fold in on himself to protect the secrets he carried and could not reveal, even to her.

"I know your leg must pain you," she said gently. "But I wondered if it could stand the trip out to Bluefield. I have something to show you."

He'd felt low all day, more than a little desolate at the thought that their adventure was over—which made not a whit of sense, but there it was.

It was also why he was happy to accept her offer now. "You

did promise me a showing of your larger pieces," he reminded her.

"Oh, yes. I certainly did."

A little over an hour later, he was leaning against a tree and watching as she stood next to a metal sculpture of a boy. The figure stood facing away from him, staring at a sculpted metal hot air balloon several feet in front of the boy. Coiled metal ropes trailed from the balloon, and the boy clutched one in his hand.

"When my father was a boy, he loved to watch the balloon ascensions in the parks," Kara said. "He told me he had a recurring dream about holding on to a rope and trailing one into the sky."

"I hope he never tried it," Niall said wryly.

"No, but he never forgot the dream. He mentioned it several times. When he grew ill, I decided to make this for him. I would sit at his bedside and work on the smaller pieces, and we talked and talked, as long as his pain allowed it." She drew a deep breath. "I would like to show it to you."

"Please," he said.

She moved to a nearby post. She gripped the handle that stood out from it and began to crank it.

Niall gasped. The balloon began to expand, as if it was being filled with gas. It wasn't, of course. But she had cleverly arranged the ribs so that they expanded, along with the mesh "silk" of the balloon. Gradually, he realized it was *rising*. The various trailing ropes actually hid supports that lifted it higher, and the balloon tilted, slightly sideways, as if grabbed by a gust of wind. It rose higher and hovered, still tilted, and the boy rose too, as if pulled aloft. His body rotated so that the viewer could see he wore a wide grin of delight.

"I...I've never seen anything like it."

"Nor have I, but it was in my head. When I sculpted the boy's face, I made it look like I feel when the heat and joy are in me and a project is coming together. Just like you described."

"Yes. It is a singular feeling, isn't it? Your father must have adored it."

"I think he did." She looked up toward the setting sun. "It's not truly what I meant to show you, though. Can you walk a little way?"

"Of course."

They moved slowly through the grounds in companionable silence. He saw the bulk of her laboratory looming in the distance and felt a stirring of curiosity. He wondered if she would show it to him. It suddenly seemed a very private sort of thing to share.

He fought back a stab of disappointment when she paused at a smaller outbuilding. Not so small, he realized, as she moved to open a wide set of double doors.

"Oh, good evening," he said.

Turner stood inside, holding a notebook and a measuring tape. "Good evening, sir."

"I'll take those," Kara told the butler. "I believe Gyda Winther is due to arrive soon. I should like the two of you to get to know each other. Cook has a pot of tea and a plate of your favorite biscuits waiting for you. Perhaps you will visit a bit with our guest while we finish here?"

Turner nodded, looking intrigued. "I should be happy to, Miss Kara."

"Thank you, Turner. We'll join you after."

Mystified, Niall stared as the butler gave over his tools and took his leave.

Kara went to the back wall and opened another wide set of doors. "It doesn't have a lovely meadow view, but it has an earthen floor and plenty of ventilation. We can fit it out however you like." At his continued confusion, she smiled. "I thought it could be a forge. For you."

"For me?" He was dumbfounded.

"We spoke of how we both missed the work, the creation," she reminded him. "Now that we are not chasing down a murderer or revealing a ring of thieves, we might find time for it."

He blinked.

"The Exhibition still has months to go. I hated the thought of you missing it—that fire in your belly—for so long. If we fix it up to your specifications, you won't have to. You can forge here, whenever you have time or inclination for it." She paused. "You can have rooms in the loft above, if you like, or stay in a separate wing in the house. Gyda is welcome, as well."

"I...I... No one has ever made me such a gift." Her generosity, her thoughtfulness—it both made his heart soar and discomfited him. He frowned. "But what happens after the Exhibition?"

She spread her hands. "Whatever you wish to happen. You can go back to Scotland without such a backlog of work. You like to travel. London might be a more convenient base for it."

"And you?"

"Me?" Her gaze grew intense. "Sometimes I feel like an automaton myself. There is a part of me that is drawn to mechanics, precision, and logic."

"Thank goodness," he said lightly.

"But I don't wish to *be* an automaton. I view myself as a more complex machine. I like travel, too. And art, music, food, and adventure—because it all feeds the creative part of me. In some ways, I do wish to be like every other girl. I want friendship, warmth—even love, someday. I need all that, too, to be a fully complete and complex human machine."

He saw her swallow before she took a step forward.

"Niall, I've never felt more my complete self than when I am with you. I know you have parts of you locked away. I do not ask for more than you are willing to give, but I'm not ready for all of this—for us—to end."

He hesitated. Would it be fair to answer her the way he longed to? She was right: there were secrets inside of him. He would always have to hold them in reserve. If they came to light, he would be in danger, along with anyone who might know. *She* might be in danger.

But they were not his secrets. And he meant what he'd told Stayme—he carried the burden, but he would not let it deny him opportunity. And this was the biggest, best, sweetest, most frightening and important opportunity of his life.

"I'm not ready for it to end either," he said quietly. "You inspire me. And leave me in awe. And you make me feel a better man. So yes. Thank you. I should love to accept your gift."

She smiled widely, her eyes huge. "Shall we see if we might accomplish something together?"

He grinned to show that he recognized the echo of the words she'd said that night, back in her rooms, when they first pledged to work together. "Yes. So we shall."

ABOUT THE AUTHOR

USA Today Bestselling author Deb Marlowe grew up with her nose in a book. Luckily, she'd read enough romances to recognize the hero she met at a college Halloween party – even though he wore a tuxedo t-shirt instead of breeches and boots. They married, settled in North Carolina and raised two handsome, funny and genuinely intelligent boys.

The author of over twenty-five historical romances, Deb is a Golden Heart Winner, a Rita Finalist and her books have won or been a finalist in the Golden Quill, the Holt Medallion, the Maggie, the Write Touch Reader Awards and the Daphne du Maurier Award.

A proud geek, history buff and story addict, she loves to talk with readers! Find her discussing books, period dramas and her infamous Men in Boots on Facebook, Twitter and Instagram. Watch her making historical recipes in her modern kitchen at Deb Marlowe's Regency Kitchen, a set of completely amateur videos on her website. While there, find out Behind the Book details and interesting Historical Tidbits and enter her monthly contest at deb@debmarlowe.com.

CPSIA information can be obtained
at www.ICGtesting.com
Printed in the USA
LVHW031925160223
739698LV00016B/56